Pick a Packet or Two

Tim Hind

Dedication

For

Emma, Mark and Millie

This book is based on actual events.
Names, locations, times and details
have been changed to protect the innocent ...
and the guilty.

The Luke Frankland Novels

In the Best Interests
Pick a Packet or Two
(Coming Soon)
Twenty-Twenty Hindsight

1

Nebraska, July 2008

Dan raised his head and allowed his eyes to open a fraction. The rest of the circle were conscientiously keeping theirs shut. Heads bowed to the ground, backs rigidly upright, knees on hard concrete. No noise, save for the hushed breathing of the circle and the screams of his own thoughts.

It was his turn today. He hadn't been avoiding it, heck he couldn't possibly have avoided it. This was a freight train hurtling down the line, with Dan and the rest of them shackled to the rails in their own black and white melodrama. Unlike the old movies, there was no hero gonna come and rescue him. His fate was inevitable. Unavoidable. Unless…

Unless he got up and walked out. He could do that. He wasn't really bound by chains or ropes. He could walk out and keep walking. The cost would be … everything. All he had ever thought he wanted would be thrown away for the one thing he knew he did want. In a single action. If he had the courage. Would it be braver to do that than to face the on-rushing train? A train that would test him, question him and force him to recognise his actions, force him to confess. Reproach him, castigate him. Demand he atone for his deeds.

Atone. Was that what he needed to do? Was his father right? His mother? His wife? They were so many miles away now, but still they were here in his head. Still they were shouting and berating him as they had since he'd made it back to the US. His lengthy recuperation in hospital accompanied not by quiet and comfort, but by his father pleading and shouting. By his mother, crying. By his wife, at first restrained from seeing him, then encouraged to visit by his parents.

'She didn't mean it. You drove her to it. You weren't yourself. It isn't her fault.'

Not one of them listening to him. Not one of them giving a damn about him. Then the men came. The dog-collared, bible wielding men. His father's confidantes. His mother's heroes. Each of them, with their selected readings and their sermons. All geared to make someone feel better about the circumstances. Someone, but not Dan.

Then came the intervention and the agreements. Made by his family, not by him, but he went along with it all. Why had he done that? Did he actually believe them? Did he abhor himself? And now, today, here he was. In the circle. He couldn't figure out if the rest of his kneeling companions really believed in the *truths* they were being told. He'd never be able to ask them. Not in here. No private conversations were allowed. Everything had to be shared with the group. Everything, but most especially, the personal testimony. He'd watched the first ones to be offered the seat in the midst of the circle crumble under the intensity of the examination. He'd despaired for them, with them. Not that those first ones had volunteered. In the same way as Dan hadn't hung back. It was simple alphabetical luck. From kindergarten to college, he had never been first pick, regardless of whether they went A to Z or Z to A. The benefits of a name like Dan Stückl.

He watched Pastor Harold, a big man of almost three hundred pounds, shifting his weight awkwardly. Kneeling on concrete couldn't be ideal for him. Dan closed his eyes again and bowed his head. It was time. One way or another, it was time.

'Let us pray, brothers and sisters, let us pray.' Pastor Harold began in his sing-song lilt. Reminiscent of every evangelical preacher Dan had ever seen on television, yet with an edge that those well-manicured, well-tailored hypocrites lacked. Pastor Harold had a history. Pastor Harold had been to the darkest of the gutters and the insides of a prison cell. The violence he had seen and the violence he had visited onto others was still there, in hard-edged vowels that occasionally betrayed his sing-song delivery.

'Let us PRAY! Let us pray to the Almighty that he may hear us and he may cleanse us of our wanton thoughts and lustful desires. For it is a sickness that you have all been suffering. A sickness as sure as if you had befallen the plagues of Israel themselves. Praise the Lord. Praise the Lord.'

'Praise the Lord. Amen,' came the response from the circle. Dan mumbled through gritted teeth. He knew what was next. A silence. A pause to allow the gathering to calm their mood. He raised his head and opened his eyes. All in the circle were looking at him. Pastor Harold walked over and put his slab of a hand onto Dan's shoulder. Then he guided him to the chair in the middle of the circle. Was it guiding? Was it forcing? Either way, Dan went meekly and sat down.

'Brother Daniel. He of his namesake's bravery. He who was thrown into his own den of lions and now rises up to cast off those animal urges, those bestial leanings. Let us say Amen for Brother Daniel. Let us say Amen.'

'Amen.'

'Tell us your testimony Brother Daniel. What is your sin?'

Dan took a breath. Get up and walk away. Do it now. Let it all go. Get on a plane and don't look back. Why are you still here? What have you got to lose? Another breath, deeper, turning into a sigh. He knew what he had to lose. Never see your son again. Never speak to your parents again. Lose your career. For what purpose? To gain the only person you have ever loved.

'Tell us your testimony Brother Daniel. What is your sin?'

Another breath. 'My name is Daniel. I was tempted by Satan and committed an abomination.'

Pastor Harold raised his hands. 'Lord, hear your faithful and repentant servant Daniel confess his sins. Praise the Lord.'

'Praise the Lord.'

'And what do you wish to tell God Almighty, Daniel?'

'I lay with another man. I am shamed by it. I am shamed by my actions and by my lustful thoughts and wanton desires. It was wrong.'

'And what will you do about it, Daniel? Tell the Lord.'

'I will renounce this abomination. I will renounce this misguided sexuality.'

'And will you return to the Lord God Almighty's way? To the bosom of your wife and the love of a man for a woman?'

'I will.'

'And will you repent of your actions?'

'I will.'

'And will you denounce this heretic, this Satanic devil who led you astray and into the wickedness of homosexuality?'

The shouting and the noise inside Dan's head stopped. He was becalmed and gazed up at Pastor Harold, who stood outside of the circle, still with his hands raised to the Lord. The Pastor, framed in the light from the room's only window, cast the shadow of a cross. It stretched out, breaching the circle and almost up to the chair in the middle. Dan had tears in his eyes.

'Will you denounce him?' Pastor Harold asked again.

Dan stared at the dark shadow of the cross.

'Will … you … denounce … HIM?' The pastor's voice was louder, more insistent. Each word laboured over. The last one cast forcibly into the circle.

'I will.'

'Praise the Lord, for our Brother is returned unto us.'

'Praise the Lord.'

The circle raised their hands, the cries of Amen and Halleluiah rang out and Pastor Harold, of the Church of the Risen Son, led them in a Psalm.

Inside his heart, or was it his soul, Dan felt something die.

2

South Shields, Tyneside, England, August 2008

The South Shields' Job Centre should have been sued for breaching advertising guidelines. A more fitting name would have been the No Jobs Centre. I didn't really care. I was only here to get my dole money. Not that it was called that. The Job Seekers Allowance was a more soothing name for spineless politicians to mouth when pressed about a welfare state sagging under the strain.

Every other week walking in here to join the queues I was reminded of the film, *The Full Monty* and was always disappointed. Sadly, the South Shields Job Centre had no taste for late 70s divas, so far from Donna Summer's *Hot Stuff* being the soundtrack, my fellow jobless comrades were inflicted with tragic piped Muzak that reflected the hopelessness of our endeavours. All this torture for fifty-two pounds and sixty pence per week. It hadn't even been my idea.

6 Months Earlier

'Luke. Get up.'

I had opened a bleary eye and gazed upon the frowning face of my father, framed in my bedroom doorway. I say mine. It was of course mine in the way all children's rooms are theirs, freely rented from their parents. Be they seven months old or, in my case, twenty-seven years old.

'Must I?' I managed from under a thick, comforting duvet.

'Yes. It's time for the talk you knew would be coming.'

I groaned and pulled the cover over my head, allowing the darkness to wrap around me. It also allowed me to realise that he was, as always, correct. I knew it, just as I knew that he wouldn't say anything more, he'd merely stand in the doorway until I gave in. Which I did.

'You're still there, aren't you?'

'Yes. Get up now.'

I raised my head, allowing the duvet to fall to my chin and arched one eyebrow at my father's now smiling face.

'Good lad. Your mum is making breakfast. You have about fifteen minutes.'

He gave me a nod, turned and made his way downstairs. I contemplated pulling the duvet back over my head, but I knew it was time too.

A shower, a shave and a plate full of my mum's perfectly cooked scrambled eggs later, I was up to the task at hand. I even had my cue for it starting when mum left the dining room and dad stayed.

'You've had your time off, you've done the travelling you wanted to and the laying around and the laying in late. Frankly, it's time to get back to the grind, Luke.'

I started to speak but my father raised a hand. A gentle gesture, as he was a gentle man, but enough to halt me.

'I know you can't talk about any of the work things that went on and I know you won't, for whatever reason, talk about anything else that happened, but you need to get your life back on track. Dan was a great bloke and yes, your mum and brother and I thought that you made a great couple, but he was married. You both knew the risks, especially for him. We didn't think it was ideal, but your mum and I both know that love has no consideration for timings or circumstances. We don't need to know why it didn't work out, that is your business, but it happened. It's like you leaving the military, it's a done deal. A career change as momentous as that is difficult at any time, I'm sure. Compound it with a heart-break and that's why we let you slump around the house for the first few months. Then you decided that a change of scenery would be good and we agreed with that. You've alternated between those two states for long enough now. You have to get up and get on with life.'

'You're telling me I need to man-up?'

'I wouldn't have phrased it like that. I'd prefer to think of it as you showing some grit and determination, which I know you have in droves.'

The intensity of his look and the emotion contained in his last sentence punched into my chest and made me catch my breath. I'd always known I was blessed with my parents, times like this just reinforced it.

'You could go out and see James if you wanted?'

'Strewth Dad, you wanna send me to the colonies too?' I said in a terrible attempt at an Australian accent.

'No, not quite. One son's enough. I don't mind his choice of country, but I do wish your brother would refrain from adopting anymore Australian idiosyncrasies. It's one thing for him to have moved there, quite another for him to go native.' My dad laughed.

For the first time in a long time, I joined in.

'Now,' he said, bringing my focus back. 'You need to get yourself down to the Job Centre in South Shields and sign on for the dole.'

It was rare for my dad to surprise me, although when he did he really did. Like when he accepted me coming out to my family as if being gay was the most natural thing in the world. Which I suppose it was. Now, he did it again. This hard-working, proud north-east Englishman had been a teenage apprentice to his own father in the construction business started by his grandfather. Years later, after graduating university in the 60s and taking on the mantle of boss, he built success upon success and encouraged me and my brother to do whatever we wanted so that we didn't follow in the family footsteps. He had told us, 'It's tough graft boys and you can do better.' Yet hard work and striving for success were core values for our family, as was paying our own way. Making money was not the be all and end all, but it was important. We had a comfortable lifestyle, but I well knew my father still held a solid foundation of working men's values, the emphasis on working. To sign on the dole was the last thing I would have thought of him advising me.

'I'm sorry?' Was the limit of my response.

'The dole, son. You're entitled. You paid your taxes and your National Insurance contributions. You are officially unemployed and you are entitled to the benefits that the country has set aside for you. You'll return to work at some stage and probably pay a lot more taxes until you eventually retire, so here and now, you are entitled to claim what is yours. You also might listen to what they have to say and you never know, they could have some worthwhile opportunities to pursue.'

I couldn't think of how to respond. Instead I heard the familiar notes of Mott The Hoople's *All the Way from Memphis* coming from the lounge stereo. My mum would be in there, swaying along to it. If my dad had been in there the two of them would have danced together. Not in some fantastically complex or choreographed number, just the two of them swaying together. It was a scene so familiar to me. Mum and Dad impromptu dancing along to music that I had always thought terribly dated, yet now found so terribly comforting. She and my dad had, for so many years, been unafraid to show the love and strength they had as a couple.

Dan was gone. Lost to me and it had made me a broken man, especially with the violence and suddenness that had befallen us, but it was done. If I couldn't have the strength of love my parents had, then I needed to be able to get up and get on with my life. It started today. 'Thanks Dad.'

'You're welcome, Luke. Are you okay?'

'No … but I'm better.'

'Good lad. Now if you'll excuse me, I think they're playing my song.'

That first morning I took the bus into South Shields, down as far as the Shields Ferry Landing stop, almost at the very mouth of the River Tyne. The old wharfs and quaysides, long past playing host to the merchant ships and trading vessels of the Empire, lay empty and somewhat forlorn. Like an elderly friend who used to be vibrant but was now a hollow remnant. The ship-shaped inlets were nothing more than a backdrop to the confusion of modern office spaces, refurbished apartments and trendy shopping units, most of which were sporting 'For Lease' signs. I walked back up the road, past St Hilda's Parish Church and onwards to my new place of fortnightly worship, the Job Centre. I had been quietly pessimistic. Prepared for a long wait and an inefficiency that I suspected would be the norm for a bunch of underpaid civil servants. Instead, I'd been pleasantly surprised. Registration was swift and they could get me in to see a consultant within a couple of hours. I went for a slow and relaxing stroll, a coffee in one of the few cafes still trading and then came back to the Centre. The consultant was a forty-something woman called Miriam. She was slim, wore flat shoes, a blue skirt and a white blouse, had short brown hair and a welcoming smile. I was beguiled into thinking that all was well in the world of the Job Centre and that opportunities were about to cascade forth. She ushered me into a small, but functional interview room. A table, two chairs and a pad of forms on her side of the desk. I sat down, still awaiting the cascade.

'So, Mr Frankland. Can I call you Luke?'

'Of course.'

'Do you have any qualifications?'

'Yes, I read law at university.'

Miriam looked up from her form. 'Oh! Really?' She said it in surprise, not sarcasm.

'Yes. I've almost finished my Masters.'

'Right. And your last job was in the Army?'

'Air Force.'

'Right. Sorry. And you were what rank on leaving?'

'A Flight Lieutenant.'

Miriam's head bobbed up again. She had that same surprised look. I wondered if she had any meerkat blood in her, as she was doing a great impression of one.

'Really? An officer?'

'Yes.'

'Right. Sorry. It's just we usually only get squaddies from the Army in here. Apologies.'

'That's okay.'

'So, do you mind me asking, what job you did in the Air Force?'

'I was an Intelligence Officer.'

'Really?'

I considered asking her to stop asking me that, as the interview would proceed quicker, but I relented. 'Yes, really,' I said and softened my response with a smile.

'Umm, and you left voluntarily?'

'I resigned.'

'Oh! Why was that, medical grounds or … ?'

'I can't tell you.'

Her head came back up from the form filling. Faster this time and with a look of concern. 'I'm sorry?'

'I can't tell you why I resigned. It's classified, otherwise I would.'

'Oh! Really?'

'Afraid so.'

'Umm, right, well, you are seeking work?'

'Yes.'

'What type of work did you have in mind?'

'I thought something at a leadership level within the roles of intelligence provision, perhaps specialising in nation state cyber capabilities or intelligence collection management. Would you have anything like that?'

This time Miriam's head hadn't ducked down to her form. She'd stayed upright, listening intently to me and now stared back at me with a strange expression that I couldn't read.

'Eh, umm, I don—, I mean I do, eh …'

'I'm sorry?' I said.

Her expression changed to one of embarrassment. She reached under the pad of forms and drew out a single piece of A4 paper. 'We have these jobs currently. A till operator at the local Tesco. A serving partner, it's what they call their behind-the-counter staff, at a local coffee shop and a sales assistant at Greggs. You know, the home bakery?'

'Yes, I know Greggs,' I replied and felt my optimism for a cascade of opportunities cascade through the floor.

'Oh, and a trainee bus driver for South Shields Transport or a barman for the George Hotel?'

I decided against telling her that putting me behind a bar would be like putting a joy rider behind the wheel of that bus. Instead I let her fill in the forms that she needed to and went on my way.

**

Now, half a year later, the fortnightly haul down to the Job Centre was a routine that saddened me. Yet I also knew that my dad had been extremely clever. It wasn't about the money, it was about ensuring I was grounded. He might have run the construction company in the end, but he always, always knew what his lads went through on the building sites. He stayed in touch with where he had come from, where his dad had come from and his dad's dad. He knew and appreciated the honest value of work.

I, like my brother before me, was a product of a public school education. From prep school to boarding school to university and then into the military. I had worked in the secret corridors of Whitehall and flown around the world on operations. I had a preferred style of suits and shirts. I had a preferred tailor. I had, until very recently, lived in a Thames-side apartment in London. My circles of society were far, far removed from the north-east of England and the unemployment lines. Yet here I was. On the dole and not at any point thinking the jobs that could be offered here were in any way beneath me. It was simply I was lucky.

I'd saved money when I'd been in the military and that meant I could wait for something better to come along. I had hopes it might and in the preceding few weeks my hopes had been raised.

The man to my front moved off and I stepped up to the window. I extracted my signing on card from its little plastic sleeve and handed it over.

'Are you still actively looking for employment?'

'Yes.'

'Have you attended any interviews in the past two weeks?'

'Eh, no. Not this time,' I said and wondered if I should have mentioned the various conversations I had been having with my former colleagues. Then again, it would hardly fit with the type of interviews this guy was expecting. I couldn't tell him I'd been in discussions with cyber warfare experts about possible new developments in the private sector.

'Okay.' He signed a form, stamped my card and handed it back.

'Thanks,' I said and turning away slipped the card back into its plastic home. Then, like each and every time I was in the Centre, I stopped and looked around. It was my promise to myself and in a way, my dad. I observed the faces of the men and women who were here and had no chance of getting out. My stay was temporary, of that there was no doubt. Some of these folk were permanent residents. My father's grounding had seeped into me.

Leaving the forlorn queues behind me, I had hardly reached the door when my mobile phone rang. I'd been expecting the call.

'Hello, Luke Frankland.'

'Hi Luke, my name is Emma Murray. John Leofric said I should give you a call,' she said, referencing my former director at the Ministry of Defence.

'And how is my old boss? Well I trust?'

'Very. He's in fine fettle. He reckons that you are the man to set up a new cyber intelligence team for Bateleur Bank.'

3

I exited Canary Wharf tube station and walked through Jubilee Park. An unseasonably cold wind played through the branches of the Dawn Redwood trees, their luscious green foliage making them look like a line of perfect Christmas trees-in-waiting.

Staring up at the surrounding buildings, with their towers of glass and shining metal, cathedrals to capitalism, I found it a little surreal that the trees would be so comfortable. Not only because they were surrounded by such intense urban development, but I recalled from somewhere in my memory, the trees were native to China. They could have been forgiven for withering in the face of such Western audaciousness, but I knew different. If the trees had inherited any of their homeland, then they'd be adaptable, quick to grow and present a face to the world that, in full bloom, looked intensely appealing.

My mind's eye saw a young woman, laughing and smiling, walking through the grounds of a Scottish house; carefree. Then a body-bag being lifted from the freezing banks of the Thames. I wondered if, at their heart, the Dawn Redwoods were equally treacherous and lethal. The anguish bubbled up inside me and I involuntarily looked around for a refuge. The glitz of Canary

Wharf wasn't limited to the headquarters of some of the world's banks, it also hosted a fair choice of dazzling-fronted bars and restaurants. A few years ago, England's restrictive licensing laws would have scuppered me, but now a quick calming shot was within reach, even at this relatively early hour. I glanced at my watch and figured there was plenty of time before the allotted interview slot. It was only the one I wanted. Purely to take the edge off for what they'd done to Lily. Going into an interview bitter and frustrated wasn't a good idea. This made good sense. A calm Luke would be better. I reached inside my jacket and felt the pack of mints. Even though it was only to calm me, the slight whiff of Tanqueray's No. Ten might not be the best first impression.

**

The room I was shown into for my interview couldn't have been further away from Miriam's little box in the South Shields' Job Centre if it had uprooted itself and moved to Mars.

On the thirty-fifth floor of a forty-floor tower the expansive and luxuriously appointed corner room faced south-east and had sweeping views across the river to the Millennium Dome, which always looked to me like some upturned balding hedgehog. Gazing past the Dome, even with the low cloud and haze of the morning, I could see to Greenwich and onwards to Grays, Dartford and Gravesend. It was stunning and, I figured, done for effect. I turned back into the room. Leather chairs and a long couch. No office desk, but low-level coffee tables, three of them in a triangular arrangement. A low-level bureau-cum-sideboard running along the far wall. High end fixtures and fittings. A massive television screen, wall-mounted, its screen blank, but its speakers playing a barely perceptible mix of light classical themes. This was designed to either make you feel luxuriously at home, or to be awestruck by the power and wealth on display.

I thought back to the various offices I'd occupied during my time in the military. 'Toto, I've a feeling we're not in Kansas anymore,' I said under my breath. The door opened and a young man brought me in the cup of tea I had agreed to when I'd arrived at the main reception. A tray, milk, sugar cubes, tea spoon, porcelain cup and saucer. As he left I checked the spoon; Garrard & Co. London. Silversmiths to The Queen, no less.

As the young man left, he held the door open for an older man and woman to enter. Apart from a pair of court shoes that must have had at least a four-inch heel on them, she was wearing much the same as Job Centre Miriam had, but it all looked a lot more expensive. As did the bob-cut of her dark brown hair. I knew nothing whatsoever about women's make-up, haircuts or clothes, but this forty-something seemed to have a good few pounds more to spend on her ensemble than good old Miriam. That said, she was also much less friendly looking.

Her companion was about a foot shorter than me, trim and just starting to show subtle highlights of grey on the sides of his dark brown hair. He was dressed in a navy suit that despite being reasonably well-fitted, looked somewhat uncomfortable on him. I got the distinct impression he'd be happier in beach shorts and a polo shirt.

'Good morning, Luke, thanks for coming in to see us. I'm Pat Harris and this is Abby Becker.'

I sat in the seat he indicated and for the next half-hour took them through what I had done within the Cyber Warfare team of the Ministry of Defence. Superficially, of course. I spoke about building the team from practically scratch, the development of our intelligence capabilities, how we sourced our information, analysed it and disseminated intelligence product. How that product was used to aid and assist the military. I never mentioned the actual threats, the attacks we'd faced or the methods we'd used to combat them. I obviously didn't mention the Chinese, nor Lily, nor the political idiots who had been running the show.

Pat Harris did little by way of interruption, other than to clarify some points. Abby never spoke until after I had taken them through my leaving the military and self-imposed sabbatical, as I had chosen to call my time in the unemployment queues.

'So why did you leave the Air Force?'

Her accent, like her hair, was clipped. A trace of London, or Essex perhaps.

Unlike Pat's American burr that reminded me a little of Bill Clinton's accent. Southern, but not *Gone With The Wind.*

I answered Abby as I had done Miriam. It was classified. Unlike Miriam, Abby bristled.

'I'm afraid we need to know. We can't employ someone who could have left under a cloud.'

Pat's face didn't mask his surprise. I almost laughed, but said nothing.

'It's okay Abby, we don't need to know. Luke came highly recommended, so we know he wasn't cashiered. Were you Luke?'

'No. Not cashiered, no dishonourable discharge, just a straightforward resignation.'

'Excelle—'

'This is most irregular,' Abby said, cutting Pat off.

'Well that's as maybe. Now, Luke,' Pat said, standing. 'I thought we could go for a spot of lunch and I can tell you about the role we are looking to create. Abby, why don't we pick this up in say, an hour and a half?' He walked away and I followed. Abby stayed sitting with a look on her face like she'd bitten a lemon.

It turned out Pat's preference for lunch was the same place that I'd visited earlier. I gave a silent prayer that the barman wouldn't yell out, 'Another double Tanqueray and tonic, sir?' as I walked in, but thankfully he had either forgotten, or more likely, he was a discreet sort. Pat and I shared a couple of Tapas plates and surprisingly, he ordered a bottle of white wine.

'You don't drink?' he asked, mistaking my expression.

'No. I mean, yes, I'm fine with that. I just thought … at lunchtime in working hours?'

'Welcome to banking,' he said and I felt a warm glow of happiness.

Over the next forty-five minutes, Pat filled me in on the fact that the UK banks were slowly coming to terms with the threats facing them in the cyber world. He was, by background, thoroughly born and raised in the American banking culture, his father also being a financier. 'The thing is, you Brits take a while to get warmed up, but now you have it's all rushing here and there to get capabilities in place. I was called in to add a bit of American steel.

I need someone I can trust to do the jobs I need doing. Sort out an intelligence team that knows what the hell *it's* doing; sort out the various centres around the world that will keep us informed twenty-four-seven. Manage the real problems we're going to have in the emerging markets of the world.'

'And they are?' I asked, genuinely not having a clue.

'What we'd have previously called Third World Nations, but more than that. It's also anywhere whose infrastructure and banking requirements haven't been a concern until recently. The new breed of emerging nations, China definitely.'

I managed to suppress a groan.

'Africa, South-East Asia, any former communist state that has taken a while to sort itself out, the Middle East and a few of the South Americans as well.'

'So all the places where thuggery and corruption are rampant?' I asked.

'Yep, that's pretty much spot on, as you Brits would say.'

'How big a problem are we looking at?'

'That's a difficult question to answer.' He paused and took a swig of his wine. 'Let's put it this way. The bank sets aside money for bad debts and fraudulent practice that it can't recover. It's all …'

I hadn't known that, but it made sense. I figured the occasional small business, or even big business, might go under and the bank would have to write-off any unpaid loans. Pat was still talking.

'… a decade ago. In this financial year they have set aside a ring-fenced amount specifically for cyber-fraud. Anything from a customer's card being skimmed to online scams to a full-on cyber theft. Based on the last two years' worth of figures they set this year's amount at five hundred.' He took another drink.

I was astounded that so much could be lost and simply written off. 'Five hundred thousand pounds? Seriously? Or is that in US dollars?'

Pat laughed. 'It's pounds. But not five hundred thousand, Luke. Five hundred million.'

I had a forkful of diced tomato and cucumber halfway to my mouth. It got no further. 'Half a *billion* pounds? For just one bank?'

Pat waved his hand in a shushing motion. 'Yes, but let's not tell the world, hey?'

'Right, sorry. But that's outrageous.'

'Yes and no. You don't really grasp yet how much money a bank like ours makes. Five hundred mill is a small pebble in a very large lake, but it isn't ideal.'

'So this is why, if I get my card skimmed and someone spends a couple of hundred pounds, banks take care of it?'

Pat nodded. 'Those couple of hundred pounds add up and you don't hear about the bigger frauds that go through, but yeah, banks set aside contingencies. Thing is, better intelligence and better awareness would make the job easier. Maybe reduce the contingency funds.'

'And that's why you're setting up this new team with intelligence-led security?'

'Yep. Exactly. So … are you up for the challenge?'

'Umm, are you offering me the job?'

'Luke, the job was yours as soon as Emma contacted you. This isn't some long-drawn-out ridiculous Government application system. If we need a capability in banking, we go get it.'

'And will Abby be open to this?'

'Abby is in the meeting because she's HR and they get frightened of lawsuits. No one gets interviewed alone so no one can be accused of anything untoward. She's a necessity, but she has no real power. I choose who works for me. I choose you.'

'I'm a little taken aback. I expected this to be a preliminary interview and, as you say, a long-drawn-out series of steps.'

'I know. If I'm honest, that's my only concern. John Leofric told both me and Emma that you were exactly who we needed, but you've never worked outside of the military. I don't need to teach you intelligence operations, Luke, but I am gonna have to show you the ropes of being commercially astute. Deal?'

'Deal,' I said and then added quickly, 'Well, deal if the salary is right and the benefits are acceptable.'

'Ha! Good. See you're thinking the right way. That bit does have to be done back in the tower with Abby in attendance, but Luke, first lesson,' he said and lifted one of the chorizo & halloumi skewers.

I waited, taking a sip of the very good French Chardonnay.

'We're a bank. A business. We're not a charity. We don't work for the fun of it. Neither do our people. Contract negotiations are a two-way street. You get an offer, you push back. Don't forget that. Oh, one other thing.'

'Yes?'

'I don't carry dead-weight in my teams. If I ask you to do something and you don't know how to do it, sing out. We can teach you. If I ask you to do something and you say yes, but you don't deliver, I fire you. Do well, reap rewards. Fuck it up and don't let the door hit your ass on the way out. Agreed?'

I felt his words blow through me like an invigorating squall. The cobwebs and inactivity of the previous months were swept away in his challenge, for that's what I heard; a challenge. A test to see if I was capable in a fast-moving, dynamic environment. My optimism and enthusiasm manifested themselves in a single word. 'Definitely.'

My upbeat mood lasted until we returned to the corner office and the sour face of Abby.

Pat lead off with, 'Luke and I have discussed the role and he is prepared to accept an offer, Abby.'

'Good,' she said with no trace of pleasure in her voice or face. She picked up her leather-bound notebook and flicked a page over before continuing, 'Given that your previous role was as a Flight Lieutenant in the Air Force, we are prepared to offer you your previous salary plus twenty percent.'

My first thought was, Wow! That's amazing! A twenty percent pay rise in one fell swoop. That's great! Thank you very much, where do I sign? Thankfully I stopped myself reacting at all and sat back, considering Pat's words at lunchtime. I counted slowly, inside my head ... one ... two ... three. As I went to speak, Pat cut me off.

'Abby, you'll have to forgive me, but I don't know what a Flight Lieutenant's salary is.'

Abby leant towards him and proffered her notes.

'Really? You sure?' Pat asked.

'Yes,' she said with that same, lemon-sucking edge to her voice. 'My husband's an equivalent rank in the Army. That's what officers at that level get paid.'

Ahh, it made sense now. Here I was, sitting in the plush office and about to be made an employee of one of the world's largest banks and she was annoyed that her old man was still digging trenches. Again I shaped to speak and again Pat cut me off.

'That's fine, Abby, but I'm not employing a military officer. I'm employing the head of cyber intelligence for a global bank. We offer the going market rate.'

He leaned over and took the notebook from her. He withdrew a pen from his jacket pocket, turned the book around and drew a one in front of Abby's original number.

'I was thinking more of this, Luke?'

I tried so hard not to make a noise, but the involuntary cough escaped my lips. 'Eh, yes. That's great, thank you,' I said and knew that the blood had drained out of my face. Abby looked peeved and Pat, making sure his expression was only seen by me, frowned a little and rolled his eyes.

Oh damn, I thought. I was meant to push back. As Abby mouthed some obviously unfelt platitudes about joining the team and a plethora of other HR and legal niceties, I managed to stay sitting on my chair and looking what I hoped was calm and collected. In truth I wanted to run around the office shouting and hollering with delight. Halfway through her proffering of contracts and places to sign, I suddenly wondered how hard Pat expected me to work for the kind of salary I had fallen into. The answer would come quickly over the next few months and it was simple. Harder and faster than I'd ever worked before. What I hadn't expected was to find myself in places more dangerous than any I'd been in with the military.

4

London, 15th September 2008

I had expected Abby to drag her feet over getting my appointment finalised, but the paperwork was tied up within days of the interview. I was told to report for my first day of employment two weeks later. A frantic scramble to get accommodation sorted in London and a hasty move south kept me busy in the interim. I realised I would be starting work on what was traditionally Battle of Britain Day. The biggest commemorative day for the Royal Air Force. I saw it as a good omen. My old firm handing me over to the new.

As I exited Canary Wharf tube station a steady stream of people were making their way past me, heading towards the station's entrance. Each was dressed in the executive uniform of dark suits and serious faces, but each also carried a cardboard box. I checked my watch; 7:30 am. This corporate life was going to be great. It looked to me like they had all been given the day off and a gift of some sort. I figured that I would have looked happier for their luck, but perhaps you became inured to this type of thing after being in this high-flying world for a while. I glanced back along the line of box-carriers and saw they were coming out of a building marked Lehman Brothers. I'd never heard of it.

Entering the glitzy foyer of Bateleur Bank headquarters, I was greeted by a smiling Pat Harris.

'Welcome, Luke.' He handed me my new ID card. 'That will get you into the building, as well as allowing you access to here,' he said, guiding me into one of the lifts to the side of the main lobby. He pointed me towards a card scanner. I held my ID next to it and when it beeped, Pat pressed a previously unlit button with the number 20 on it. The lift rose smoothly and quickly.

Reaching into my wallet I took out the plastic sleeve that had once held my Job Centre signing-on card. I'd kept it for some strange sentimental reason that I hadn't quite understood myself. I slid the Bank ID into it.

The lift door opened to reveal a scene reminiscent of a science-fiction movie. An open plan office with a scattering of desks, most topped with an array of computer screens, sat to the front of a glass wall that ran the complete width of the building. A single glass door and a complex electronic keypad were located at the midpoint of the wall. Behind the glass, the rest of the twentieth floor was home to five lines of double-sided racks, each one extending all the way to the building's far wall. Each rack was crammed full of black boxes and each box had a single blue light illuminated on its front panel. It could only have looked more like *Terminator* if the lights had been red lasers.

Two men got up from their seats in the office space. Pat made the introductions.

'Luke, this is Steve Bryant. The caretaker of our castle keep,' he said, whilst sweeping his hand towards the glass wall and the bank's main server farm.

I shook hands with a man who, had I passed on the street, I would have thought was a market trader or maybe a docker on the few remaining real wharfs in London. He was short and stocky if I was being generous. Fat was more accurate. He reached for my hand with one of his own that looked like five pudgy sausages sown onto a blown up balloon.

'How you doing, La?' He asked in a Scouse accent that was so thick as to make you think he'd left his native Liverpool for the first time that morning. His suit jacket was hanging on the back of the chair he'd vacated and his white shirt was more out than in the waistband of his trousers. The red tie he wore would have been an appropriate length had it not had the major circumference of his belly to overcome.

'I'm good, thanks. Pleased to be here.'

'Yeah, well that might not last.'

'Sorry?'

'Only joking, mate.' He laughed and his man-boobs jiggled up and down. The smile that spread across his reddening face was contagious and I couldn't help but instantly like him. He reminded me of the old comedians I'd seen on TV. The ones who had honed their skills in the grimy working men's clubs of the north of England. Beer stains and tobacco and darkened rooms echoing to the sound of dubious jokes and raucous laughter.

'And this is Paul,' Pat said, waving a hand at the young man next to Steve.

Laurel and Hardy, or Big Bird and the Cookie Monster were the first two comparisons my mind jumped to. Where Steve Bryant was short, fat and middle-aged, Paul Malone was tall, fit, lithe even, not a day over twenty-five and would not have looked out of place in a boy band playing the Wembley Arena. I shook Paul's hand but it was Steve who kept talking.

'I'm what you would call the continuous face of our IT at the bank, Luke. Been here since before online banking. Back when we had tellers and real banks and no one knew how to spell ATM. Back in the good old days when you could do this job without a degree in basket weaving. This youngster,' he pointed a rotund thumb at Paul, 'is my apprentice graduate. Aren't you son?'

Paul nodded and managed a, 'Yes, Steve.'

'He's quite bright for a Manc,' Steve said, his face losing all colour and the smile disappearing.

I wondered for a split second if I'd inherited a massive HR problem. It was well known that Liverpudlians and Mancunians were not the best of buddies. The antagonism between the cities was legend, but as I began to wonder how I would resolve the likely issues, Paul raised a middle finger towards Steve.

'And he's an old fart with fat hands that can't reach the keyboard because his gut gets in the way,' Paul said. 'Good job he's quite clever for a Scouser, really, but don't leave anything lying around that's a bit valuable. He'll have it away quick as look at it.'

Then the two of them beamed at each other, before turning around and waving Pat and me into the main office area.

Pat put his hand on my forearm and slowed my step, allowing Steve and Paul to walk ahead a little.

'Steve's never kept a graduate for longer than three weeks. We send him a new intake each spring and they never last. He weeds out the slow, the stupid, the pretenders and the fly-by-the-seat-of-their-pants programmers. He's been my saviour for not allowing wildcards into our system. He's had Paul working for him for a year and a half. Still calls him an apprentice just to wind him up, but in private, he told me after one week that Paul was as good as we were ever going to get.'

'Is this all we have?' I asked, perplexed at two men and me being the whole of an intelligence cell.

'For now,' Pat answered. 'I brought Paul and Steve over from our main IT section as they're the best operational programmers and system engineers we have. I figured they'd be a good base to build on, but I also thought you would want to add some others? How many do you need?'

'Seriously? I get to choose with that amount of freedom?'

'Like I said, Luke. We're a business, not a charity. We do what needs doing, even if the likes of Abby get in our way at times. So how many do you need.'

I already knew the answer, I'd thought of little else for the preceding two weeks as I'd waited for the employment contract to go through.

'Two,' I said.

'Is that all?'

'Yeah. Two.'

'And you know who you want?' Pat asked as we walked forward to join Steve and Paul.

'Absolutely.'

'Do you have their numbers on you?'

'Eh, yes. In my phone.'

Pat reached across the nearest desk and slid a landline phone across to me. 'Your cell phone won't be able to dial out from in here, but as soon as we're done, you call them up and offer them both a job.'

'Really?'

'Really,' Pat answered. 'I told you, we try to be dynamic.'

'And what do I do if they ask me how much the salary is?'

Pat lifted a sheet of paper from the desk and scribbled a figure on it. 'What do you reckon, fair enough?'

I nodded. 'But what about Abby? You said she needed to be in on hiring?'

'And she will be, if your guys accept your invite to come work for you. That's when we tell her all about it. She'll be her usually prissy self, but she'll still fast-track them.'

'She will?'

'Oh yes. She is, as you Brits would say, a royal pain in the pro-verbial, but she also knows what she needs to do to keep her own ass employed. Right,' he said, switching tack, 'Steve, what do you have for us?'

I was astonished. Just like that I had requested to double the size of my intelligence team and just like that it was a done deal. I mean I still needed to call the people I had in mind and they still had to say yes, but the hurdles that would have been placed in my way within the military were simply non-existent here.

'Luke?'

I refocussed and saw Steve waving us over to chairs that he'd set around one end of a conference table away from the clusters of workstations and desks. A flat screen display that had to be at least four feet across descended from a ceiling mount and came to rest at the far end of the table. On its otherwise blank screen was a stylised eagle holding a circular motif in one of its talons. Within the circle was a red, white and blue "A2E".

As soon as I had taken my seat, Steve began. 'Welcome again Luke. Pat's asked me to run you through the bank's IT systems and structures and the threats we are currently facing.' He gestured to-wards the screen. 'This is the Amalgamated Bateleur Corporate

Digital Environment, or A2E for short.' The eagle burst into a thousand pixels, only to be replaced by a picture of the server farm that was behind the glass wall. Smaller pictures of other, smaller, server farms popped up on screen, the lines interconnecting them labelled with national flags.

'We have a distributed server environment split across fourteen nation states and each one not only looks after their own banking affairs, but can, in times of crises, be called upon to provide dynamic backup to each other.'

I nodded and thought that so far, I had understood every word he'd said. I didn't know how the server farms worked and I certainly had no clue exactly how they could come to each other's rescue if needed, but then again, I didn't have to. That's why I had people like Steve and Paul.

'As of this morning, four of these server environments have suffered intrusive and sustained cyber-attacks. As for the—'

The confused expression on my face stopped Steve in mid-sentence. 'You mean they've suffered attacks in the past?' I asked.

'Uh, no. Well, yes they have, of course, but I mean they are currently under attack.'

I looked across to Pat but his face remained neutral. Placid even. I tried to evaluate the level of threat Steve had indicated. 'You're telling me that four out of fourteen server farms within the bank are currently being compromised?'

'Not completely compromised,' Paul interjected. 'We're in the process of shutting the breaches down, but yes, they are being probed and attempted hacks are in progress.'

'And this is a normal day?' I asked.

'No,' Steve answered.

'Thank God for that,' I said.

'This is a quiet day. It's usually worse than this, isn't it Paul?'

Paul gave a sigh in confirmation.

'Now can you see why I want you and your team to be up and running as quickly as possible?' Pat asked.

I managed a nod. 'Is the whole of the banking sector like this?'

All three of them shared a look between themselves, but it was Pat who spoke. 'No Luke. That's the thing. Compared to the other top UK banks, we're getting hit at a much higher frequency and losing about as much money as the other top four banks put together. Most times we have no clue who or what is attacking us. To put it into terms from your last job, we are wandering around a minefield wearing a blindfold.'

Steve leant forward and laughed. 'Still pleased to be here?'

I was about to answer when an icon popped up on the lower right of the conference screen. It showed a small telephone in red, vibrating from side-to-side. Paul slid his chair backwards and picked up the nearest phone before it had started ringing. He listened for a few moments, his face taking on a look of mild interest that rapidly morphed into mild shock and then grave concern. He hung up.

'Turn the screen onto live TV,' he said and I was somehow reminded of a day years before when the news of the twin towers had come through. The sudden demand to see events happening half a world away.

'Which channel,' Steve asked reaching for a remote control.

'Any of them,' Paul said, then added, 'Bloomberg maybe, CNN, BBC.'

'What's going on?' Pat asked.

As the screen flashed once and the sound came through, we watched events unfolding not half a world away. In fact it was less than half a block away. Television cameras followed a stream of people moving through Jubilee Park towards Canary Wharf Tube Station. A ticker stream running under the main picture reported:
LEHMAN BROTHERS BANKRUPT – INTERNATIONAL MARKETS TRY TO STOP DAY TURNING FROM DARK TO BLACK ***UK'S BATELEUR BANK SAYS NO TO POTENTIAL BAIL OUT PACKAGE***US MARKETS OPEN IN FIVE HOURS***ANALYSTS SAY IT COULD BE A REPEAT OF 1929*** ***LEHMAN BROTH—

Pat stood up and turned the screen off.

Steve and Paul said simultaneously, 'Fuck.'

I wasn't quite sure how or why, but I was certain that this 15th of September wouldn't be remembered for Battle of Britain Day.

5

Dan stood to attention as the Army Colonel walked in.

'Captain Stückl?'

'Yes, Ma'am.'

'Good, I'm Colonel Francois. Follow me.'

Dan did as instructed and found himself being led into the heart of the headquarters building. A couple of sharp turns and corridors later, he arrived in the Colonel's office. She indicated for him to take the seat in front of her desk while she made her way around to the other side.

'Your psych and evaluation reports are through and I'm pleased to say you've been given a completely clean slate.'

Dan knew the announcement warranted a smile. The same one he'd been faking every day for almost a year. 'Thank you Ma'am.'

'You've also done well on the course. I'm impressed. Not many Army Intelligence types would be able to pass basic infantry training. Even allowing for the dispensations granted, what with you only being attached into the headquarters team. It's still an achievement.'

He knew it was. He'd worked harder and given more of himself physically than at any other time in his career. He also knew he was lucky to still have a career, of sorts. It was obvious the Army wanted him out of sight and out of mind. As soon as he'd returned from the eight week furlough that his family had insisted he spend at the Church of the Risen Son, he'd faced a disciplinary hearing. Having a domestic incident wasn't unusual for serving military, but having one whilst serving abroad in a host nation like the United Kingdom was not the done thing. He and his wife had drawn attention to themselves. He had potentially caused embarrassment to the US Government, but there was no real proof of any wrongdoing on his part and the UK Ministry of Defence had given him a glowing write-up and recommendation. His stint at the Church had proved there was nothing, as Pastor Harold had put it, *perverted in his soul,* which was important in the eyes of a military that officially didn't ask and didn't tell, but who also officially viewed homosexual men as *creating an unacceptable risk to the high standards of morale, good order and discipline, and unit cohesion that are the essence of military capability.*

He had dived and ducked and done what was necessary. The hearing came back with no case to answer. He thought all was going to return to normal, but less than two weeks later he'd been summoned to his CO's office.

**

'We think you need a change of scenery, Dan.'

'Sir?'

'We know you and you wife, Shirlene, isn't it?'

'Uh, yes Sir.'

'We know you've all been through a trying time and we reckon giving you a goal to work towards will refocus you. A bonus at the end as well. Maybe even help her too.'

'A bonus?'

'You did well on your last tour in the UK, even allowing for the difficulties in the end. I think you'd thrive with another tour in that part of the world.'

'You're sending me back to London?' He hadn't managed to keep the thrill out of his voice.

'No. Not London. Europe, yes, but not England. You're going to a place called Vicenza, in Italy.'

Dan thought it was too good to be true. He was right.

'The 173rd Airborne Brigade have requested a cyber intelligence liaison officer. It does mean going to Fort Benning and undergoing a conversion course. Not the full infantry training, but enough to keep you safe when you're with them.'

'In Italy? I need to be safe in Italy?'

'Well … you know how these infantry boys are. They think everyone needs to know how to fight first and be a specialist later. It'll be a cake walk.'

**

It had been far from a cake walk, but he'd done it. He was passed fit to serve on attachment. The last few tests were some mandatory psychological assessments and now Colonel Francois, the CO of the training regiment at Fort Benning, was telling him he'd passed those too. Vicenza, Italy was the next stop and it would be good timing. Shirlene had just announced she was expecting again, a little brother or sister for Ryan, who at four years old was not yet in school, so the perfect age to move.

The pregnancy wasn't a surprise. Since he'd got back from the conversion therapy Shirlene had made him fuck her every other night. He figured it was her way of reclaiming her man. He'd done his duty. Physically at least. They would move out to Europe and have two or three years there.

'Is that all Colonel?' He asked beginning to rise out of his seat.

'I'm afraid not Captain Stückl. Are you aware that US troops came under fire from Pakistani forces last week?'

'Yes, Ma'am.'

'Well, the Pentagon is far from happy.'

Dan felt his heart sink.

'We're being tasked with ramping up the numbers in some key locations. Problem is we're short on certain specialisations.' She paused and Dan felt his heart sink further.

'I assume intelligence officers are one of those shortfalls, Ma'am?'

'They are. Especially any intelligence specialists that have passed infantry selection. It makes you a wanted man, Captain.'

He knew he had to ask. 'And who in particular wants me?'

'The 1st Battalion of the 96th Infantry Regiment.'

'And Vicenza?'

'You'll go there on your return, just not right now.'

'And my wife and family?'

'They'll stay in the housing here at Fort Benning. Until you come back.'

Dan figured that Shirlene would at least be happy with that. She had liked the idea of Europe, but would have given him sheer hell if she'd had to manage the move on her own. She was also quite content living in Georgia. More than a thousand miles from their childhood home of Nebraska, Shirlene was fitting right into the southern ways and anyway, she could hardly complain if his work took him away. She'd wanted him to stay in the Army; to save his career. This was one of the consequences of that decision. You went where they sent you, without question. He realised the Colonel hadn't actually told him where that was yet.

'Come back from where exactly, Ma'am?'

She referred to a piece of paper on her desk. 'The Korengal Valley, Kunar Province.'

'Ma'am?'

'Afghanistan, Stückl. North-east Afghanistan.'

She had said it with a trace of sympathy he hadn't expected. He wondered why. What had he missed? Then he realised. 'How long am I going for?'

'Twelve months.'

6

London, November 2008

Former Flight Sergeant Mark Donoghue had left the Royal Air Force two weeks after me. Acknowledged as the UK military's top cyber counter-intelligence and computer security expert, he had become increasingly disgruntled with the government's negligence and lack of response to nation-state cyber intrusions; especially those instigated by China. As he'd served nearly thirty-one years he was able to walk out with an immediate pension. I'd attended his leaving drinks and halfway through the evening he'd told me he was heading north to the wilds of Yorkshire to do, as he put it, bugger all.

Former Warrant Officer Rachel Kennedy had left the Army about three months later. She hadn't travelled far though and was working as a civil servant in the Ministry of Defence, two offices down from where we had previously worked together.

Less than five minutes into my calls with both on the same day as the financial markets around the world had crashed, they had agreed to come back to work with me. Mark was insistent that he could start immediately.

'Luke, this retirement lark is not all I imagined. I'm bored senseless. Please let me start as soon as possible.'

Rachel took four weeks to get out of the Civil Service. They made her work every last day of her notice period, but for the past month me and my new team of four had been coming to terms with the cyber threats that faced the Bateleur Bank. I was appalled and it was only getting worse.

As the markets continued to collapse throughout September and more financial institutions went belly-up on a daily basis, the executives at Bateleur, cash rich and stable, decided it would be a good idea to buy up vulnerable banks globally. The strategy, communicated to us via emailed newsletters and official company communiques, was a simple one. Buy low now and eventually sell high after the recession had passed. It also seemed, according to Pat, that to get banking licences in some nations was difficult if not impossible, whereas buying an already established bank gave you a straight shot into a country's domestic banking market. From the little financial sector acumen I had gained to date, it appeared sensible enough, but it came with a massive problem for me. Vulnerable banks in developing markets did not have robust security measures. With each new Bateleur purchase and each new avenue into banking markets, I inherited some of the most insecure networks I had ever seen. I needed to implement an intelligence-driven cyber security plan, on a global scale.

Added to that, what Steve had told me on my first day was true. Bateleur was being attacked on a daily basis and losing more money than all the other top four UK banks put together. We were leaking *invisible* money and were mostly blind to what was coming at us. More worrying, the attacks were so sophisticated and adept that we were not managing to defeat any of the incursions.

Halfway through November we had started working six-day weeks, but were still under siege. I was beginning to wonder how long before Pat Harris carried through on his promise of firing people who didn't perform. I checked my watch. Lunchtime.

'I'm going for a walk and a bite to eat, anyone care to join me?'

Rachel and Steve were standing before I'd finished the sentence. Paul and Mark glanced up, both pointed at the screen they had been staring at intensely, before mumbling something about wanting to finish running a blocking program. They'd not move for hours, so it was best to leave them to it.

**

The team's go-to venue was All Bar One, the place I'd visited twice on my first day and what I had rechristened "Meeting Room AB1". By the end of my first week the bar manager, a Spaniard called Sebastian, knew my preferred tipple at lunch times, a good South African Chenin Blanc, and my favoured post-work beverage, a stiff G&T. He had even mastered how little tonic needed to go into the Tanqueray No. Ten to make it palatable.

Although it was Saturday and busy, I knew Sebastian would fit us in. The day was crisp, but far from cold, so we took an outside seat and chatted casually whilst watching the world saunter by. I was always amazed at how beautiful London could be on a late autumn day. I really did love living in a city so packed with diversity and variations of culture, but Canary Wharf on a typical weekday was far from that. It was a male-dominated, homophobic throwback to the worst excesses of the eighties, but on a weekend it softened, if only a little.

Alongside Jubilee Park, with its Dawn Redwood trees whose foliage was now a deep rustic red, twisting and turning in the wind, desperately fighting the inevitable will of nature to fall, there were families of all hues and compositions. I watched a near-nuclear mum, dad and two kids, strolling along hand in hand and felt the familiar twinge of deep regret.

The waitress came with our food and drinks and as I bit into my chicken quesadilla I continued to watch the passing families. My regret threatened to turn into a wave of sadness and despair that would engulf me. I couldn't let that happen in the midst of a working day, even if it was a Saturday. That pain had to be kept for when I was on my own, cloistered within the walls of my new home. A penthouse apartment in the Oxygen Building on the Royal Victoria Dock was my extravagance thanks to the Bank's salary. Less than half an hour's walk from work, affording amazing views out over the city and of aircraft on approach to London City

34

Airport, it was beautiful, but it couldn't stave off the deep depression that encroached on most nights. Dan and I would likely never have the chance to fulfil our once longed for dreams. We'd never live as a couple, openly and without fear. A once believed in and most wished for pathway that we would probably never walk. I reached for my wine, took another bite of chicken and forced myself to concentrate on the families passing-by.

I couldn't let myself be swamped with self-pity. Instead I watched a little boy on a bicycle being steadied by his father. Both moved forward together on the flat grass of the park before the father let go and the boy made one, two, three revolutions on his pedals before falling sideways. He was well protected with helmet, knee and elbow pads, but I was still surprised to see him jump up laughing. I couldn't quite hear his shouts, but as he grabbed the bike and his father joined him, it was obvious he was straining to try again, straight away. They set off and this time the boy managed a little further before succumbing to gravity. A girl, older, came riding up. A woman joined the group. The woman hugged the boy and the girl, the older sister I guessed, rode ahead a little and then turned, encouraging her brother to try again. This time he nearly made it all the way to her. She reached down and gave him a high five. In that instant I felt the sadness leave me. It would come back, of that there was no doubt, but not today.

'What are you smiling at Boss?' Rachel asked.

I brought my attention back to the table where she and Steve had been in deep discussions about the problems we were facing in the bank.

'Oh nothing really, just watching that little boy over there,' I said, pointing past her, 'Try, try and try again.'

Both she and Steve turned to look where I was indicating and for a minute or two we were casual observers to a fast-approaching moment that the little boy would remember for the rest of his life. The day he learnt to ride a bike. Quite surreal really.

'I remember doing that,' Steve said. 'My Grandad and me down on the side of the Mersey Estuary.'

'My best friend and me on a hill that was almost vertical. My mum nearly killed me when I got home because I was covered in cuts and bruises and had scuffed my new school shoes,' Rachel added.

'My dad. In a park on the outskirts of Sunderland. Freezing cold and fabulous.' I said. 'I'm not sure how many attempts that young boy's made, or how many times he's fallen over, but he's almost there. Strange to think, had we come here only half an hour later we'd never have known the trials and tribulations that he's gone through to succe—' I stopped short, still looking towards the boy. Rachel and Steve turned back towards me.

'Boss?' Rachel asked.

'Steve, how many attacks have we had in the last month?'

His face reflected the confusion over my abrupt change of topic, but he went with it. 'Eh, one hundred and fifty-six.'

'How many unsuccessful?'

'You know that, Luke. None.'

'Exactly. Each one is a new attack vector that comes in at us and each one is always successful.'

'Eh, yeah,' Steve said dubiously. 'That's our problem, we can't get a read on them. Where's this going, Luke?'

'You don't get on a bike and ride it for the first time with no failures. You have to practise.'

'Okay. Not sure of the relevance, but go on. Where you headin'?' Steve asked, the dubious tone still in his voice.

'They have to be practising those attacks somewhere. Against other banks? They have to be failing and perfecting and testing against something,' I said.

Steve considered my logic and I watched the internal cogs of thought play out on his face. In the end he gave a small sigh of satisfaction. 'You might just have nailed it. That would explain why we're losing so much more than the others. They're fending off each attack until the penetration is perfected and then we're copping the full force of a precisely engineered piece of code. No wonder we can't stop them.' He looked crestfallen as he took a swig of his lager.

'But we can,' I said.

'Can we?' Steve asked, looking a little more upbeat.

'Yep. We need to information share. Just like I used to do in the military. Any attacks on us, or the Americans, Canadians, Aussies or Kiwis were shared. We need to set up an inter-bank liaison group. Share the intelligence on the attacks coming into our networks and together, work out defences to them. In that way, we can all be better prepared to fend them off.'

The happy optimism left Steve again. 'This is the banking world, Luke. No one shares anything with anyone. It's cutthroat and especially within IT networks. Better tech and better intel gives a competitive advantage. Reacting a fraction of a second sooner gives more profit. There isn't a hope in hell of them allowing any access or sharing any information. We're losing the most and they're probably quite happy with that particular state of affairs. There's no way they'll set up a liaison group, and even if they do, just to pay lip service, there's no way they share anything meaningful.'

I gave him a broad smile and raised my wine glass. 'Ah Steve, you may well have been right in the past. But … they haven't met Rachel.'

While Steve looked on bemused, Rachel raised her glass of sparkling water and chinked it with mine. 'No, Boss. That they have not.' She winked at me and even I felt a slight flutter in my heart.

7

Firebase Phoenix, Korengal Valley, Afghanistan, 1st January 2009

Sweat trickled into his eyes blurring the kaleidoscope view of shimmering green haze. Without Night Vision Goggles, he would have been blind, save for the bright tracers streaking out to the surrounding hills and the scant flashes of incoming ricochets. The Afghan night was pitch black. Not just dark, like the nights were at home, but pitch, in the truest sense of the word. A deep tar black that offered no way to sense direction or orientation. On his first night here, he had wondered how anyone without NVGs could ever hope to find their way, but of course that was naïve. The Taliban fighters lived in the mountains and valleys. It was their home, as it had been for generations uncounted before them. He and his comrades were interlopers, in need of technology to see through the darkness.

As the resonating thud-thud-thud of the .50 calibre Browning M2 heavy machine guns played out their bass drumbeat in body jarring bursts of fours and fives, the lighter beats of the medium M240s guns and staccato rattle of the M4 assault rifles added mid and treble overtones into a combined orchestra of death and destruction being unloaded into the valley. Up above the whop-whop of invisible helicopter gunships provided a separate soundtrack, occasionally punctuated by a screaming ground-attack jet whose ripping of the night ended in half a mountainside lighting up with flame and phosphorous.

Dan shouldered his rifle and gazed through his green-scoped world. The rules of engagement at night-time were simple in the extreme. Anything moving anywhere in the valley, on the slopes of the now snow-tipped mountains, near or far, in a 360-degree arc around Firebase Phoenix was fair game. *Open Season* was how the boys of the 96th Infantry Regiment called it. A Taliban Turkey Shoot. He smiled at the sight of little figures, light against the darkness of the trees, running through his vision. He loosed off a couple of rounds.

One of the figures ran into the cover of a rocky outcrop and hunkered down. The other fell in a crumpled heap. Dan had no clue if it was his bullet or one of the hundreds of others that had hit home. Snipers might be able to tell if they had a kill, but in a full-on night time firefight like this, the rest of the mere mortal soldiers had to go with a share of the spoils. He ducked a little as the heavy crump of a Taliban mortar sounded somewhere behind him. Raising his head, he pushed the brim of his helmet back and smiled to himself. The luminous dial of his watch showed one minute past midnight. Happy New Year. Three months to the day since his arrival. How strange it was that he had become used to this madness so quickly.

The first night he'd come under fire, on his second day in-country, he had dived down as close to the ground in his living space as possible. He'd been comforted by the knowledge that he was surrounded by walls of HESCO 'concertainers' whilst above him was a corrugated steel roof, surmounted by four feet of sandbags, reinforced steel and concrete. Comforted, but for the sound of the tick-tak-tick of the incoming small arms and the heavier crump of RPGs and mortars. The surrounding high mountains allowed the insurgents to shoot down into the firebase from a myriad of firing positions. In turn, the enemy were being engaged simultaneously by every soldier in the 1st Battalion. Well almost every soldier. Dan hadn't fired a single shot. He'd been overwhelmed by the cacophony of battle.

Staff Sergeant Lieberman had come to check in on him and been very understanding. 'It's okay, Sir. Y'all not used to this. You intelligence guys are used to being REMFs, ain't ya?' He'd said it in a good-natured way, adding a laugh to the end of his remark, but he'd been right. Dan's army career had been completely spent as a Rear Echelon Mother Fucker. Now here he was, less than a hundred yards away from a tenacious and resilient enemy.

Lieberman had helped him up. 'You stick with me, Sir, and we'll go give those Afghani fuckers a bit of our own death and destruction. It'll make you feel a whole helluva lot better.'

Dan had followed along, doubting that putting his head over a sandbagged parapet and squeezing off a few rounds would help in any way, but he'd been wrong. It had been liberating.

Now, a short ninety days later, he was accustomed to his new way of life. His daily routine was to brief the platoon commanders in the pre-dawn. Then he'd watch the patrols head out to the local villages, a task that rarely ended in them reaching the designated village as it was more likely they'd be ambushed on the road and have to fight their way back into the firebase. In the evenings, around the time of the soulful call to prayer that would echo up and down the Korengal Valley, there would be a lull. Like a drawing in of breath and a collective sigh that hushed its way along the steep-sided mountains. Then the night would come down and the Taliban would emerge to fight and die. In the mountains, there was no break for the regular 'fighting season'.

It never ended for them. These Afghans. Only the people they fought changed. British, Russian, American. The rock on which Empires suffered and bled was hewn in the Afghan mountains. Dan remembered the history Luke had taught him and he knew that the British Empire had fought battles just like he was doing now, not that far to his south in the famous Khyber Pass. The thoughts of those conversations brought the image of Luke to his mind.

He felt his heart lurch in a familiar way. His eyes lost focus on the haze of green in his NVGs and he saw the features of the man that he still loved, despite all that had been placed between them. A wave of regret swept over him. He took it and moulded it into anger. Then he refocussed and poured round after round into the running figures down in the valley.

8

I first met Rachel Kennedy in 2001, when I'd been sent, as a most junior officer, to the UK's Ministry of Defence Debriefing Team. It was what they called a holding post. Somewhere to send you between Initial Officer Training and professional intelligence training. I fully expected to be the office tea-boy and for a while I was, but then Rachel started letting me sit in on the interviews she was conducting with Middle Eastern refugees.

The task was simple, in theory. Debrief Iraqi refugees coming into the UK and try to get as much information about the weapons of mass destruction Saddam had stockpiled. Problem was that some of the refugees were genuinely fleeing from Saddam, while others were actively working for him. Trying to discern between the two meant subtle and precise interrogation techniques centred on finding a way into a person's lifestyle, establishing a rapport, building on that and eventually garnering trust. Rachel Kennedy was the absolute master at it. As I'd once had said to me, there wasn't a man, nor most women, who didn't melt when she walked into a room. Yes, she was extremely attractive, her body was lithe and athletic and her bearing that of a ballet dancer, but it was more than that. She put you instantly at ease and mirrored your movements, inflections and moods until you quickly felt like she was your most trusted confidant. Against the tough, cynical butchers that were some of Saddam's henchmen, she had to work hard to get her information. Against the banking executives of Canary Wharf it would be child's play. I almost felt sorry for them. Almost.

With her help we held the inaugural meeting of the Inter-Bank Task Force four weeks after coming up with the original idea. By Christmas, Steve, Paul and Mark, through the communication channels managed by Rachel, had begun to defeat a quarter of all attacks being launched against us. As we went into the new year all of the banks were reporting a notable reduction in successful penetrations. The reason was simple. When a new attack vector occurred, we all responded together and implemented security patches that shut down the gaps in our systems. By mid-January and for the first time since I had started the job, I could afford to relax and take in the bigger picture. I could start building up a world view of what else was occurring within our bank. Like when I had first started, I was appalled at the reality. This time I went to Pat Harris.

'Congratulations,' he said as I entered his office.

'Eh, thanks. I think. What for?'

'You saved the bank an estimated three million pounds in the last two weeks.'

'We did?'

'According to the people who do the calculations, yes. That's quite a good return on our investment for your salary!'

'Do I get that as a bonus for my team?' I said jokingly.

He laughed and beckoned me over to the soft chairs next to his office window. The view out over London was obscured by snow flurries and low clouds. 'No. I'm afraid it doesn't work like that, sadly. Otherwise, you'd be outta here and lying on some beach somewhere and then where would we be?'

'Not sure about you, but yes, I'd be on a beach.'

'Exactly.' He sat down and waited for me to do the same. 'So what can I do for you, Luke?'

'Now that we're no longer fighting fires reactively, Mark and Steve have been able to analyse some trends, to be more proactive in our security. We're beginning to identify some localised hot spots.'

'Okay. Localised by type, mode of theft, what are we talking about here?'

'Geography. We have definite blips where the required data and reporting of our networks' status is not being carried out. It could be nothing or it could be being done to mask internal system vulnerabilities.'

'Internal fraud, you mean?'

'Yes. As a worst case. We couldn't see it before as it was being lost amongst all the noise of attacks on the bank's systems, but now they're emerging out of the background.'

'What and where exactly are we talking?'

'The what, like I say, we don't know yet. The where is spread out over a few places but mainly in Africa. South Africa is the principle one. I think we sh—'

'When are you going?'

'Pardon?'

'You're my head of Cyber Intelligence. You're telling me we have a location not telling you the data you need to better protect our systems. So get on a plane and find out what's going on.' He stood up. I figured I'd get used to Pat's dynamism at some point, but it still came as a rude, if pleasant, reality. I stood too.

'We good?' He said and grinned. 'I love seeing that look on your face. I keep telling you, we're a business and we have funds that we can spend to solve our problems. We don't need to put in requisitions in triplicate to make things happen. You say we have missing data, but you're not sure how or why … so go find out. Okay?'

'Eh, okay,' I said, as he guided me back towards his office door.

'Great, you'll love it. Jo'burg in January is beautiful. Better than this,' he said, nodding towards the window and the snow scene beyond. 'Warm and dry, with non-stop sunshine. It'll do you good. But Luke, stop by William Carmichael's office for me and tell him what you're up to, will you?' He stopped at the threshold and gave me a nonchalant wave of farewell.

**

William Carmichael was the head of physical security for Bateleur. The man responsible for preventing what I always thought of as the traditional threats to a bank. Hold-ups, heists, robberies, burglaries, deposit-box snatches and whatever else my limited, TV-movie imagination could come up with. He was as tall as I was, but about as wide as two of me. A bald head and thick neck made him seem intimidating despite being dressed in a standard business suit, white shirt and conservatively dull rust-coloured tie.

I told him that Pat had asked me to drop by and that I was off to South Africa.

'Ever been there before?'

'Yes, on holiday visiting friends who live there,' I said. Which was true. In a break from university, I had spent a few weeks with very close family friends who lived on the Western Cape. I really liked the country and the people.

'I'm guessing they don't live in downtown Johannesburg?'

'No.'

'Well, you are ex-military. You can look after yourself.'

I didn't wish to dissuade him of his illusion. A fist fight was the last thing I figured I'd do successfully, although my height and weight would probably make a few people hesitate. Hopefully long enough for me to run in the opposite direction.

Carmichael continued, 'Just keep your wits about you and don't be out on your own after dark. I mean it. We do not need a bank employee going missing in South Africa to add to our already mounting problems down there.'

'Problems? What problems?'

'Nothing you need be concerned with. Nothing to do with all your computer stuff. Just physical things. My concern. Oh, I suppose I should give you the standard warning; don't fuck anyone while you're down there. The women are riddled with HIV. And not just the prostitutes.'

I was surprised at his sweeping write-off of a whole country, but somehow it was tinged with a modicum of self-satisfaction that he, and obviously everyone else in the bank, still figured I was straight. That was no bad thing in its prevailing culture of testosterone filled, masochistic-male dominance.

'And if you do want to go with some slapper, use protection and don't get caught with a prostitute. It's a dismissible offence. The bank will fire you as quick as you can get your dick back in your pants. Especially someone in your position within security. All clear?'

I hadn't realised the bank had such a moral outlook on life, but it didn't surprise me, nor did it concern me.

Carmichael ended with an abrupt, 'Have a nice trip.' He said it as a definitive close to our swift meeting and I walked away, not really feeling one way or another toward William. He was a bit gruff, no doubt busy and he was protecting his domain. Suited me. I was equally okay with him ending things quickly as I couldn't see what he and I would have to share workwise anyway. Two hours after arriving into the heat of Johannesburg, I realised I'd been wrong.

9

Johannesburg, South Africa, January 2009

London to Jo'burg direct in business class seat 62A on the upper deck of a British Airways Boeing 747-400. It had made the eleven hour flight more comfortable than some thirty minute trips I'd taken on the London Tube. My preference for seats had been a well-considered one. Seat 62A was rear facing with storage lockers along the side that doubled as a full length table. It meant I could reach my constantly refilled G&T with my right hand. Much less clumsy than if I'd been in 62K and having to reach for my drink with my left. Small things mattered. Attention to detail was important. As did knowing I'd be met at arrivals by a driver. No need to deny myself a last G&T before touchdown.

A very heavily-muscled, tall and I suppose what I'd have called ruggedly handsome man, dressed in jeans and a tight-fitting black polo shirt with our bank's logo on it, was waiting for me outside the doors of the customs hall. The cardboard sign he held showed, in very neat block print, Bateleur Bank - Lick Franclond. I figured it was close enough.

'Hi, I think that's me,' I said pointing to the sign.

'Hello. I am Thato. I will be driving you into town.'

'Excellent. You work for the bank?'

'In security, yes. Please come with me.'

Ninety minutes later, I had been driven to my hotel, checked-in, had a shower, changed clothes, met Thato in the lobby and was now walking up to the front doors of Bateleur's main corporate office in downtown Johannesburg. A rotund man, also in jeans and a polo shirt that was tight-fitting, but not in the way of Thato's, greeted me.

'Hello, I am Graeme Bakkes.'

I recognised his name and knew he was the head of Information Technology for our South African operations. I'd seen his signature block on many an internal communication, but I'd never actually spoken to him. We shook hands and I expected to follow him into the office. Instead he started down the steps I had just come up.

'Come along, please Mr Frankland. I wish to show you something.'

'Call me Luke, please.'

He glanced behind, 'Okay, but follow me please.'

His South African accent, like everyone I'd ever heard, was terminated by clipped edges and made it sound like he was impatient. His bustling down the steps and back to the car I'd just alighted from underlined his haste.

'Where are we going, Graeme?' I asked as I climbed into the back seat beside him.

'I want to show you why you have not been receiving regular threat assessments and reports from us regarding cyber security issues.'

'Okay,' I managed, but was at a loss as to why I was in the back of a car driving away from the bank. I may have been happy to acknowledge that my technical skills in coding and computer design were not a forté, but I did know that the bank's main servers for the country were on the ninth floor of the office building now behind me. 'And that means we have to go exactly where?'

'Please, Luke,' he said and I noticed he pronounced it like it had been written on the arrivals card at the airport, 'You will see when we get there. For now, enjoy the view.'

He took out a Blackberry and dropped his gaze to the screen, his fingers fluttering across the keys faster than my eyes could follow. I figured I wasn't going to get much in the way of a tour guide commentary from either Graeme or Thato, so I did as suggested and looked out the window.

The CBD buildings fell away quickly and were replaced by a large parkland to the left, which in turn was replaced by more buildings and on the right, one of the biggest train marshalling yards I'd ever seen. Its size seemed to expand as we gained height on an approach to a bridge and then we turned onto a multilane highway, which looked as non-descript as every other one in every other country.

Half an hour of relatively light traffic later, we pulled off the highway following a signposted arrow for Alexandra and two minutes later I was being driven into a different planet.

'Welcome to Alex,' Graeme said. 'We'll be at our destination shortly.'

The roads were laid out on a grid system with streets running east to west and avenues north to south, like Manhattan Island, New York, but that was where the similarities ended. Alex was light years from Central Park. It once would have been called, a 'Shanty Town' but was now referred to as an 'Informal Settlement'. The political correctness of the term did little to change the reality.

Low-level, tightly packed buildings crowded either side of rubble and rubbish strewn roads only to open into barren and derelict wasteland on occasion. Then the ramshackle buildings would crowd in again. Numbers, painted in broad brushstrokes and garish colours, but with little artistic merit, signalled that we were on 10th Avenue. I gazed out at street-side, metal-racked market stalls, open to the elements save for a rough tarpaulin roof held in place with the precarious placement of corrugated metal sheets and breeze blocks. The racks held glass bottles that had 'Petrol' scrawled on them in black marker. These take-away gas stations, or Molotov cocktails, depending on your viewpoint, squeezed in next to fresh vegetables, fresh bread, fly-covered meat and various other commodities including, on one wishful thinking entrepreneur's racks, a row of what looked like partially broken plastic tricycles.

Each stall leant against and beside houses that were little more than raw bricks hanging together by will power more than construction skills. Where there weren't market stalls lining the roads, cars, old, dented and scratched were parked haphazardly on the verges. Some had cracked windows, some had no wheels, all of them, even those that looked like they might make a journey, were far past their best days. If inanimate objects could look sad, the cars of Alex did.

Every face I could see, apart from Graeme's, was black and everyone, regardless of their actual age, looked wearied and hard. Just as I was wondering how anyone could live in a place like Alex, we passed a brightly coloured, obviously new sign, painstakingly and beautifully painted with meticulous lettering announcing that the building crouching behind, barely more than what I would have called a tin-roofed slum, was the home to a Childhood and Literature Early Learning Centre and Day Care. I felt the emotion rise in my throat as a snake of small children, all hand in hand, all no more than five or six years old, made their way up the lane towards the centre.

Then they were gone from my view and the car was slowing next to a series of buildings equally as run down as the rest I'd seen, but whose construction heralded an attempt to be more permanent shops than the market stalls. One sported a couple of metal advertising signs for beer, including to my amazement a bright Guinness roundel placed, albeit crookedly, atop a heavily shuttered main entrance.

Next to the liquor store was a small convenience outlet, akin to a 7-Eleven but the Alex version. Every door sported heavy metal-barred gates and every window was framed with more bars. I looked across the street to a house and realised it too was secured like a fortified version of an Alcatraz cell.

The car came to a stop just past the store and in front of a tall wall which had a tarpaulin draped from the top and angled down to the fractured pavement. It formed a hastily and badly constructed tent. The heavy green material was held in place by a couple of breeze blocks on the top of the wall that looked like they would come down with a reasonably light tug. More breeze blocks weighed down the tarpaulin on the ground. The open sides of the triangular affair flapped in the wind.

I looked past Graeme to the shops. 'We've stopped? Here?'

'Yes, Luke. This is what I need to show you. Just stay in the car a moment,' he said and tapped Thato on the shoulder. Thato leant over and opened the front glove box. I wasn't frightened or shocked as he withdrew a shoulder holster and a Glock 17 handgun. In truth, I felt quietly relieved. Thato was a big man, but the surroundings of Alex made me quite pleased that he had brought more than his fists and feet to look out for me. Once Thato had slipped the holster across his broad shoulders and secured the Glock in place, he stepped outside, took a wander around the car so that any onlookers could see he was not to be messed with and then opened my door. I climbed out into a warm, but not blisteringly hot, day. Still, the glare of the sun against the white, cream and red bricks of the nearby buildings made me squint.

Graeme ushered me over to the tarpaulin and held one of the sides to stop it flapping. He nodded for me to duck under his arm. I went inside to find a gaping black hole in the wall. It was roughly rectangular and had jagged bits of metal protruding from the concrete and breeze blocks on all four sides. Under the confines of the green tarp, there was a faint smell of burnt plastic and a sweeter fragrance that I recognised as cordite. The type of smell I'd encountered on firing ranges during my time in the military.

Graeme stood next to me.

'What am I looking at?' I asked.

'An ATM.'

I took a pace backwards and it became apparent. The metal frame of the ATM's case. The twisted wreckage of the customer interface. 'What happened?'

'It was blown up with two sticks of mining-grade gelignite.'

'Seriously? Why on earth would you blow up an ATM?'

'Because not all the money gets destroyed. It blows the machine apart and it falls out of the wall easily. The thieves probably make a couple of hundred rand, unburnt. A thousand if they're lucky.'

The South African economy and its currency had suffered during the financial meltdown of the previous September. It was now holding at just shy of ten rand to the US dollar. At best then, a thousand rand was only going to be a hundred US, if that. The obvious question was why on earth would anyone blow up an ATM for that small an amount of money? Why would you risk the dangers of using gelignite, which presumably you also had to steal and why would you risk the prison sentence if you were caught? All for less than a decen—

I halted myself in mid-thought. It made sense now. All of those questions would have poured out of me and I would have been incredulous, unbelieving, probably suspicious of what Graeme was trying to tell me, if we had gone for what I had been expecting, a meeting in the main bank office. Instead, here I was under a green tarpaulin in Alex.

I walked out from under the tarp and stood on the fractured pavement. A small, yet interested crowd had gathered across the road, staying respectfully far enough away from Thato as to be of no concern. I allowed my gaze to traverse them, quickly and without catching any of their eyes, but the answers to my questions were written as clear as day in their heavy-set expressions, slumped shoulders and wearied looks.

A couple of hundred rand would make a difference. A couple of hundred rand would buy the bottled petrol to put in one of the sad cars. Perhaps buy vegetables or meat from the market, or a toy for a child, or perhaps, pay for the day care to give a little one a bit of hope. Hope that could carry them out of this place. I looked down at the dust and concrete and fractured pieces of brick between my feet.

'We have had seventy ATMs attacked like this in the past three months,' Graeme said, coming out of the tarpaulin tent behind me. 'We have neither clever skimming devices, nor clever credit card fraud nor bank hacks. We have armed men, desperate men, using old and dangerous explosives from mine sites to blow up cash dispensers. I am the head of IT security for the bank in South Africa. That is both physical and cyber threat security. There is only me. The emails from your team in London are constantly barraging me for details of what cybercrime we face. Reports that I am meant to write about possible computer intrusions and trends and methods. This,' he paused and swept his hand out towards the green tarp and the arc of his gesture encompassed the little group of onlookers, 'this is my trend. This is the method. Seventy in three months. Each one has to be investigated, each one needs Thato or one of his colleagues to accompany me to the sites, each one needs a police report, that may or may not be coming from a corrupt officer, or even if not corrupt, an officer who is dealing with murder, rape, kidnapping and a thousand other crimes that fester in places like Alex and all over my country. Now do you understand why you have not been getting reports?'

I nodded and allowed Thato to open the car door for me.

Graeme retook his seat alongside me. 'Last week we had a hold-up in Soweto. The cashier didn't give over the money fast enough for them, so they chopped his hand off with a machete.'

There was no response I could make that would not sound trite, so instead I said nothing. In my head I understood something I hadn't half an hour before. The usual people and processes model that I had always used to understand how anything worked within the world of intelligence, cyber or otherwise, needed a new frame of reference to take into account Graeme's world. We might work for the same bank and he might be the head of IT security, but his realities were vastly different from my own. It was a lesson I needed to learn.

As if reading my thoughts he said, 'You know something that you will have to realise?' He'd asked it as a rhetorical setup for whatever he wanted to share with me.

'Go on.'

'We have all of this trouble now because our criminals are not as sophisticated as the cyber thieves in London and the rest of the world, but if you keep improving your security, if you counter every move they make with their skimmers and their card readers and their cloning technologies, one day, they will revert to tearing your cash machines out of the walls too.'

**

I had dinner with Graeme and his wife, Marelize, that night in one of Johannesburg's best known restaurants, situated in Nelson Mandela Square. We were joined by a couple of the other executives from head office. It was a pleasant evening, with good food and better wine. As I was leaving to be driven back to my hotel by Thato and under strict instructions not to go for any tourist walks around the Central Business District in the dark, I drew Graeme aside and apologised.

'You won't be getting any hassles from me about cyber trends or reporting anytime soon.'

'Thank you, Luke. I am sorry you had to come all this way. I tried to tell Will that I was not trying to be awkward.'

'Will? William Carmichael?'

'Yes. Did he not tell you?'

I diverted Graeme's question by thanking him for changing my perspective. After taking my leave I went back to the hotel. The in-room mini-bar had a single bottle of wine that looked as if it might be reasonable, but instead I rang room service and ordered two glasses of tonic water. The bottle of Tanqueray No. Ten that I had bought at duty free would be much more suitable for my immediate needs.

Settled with a glass mixed exactly how I liked it and my iPod playing a mix of the Pet Shop Boys, I settled back on the bed, only to be startled by the in-room phone warbling.

'Hello?'

'Luke? It's Mark. Sorry to ring you so late, but we have a bit of a situation and Pat said we should act on it straight away.'

I swung my legs off the side of the bed and sat up. Mark's voice was calm, but to be ringing me at almost midnight was a concern. 'A situation?'

'You know we've been running deep diagnostics against all the outlying international bank systems, now we have spare capacity?'

I did know. Steve, Mark and I had discussed the concerns we had. Most centred around the acquisition of other banking networks that Bateleur had been making over the preceding months. Since my first day in the bank, coinciding with the financial crash, Bateleur had bought fifteen regional banks stretching from South

America to Indonesia. The problem with all of them was that their systems tended to be older and the legacy architecture of security they brought with them was not in any way as robust as we wanted. Steve and Mark had drawn up a list of potential vulnerabilities and had been working their way through them. It seemed from Mark's phone call, they had found something.

'Go on, Mark, I'm listening.'

'It's Ukraine. We've had a massive intrusion through a CPP. Thousands of card details have been hoovered up. Steve and I found it late this evening. Pat wants me to go to Kiev on the next flight. He wants you there too.'

'CPP?'

'A Common Point of Purchase. Basically, it's a website that has been compromised. In this case the biggest commercial site in the Ukraine. Twenty-two lines of code were added to the back end that allowed every credit card entered as payment to be electronically skimmed.'

'How's that to do with us?'

'Because eighty percent of those cards were issued by the newly purchased Bateleur Bank of Ukraine.'

'Ah, I see.'

'Well, I say Bateleur, obviously these are legacy cards that were issued by the original bank, but they're our problem now.'

'Quite. So what do you need?'

'I need to get access to the local servers in Ukraine. Some of the things we need to check can't be accessed across the network.'

'Okay. How can I help?'

'Pat wants you there with me. Just in case there are any complications or obstacles put in my way.'

'No problem. I'll see you there.'

'Thanks Luke.'

The line went dead and I took a large swig of my gin before pulling out my laptop. I'd fly back to London as planned, then onto a British Airways A320 that would take me on the short hop to Kiev. I needed a couple of hours in Heathrow to be able to buy some winter clothes. From a South African summer to a Ukrainian winter would need a change of attire; my cream, three-piece, Irish linen suit wouldn't be up to the task.

I knew the seat layout of the A320 as well as I did the rest of the BA fleet. Pulling up the booking form, I clicked into the seat map and chose my preferred option. Travelling Business Class had many benefits but for me, being able to choose my own seat was up there with the best. Almost comparable with the unlimited premium gin in the lounges.

I lingered over the Airbus profile image on screen and considered how strange some of my former colleagues had thought me. As an air intelligence officer I'd had to be adept at equipment recognition, but I always struggled telling my Abrams Main Battle Tank from my Challengers and on occasion the differences between a Rafale fighter jet and its close lookalike, the Mirage had passed me by, but when it came to civilian airliners I could instantly recognise each one. They were as different and unique to me as chalk and cheese and since I'd been a boy, I'd loved them.

It was my secret geekery. Secret because I'd learnt over time that my interest in airliners, akin to that other geek-niche hobby of train spotting, which I didn't indulge in, was better kept to myself. It only stalled conversations at dinner parties and garnered me embarrassed looks when I launched into the design niceties of a Boeing or an Airbus. Over the years it had become something I kept to myself. I looked from the screen to my glass. My two secrets in life.

I refilled the glass and considered how wrong that thought was. There was a much bigger secret at my core. One that although my family and some close friends knew, the world in general did not. I wondered if that would ever change.

Closing the seat map browser window, I plugged in a USB stick and opened the pictures stored on it. Draining another drink in rapid time I scrolled through images of me and Dan in happier times. I wondered what he was doing and if he ever thought of me.

10

Kiev, January 2009

The man waiting for me at Kiev's Boryspil International Airport had a card with my name spelt properly and wore a dark suit and white, open-necked shirt. I imagined it was open-necked as I doubted they made shirts big enough to allow him to fasten a collar button. Maksym, as he introduced himself in heavily accented English, was both taller and wider than Thato and where my South African driver-cum-minder had been ruggedly handsome, Maksym was what I could only describe as mean looking. Bald, heavy browed with a nose that was decidedly crooked, he raised one of his huge hands and waved for me to follow him. I mused on what it was they fed young men round these parts, as the only other Ukrainians I was aware of, the boxing Klitschko brothers, were equally massive. They were at least better looking.

**

As we drove into Kiev on the Naberezhne Highway alongside the Dnieper River, I was astonished to see a massive billboard of Elton John, resplendent with an equally massive graffiti scrawled across it. Both the image and the graffiti were faded and the text of both the black aerosol and the original poster was in Cyrillic, but I could work out the date of Elton's supposed appearance, the 17 June 2008. I leaned forward, resting my arms on the back of the front passenger seat and asked Maksym what the poster was about. I couldn't believe Elton John had played a concert in Kiev.

'Yes. In Independence Square,' Maksym confirmed without looking around. 'Very big. Free. Over two hundred thousand turn up. Including President. For charity. For ides.'

'Ides? I don't understand.'

'Ides. The disease. Lots of people in Ukraine have it. Not just the faggots.'

The word sounded abrupt and coarse, and immediately took me back to the last time I had heard it. Shouted by Shirlene as she raced towards me with a knife in her hand. More than three years had gone by, but the memory was visceral and as clear as if it had been three minutes. Despite the Ukrainian weather I felt a hot sweat bathe me. I glanced at the back of the driver's head and the logical part of my brain processed that Maksym's tone in pronouncing the word had not been harsh. It was neutral, almost said in a matter-of-fact way. I took a breath and wondered if I should call him on the use of the word. State that I was not impressed by his language. Where would that take us? What if he asked why not? What then? Instead I swallowed my irritation and responded with a meek clarification. 'Ides? Do you mean, Aids? HIV, yes?'

'Yes. The faggots give it to the drug addicts. Addicts give it to the normal people. Now big problem in Ukraine. He came to play concert. Say that we need to stop ides before it stops us. His charity opens, eh, how you say? ... a shop for medicines and doctors?'

Desperate to correct Maksym's choice of words regarding gay and straight members of Ukrainian society, I again ignored it and figured it was best to do the simple tasks first. 'Umm, a clinic?'

'Yes, a clinic. He starts a clinic to help people.'

We were almost past the huge billboard now.

'What does the graffiti say?'

Maksym ducked his head down to look. 'Eh, I am not sure of the words in English. Some people, religion people?'

'Religious?'

'Yes, religious people. They are not happy he come. Call him evil and say he was trying to make everyone into faggots with his music and helping the addicts and others with the disease. They call him a bad person. A devil who is guilty of saying bad things about God.'

'A heretic?'

'I am not sure of that word. I don't think so. Like when in the old times you say God is bad and not real. You know? And then they stone you?'

I could only think of one possible word. 'Blasphemy?'

'Yes!' Maksym almost shouted his approval at my choice of language. 'Yes, this is the word. My English is not as good as I want it to be. I will try to remember blas-fer-me.'

I repeated the word, sounding out the syllables and after a couple of goes he had it mastered. 'I'm not too sure how often you are going to need to use blasphemy in a sentence,' I offered once he was satisfied with his pronunciation.

He laughed and his thick shoulders moved up and down. 'Perhaps you are right. But I teach my girls English at home and you never know what children will want to know. One day I will teach them this singer was not a devil and was trying to do good for our people.'

That surprised me on a number of fronts, but I figured getting into a discussion about gay rights might not be the best use of my time. I opted for an easier question. 'Your girls? How old?'

He glanced round to me with an unexpected smile across his face. 'Twin girls. Now five years.'

The big, bald and frankly quite frightening looking Maksym had transformed in the single sentence. His eyes softened and his whole demeanour mellowed. It was another major surprise to me.

'Do you have more children?'

'No. Just my girls. My wife died in car accident. So now just me and them.'

Once more his voice carried a neutral tone but the impact of his words was no less. I said the things I was programmed to say in the circumstances.

'Oh. I'm sorry for your loss. That's a terrible thing to happen.'

His heavy shoulders moved again in a shrug. 'Thank you, but it is nearly four years now. She did not suffer and our girls were too young to know. I talk to them of her and tell them about her, but they will grow up knowing only a memory. Like a favourite story to comfort them at night.'

I thought Maksym's English might be limited but somewhere inside this huge man was a poet.

'Do you work for the bank, Maksym?'

'No. Not directly. I run my own security business. The bank is one of my regular clients. They use me and my men to pick people like you up from airport. Or if you stay in town. We look after you. Keep safe. But you must not be staying, no?'

I had no idea how long I was staying. I had no real idea what I would find on my arrival, but it seemed Maksym knew better than I. 'Why do you say that?'

'No one has asked me to be with you this evening. If you go into town. Usually, I would know already.'

'Would I need you to be with me? I thought Kiev was safe?'

'It is. But ...'

His voice trailed off. I could see the twist of his mouth in the rear-view mirror.

'But?'

'But we have gangs. They have been known to kidnap Western executives. Americans mostly, because they know they will get paid the ransom with no arguments. The big American companies do not like their people coming back with pieces missing from them. So they pay up.'

Inwardly I wondered what the hell I had let myself in for by coming to Kiev. Outwardly I thought a brave face was called for. And a degree of practical preparation. 'Right. Well it would seem sensible then if I do stay overnight, or longer, and want to go out for a meal, I would have someone like you looking out for me.'

He reached into the top pocket of his jacket and produced a business card which he handed back to me. 'My number is on there. If your plans change and you need me, call. Maybe an hour before. So I can get babysitter. Yes?'

'Yes. Thank you.' I pocketed the card and settled back in my seat. As I looked out of the window at the piles of snow lining the road, discoloured to grey and black by the traffic's pollution, I was grateful I had bought warmer clothes.

The car emerged from a short tunnel and into the docklands area of the city. Unlike London, these docks were still bustling with ships. The skyline was dominated by warehouses and working cranes, none of which had been redeveloped by oligarchs' money and turned into high-priced apartments and industrial sculptures.

We slowed, turned off the highway and soon Maksym pulled the car up to the front of a five-storey building. The frontage was symmetrically designed, with two pairs of rectangular windows centred between larger arched windows off to each side. Each window was barred with exquisitely turned and shaped metalwork that looked more like an art installation than a security feature. It was a long way from the Alex shop fronts.

On the fifth floor all the windows had a domed top sill and the overall effect was beautiful. I didn't know enough about architectural styles but I recognised bits of what in England would have been called Edwardian, with a dash of Art Nouveau. Impressive and grand were my initial thoughts, but as I gazed up I couldn't help be a little surprised at how the bank had stamped its mark on the building.

Bateleur's main iconic symbol was the Bateleur Eagle. It was usually depicted in a 3-D rendering within the company logo and mounted in a large plastic sign halfway up any building the company owned. The sign on Bateleur Tower back in London was much the same, albeit much larger and mounted at the very top to compete with the other conglomerates, each of whom had an equal fascination with proclaiming their presence. Except here in Kiev there was no plastic sign. Instead, two bronze sculptures of eagles, their talons raised like they were about to strike a prey, sat, one each atop the arched sills on the second-storey. They looked imposing and dramatic certainly, but they also were styled a little too much like another eagle symbol used during the middle of the 20th century. Given what I knew of World War Two and the devastation suffered by Kiev during the Nazi capture and occupation of the city, I was amazed anyone would have thought those eagles were a good idea.

However, I wasn't here to redesign buildings, nor give lectures on the potential offence caused by aesthetically questionable sculptures, not to try to school Maksym on his inappropriate descriptions of gay people. I was here to investigate credit and debit card fraud.

In retrospect, the first two tasks would have been easier. And safer.

**

Mark was waiting for me in the basement level of the bank. Down here, the original infrastructure of what had been the Tisza Bank of Ukraine prior to its buyout by Bateleur, was still very much in evidence. He had commandeered the office of the in-house IT team, situated next to the bank's less than modern looking server room.

He greeted me with a roll of the eyes and a handshake.

'Oh boy, am I glad you're here.'

'That good?'

'It's a disaster, Luke. I have no idea if this buying up old banks to get into their markets is a good idea or not, but from a network security point of view, it's like we've booked tickets on the Titanic because we prefer ice in our cocktails.'

'So what have you found out?'

'The CPP attack was on the main commercial web platform in the Ukraine, Tarazatko dot com.'

'Never heard of it,' I said, taking a seat across from him.

'Imagine a locally produced version of Amazon. We only noticed the problem when Steve, Mark and I began to see spikes in reports from credit and debit card holders. It was obvious the cards had been skimmed, but we were looking at a central surge of fraud spread across customers located right across the country. That meant it had to be online. A quick check of the transactions all led back to the Tarazatko site. Steve got access to the back end and sure enough it had been compromised.'

'Do I want to ask how Steve got access so quickly to a commercial site?'

'No, of course you don't,' Mark said with a comical frown.

'Okay, so why did you need to come here, if we can access all we need to from London?'

'Ah, well. There are two ways of running a Common Point of Purchase skim. You compromise the site, hoover up all the credit card details and then leave a backdoor to exploit later. That way you can go back in and take the details at your leisure.'

'Like the backdoor access we found in the MoD laptops?' I asked, referring to an old situation Mark and I had worked on whilst still in the military.

'Exactly. Tough to find and almost impossible to trace, but if it is discovered, then a simple patch solves the problem and the bad guys lose all access to their hard won data.'

'And the second way?'

'You hoover up all the credit card details and bounce them out around the world, via various dummy locations until you can store them safe on your own systems.'

'Which I shall assume from the thieves' point of view is better as they have the data, but worse because no matter how smart they are, someone, like you or Steve or Paul, can follow the trail of IP addresses across the globe?'

'Exactly,' Mark said and turned the open laptop that sat on the desk between us so that I could see the screen. 'Our bad guys did a combination attack. They bounced the data, but only to one other server and then they put a backdoor into that. A sort of best of both worlds attempt.' He pointed to a world map on the screen and a small red circle that was sitting over Kiev.

'Okay. So they didn't bounce it far then. Who owns the server that they put the data onto.'

'That's the reason Pat wanted me to come here, Luke. We do.'

I looked over my shoulder to the racks of rather antiquated machines sitting in rows within the bank's server farm. 'You mean, in there. The data got stored in there?'

'Yep.'

'How the hell can that happen?'

Mark said nothing and looked back across the table towards me. I recognised his expression. He was giving me time to process the possibilities. It didn't take long. There weren't many ways to negate a bank's security protocols, even if the Ukrainian legacy systems were not as robust as I would have liked. I sighed. 'They have an insider?'

Mark nodded.

'Are we sure?'

'Oh yes. We know the data made its way onto our system in there,' he said, hooking a thumb towards the racks of machines. 'Because we found it nestling within one of the air gapped servers.'

My shoulders slumped. Now I understood why I was here. The fact that the stolen data made its way onto a bank server was complex enough, but for it to be transferred from the public facing, network enabled machines and onto a bank accessible only machine, with no external connections to the outside world, definitely meant an inside hand.

Mark sat back in his chair. 'It's clever. Bounce the data from the commercial site to a bank server that is extremely hard to penetrate. It makes it look like the data simply disappears. Then store it in an offline location for later physical download and collection.'

'But if this is the work of an insider who can access our servers, surely they could just download all the original card data and save the back and forth to the commercial site?'

'Not really. All the data on the bank servers, even on the legacy servers of the original Ukrainian system, is heavily encrypted. It would take a super-computer and a couple of years to break the keys into that and we change the algorithms every six days.'

'Whereas the customers entered their card details in clear onto the commercial site?'

'Yep,' Mark nodded. 'Well, they shouldn't have, but those twenty-two lines of code made the site look secure, but it wasn't.'

'This all sounds extremely sophisticated. Is it?'

'Not really. Not if you know the access network codes for our servers. Without them, yes, it's a massively complex operation. With them, the coding becomes low-level and the re-routing of

the data is, at best, talented amateur status. The clever twist is to hide it on our own bank server. The last place you'd look for it.'

I stood up and moved towards the racks of computers. 'So how did we find it so quickly?'

'Because Paul followed the single bounce from the Tarazatko site and then didn't believe that any coder out there could have made the data disappear from his tracking software. So he did a full search on the local Kiev systems.'

'You're telling me Paul's ego is responsible?'

Mark laughed. 'Yeah, I guess I am. To be fair, the boy is outstanding.'

'Don't take this the wrong way, Mark, bu—'

'But why isn't Paul here?' He asked, cutting me off.

I nodded.

'He's got a cold. His sinuses are loaded. Doctor said he shouldn't be flying.'

'Oh, okay. So who is the insider in the bank, do we know?'

'Oh yes. That was easy. To finally download the data and remove it from the bank, someone had to physically plug in a USB drive. All the bank's systems have still got USB drives but they are electronically disabled. You can, if you have local permissions, reset it and to do that, you need to logon with an authorised account. We found the logon and the USB enable command, then we compared that to the server rack CCTV. Turns out the man responsible didn't bother masking his face or his logon.'

'And?' I asked, turning away from the computers to face Mark.

'Bohdan Ravansenko. Deputy of IT Security.'

'We're sure?'

'One hundred percent. He's removed two sets of skimmed data in the past few weeks. The latest set is still on the bank's server, waiting to be downloaded.'

'Okay, then I guess I finally know why you wanted me here too. I'll go speak to his boss and get him fired, while you clean up whatever data and holes are on the local systems.'

'Yeah, we could … and that was the plan when I left London, but I got a phone call about half an hour ago.'

'From?'

'Pat Harris. He wanted me to brief you up to this point and then get you to give him a call. He's had a change of mind.'

'Oh, that sounds ominous. What does he want us to do?'

'Honestly … You'll want to hear it from him, Luke.'

I picked up my encrypted Blackberry and dialled Pat's number in London. Ten minutes later and out of arguments, I was convinced of a few things. Pat would indeed fire people who didn't do the jobs he wanted doing and more crucially, the American banker, who had been the son of an American financier, had never worked with or in the military and because of that fact he had a huge misconception of the skillsets that Mark and I possessed. Despite trying to point this out to him, he was undeterred.

He had closed with, 'You're being too modest, Luke. Now get it sorted.'

I hung up and faced Mark. 'We're going to need some help.'

**

Petro Zelensky, the Vice-President of Bateleur, Ukraine, ushered me, Mark, his senior managers and all five of the in-house IT specialists, including the Head of IT Security, Oleh Kuchma and his deputy, Bohdan Ravansenko, into the beautifully appointed conference room on the fourth floor of the bank's headquarters. The neo-classical design of the room and the exquisite, solid oak of the oval meeting table belied any notion of a dour, Eastern Bloc, impoverished financial institution that had been bought out and *rescued* by Western capitalism. Despite the surroundings, the fact of the matter was that the Tisza Bank of Ukraine had been less than five days from receivership and collapse before Bateleur came in with an offer it literally couldn't refuse. Perhaps the resentment of the takeover was why Ravansenko had done what he had done. His motivation was something I'd have to ponder later, it could be a factor for other new employees of ours around the world. For now though, I had a presentation to give.

When everyone had taken their seats, Petro introduced me and I stood. Mark turned the in-room projector on and an image of a network diagram appeared on the wall. It took me less than five

minutes to brief them on the Common Point of Purchase skimming scam and how we had no idea where the data had been moved to. I ended by saying that with our swift response to the initial reports of fraud we had, at least, discovered the original CPP attack, suspended all cloned customer cards and, despite not being required to under Ukrainian law, we had nonetheless refunded all unauthorised transactions for the affected customers and finally, we had discovered, in an in-depth sweep of our systems, a potential flaw in our own security. To explain that, I handed over to Mark. He stood while I retook my seat.

The next ten minutes were spent with Mark outlining a potential backdoor into the Tisza Bank legacy systems. I kept my face neutral, but watched Ravansenko without directly looking at him. The man was no poker player. Small beads of sweat were appearing on his upper lip as Mark detailed the factually correct methods that could have been exploited by a clever hacker. He went on to detail how the cyber security team in London would begin to shut each frailty down. By tomorrow, all the gaps would be patched and the bank systems locked down tight.

As Mark finished, Bodhan Ravansenko was wide-eyed and the beads of sweat on his lip had been joined by a sheen of glistening fear across the width of his brow. I wondered if he was going to blurt out, 'It was me, it's a fair cop, Guv,' but sadly he wasn't that shaken, or he'd never been an avid viewer of *The Bill*.

I thanked them for their attention, told them they could relax and ended by asking Petro Zelensky to reassure all his other staff that the security breach was being dealt with. Smiles and handshakes were exchanged, I noted Ravansenko's was particularly clammy, and Mark and I departed for a flight home to London.

Or at least we would eventually, but not just yet.

**

Maksym Viktorovich Ponomarenko's twin girls were called Ksenia and Anastasia. Their long dark hair hung in ringlets and framed pretty faces, set with happy eyes. Their initial shyness of the two strangers their father had brought into their home was gone in minutes and they were now laughing uncontrollably as Mark ducked behind his open laptop screen before popping back up and sticking his tongue out at them.

In between his appearances over the top or round the side of the screen, he continued to give me a running commentary on the progress of the plan. Maksym, yet again befuddling any stereotype I might have had of the man, was serving up what looked like potato dumplings and what he called *varenyky*, onto four dinner plates and two children's bowls. The fourth plate was for Yulia, a stunningly attractive twenty-something blonde who was apparently Maksym's go-to babysitter. I could understand why she might well be his preferred choice. Even I could see the merits of Yulia.

We ate and then Mark and I continued our monitoring of the laptop, while Ksenia and Anastasia were bathed before being brought out in matching pyjamas to say goodnight in their best practised English. They were adorable, as was the big man's obvious love of his girls. I found myself thinking again of Dan and part of me lost the joy of the domestic scene I was a spectator to. I felt a wave of melancholy threaten to overwhelm me, but it crashed and floundered against the sudden ringing of my mobile phone.

'The data has been transferred off the system,' Paul said from the office in London.

I looked across to Mark. The CCTV feed he was watching confirmed it. 'It's Ravansenko,' he said.

I stood. 'Okay, Maksym. It's time.'

He kissed both of his daughters and handed them across to Yulia. Then he pulled out his own phone and made a short call. 'It is done. My colleague will track him and report. We should go now,' he said, reaching for his jacket.

Mark closed the laptop and he and I followed the big Ukrainian out of the door and down to his car.

11

Kiev, January 2009

When Pat Harris learnt about the initial skimming operation he was keen to catch the bigger fish. A call to some people he knew at Interpol had not gone well. They'd rapidly disavowed him of the notion that they would, or could, help. Without any evidence, other than the data, all they could do was arrest Ravansenko. He'd clam up and that would be that. They would not mount a major surveillance operation on a hunch that he might hand the data over to a bunch of unknown criminals.

Annoyed and frustrated, Pat decided to send Paul and me to Kiev. I would fire Ravansenko, while Paul deleted all the stolen data and secured the system. However, in the time it took me to get from South Africa to the Ukraine, Pat had come up with an alternative plan. As Mark was here because of Paul's sinus issues, Pat had mistakenly thought that two former military guys could be more dynamic. Do more than just delete data and fire people.

Despite my phone call to him, when I tried to dissuade him, it was a clear choice: do what he wanted or walk away from my job. I liked my job. I liked my apartment and I liked the money. I really liked the money. There was no room left for manoeuvre and anyway, it wasn't such a bad idea.

Not now that I had Maksym to help me out.

Before Mark had left London, Paul and Steve embedded code into the data set that was still on the bank servers. As soon as it was extracted by Ravansenko the tracking code would go along for the ride. If he forwarded the data via any networked method, be it email, file transfer apps or cloud hosts, encrypted or otherwise, we would be able to follow it like a trail of breadcrumbs. The plan then was to eradicate the sites that we discovered by destroying them with embedded malware. Reverse hacking to take down the bad guy's networks.

However, Paul reckoned that Ravansenko would sanitise the data and there was a high chance the tracking software would be deleted. Our breadcrumbs would be no more and we wouldn't know where to look. The only fool proof way to find out who Ravansenko had sent the data to, was to get our hands on the computer he would use to do it.

Pat's mistake was thinking that because I was a former military intelligence officer and that Mark was a former military policeman, we would have certain skills. We didn't. But then again, we didn't necessarily need them if we could hire them.

Maksym, Mark and I would head to Ravansenko's home, while Maksym's man would follow Ravansenko when he left the bank, just in case he went somewhere else. I was in the passenger seat, Mark in the back and a steady commentary was coming out of the hands-free speaker connected to Maksym's mobile phone, but it was in Ukrainian so I was none the wiser. Every so often, Maksym would offer a word or two in English. 'He has gone east. Over the Moskovsky Bridge.'

My mental map of Kiev wasn't great but I'd looked up Ravansenko's address earlier and east was the right direction. 'That's good?' I said.

'Yes. He probably heads home. At least he is not going to Minsk Massif or Borshchahivka.'

'Are they dangerous places?'

'Gang territory. But ...'

'But?' Mark asked, before I could.

'This man's home, in Troieshchyna ...'

I would have stumbled over the correct pronunciation of the word Maksym had just said, but the tone in his voice wasn't lost on me. 'What about it?'

'It is not best place.'

I wasn't quite sure what he meant, but it didn't take that long to discover. Our car headed over the more southerly Paton Bridge. I had wondered if it was named after the famous general, but Maksym assured me it was named after a famous Ukrainian.

Twenty minutes later we were heading into Troieshchyna. The area was bisected by wide, six-lane boulevards that at first glance looked affluent, but as you progressed into the suburb, wave after wave of Soviet-era, high-rise blocks began to dominate the horizon. Sunset had come and gone an hour ago, but the boulevards' tall streetlights threw a broad canopy of illumination far to the sides. The blocks, with their thousands of lit windows, added to the perpetual man-made twilight. It revealed some of the high-rises had been painted in blues and yellows and deep reds, no doubt trying to mask the drab greyness of the Soviets, but the hundreds of blocks in row after row looked to me like a dystopian nightmare.

Mark, peering out of the rear window said it best, 'My God. What mad man designed this?'

Maksym laughed. 'The same mad men who thought everyone was equal. Except for our leaders. They were not living here. They were in private homes in Moscow and on outskirts of Kiev, in their dachas.'

I couldn't imagine how many people were squeezed into this vertical living space, but I could imagine that the vision of social comradery probably hadn't worked out. The fabric of the side streets and the overall feel of the place was quickly reinforcing my assumptions. Maksym sensed my unease.

'You are right to be worried. There is a lot of trouble, violence, bad people here. It costs cheap to buy and rent. So many, many migrants come but then people who do not want migrants also here. Nazi thugs who forget what our forefathers did against the Nazis.'

'Standard stuff across Europe,' Mark said. 'Breeding grounds of low-cost housing that attract immigrants and xenophobia. I wonder if we will ever learn?'

I was about to answer, but another report came in across the mobile phone.

'He has gone home. My friend waits for us.'

We turned off the wide boulevard and down one of the feeder streets, twisting our way around separate rectangles of open ground. Some were filled with forlorn thickets of ragged trees struggling against the Kiev winter. Most were barren tracts of crushed gravel. In one, the car's headlights picked out a children's play area of concrete climbing shapes, the long ago bright paint now peeling in a sad bow to an audience of none. That was when I realised what was wrong.

'Maksym, where are all the people?

'It is after dark. You either drive or you do not go out in Troieshchyna. Well, not unless you are with them,' he said, inclining his head down a side street towards a gathering of about twenty skinheads. They were languishing up against a separate low-rise block of garages and a steady stream of cars were pulling up to them.

'Drugs?' Mark asked.

'Yes. And other things. Guns, knives, girls. Whatever sells,' Maksym answered. His tone a mix of sadness and anger.

The view fell away behind us and we turned into another side street a little further on. A W-shaped tower block dominated this latest rectangle of ground. We slowed next to a car pulled up on the verge and Maksym spoke a few words to his colleague. Then we pulled past and parked in front of the block.

'My friend waits here. To make sure car not stolen. We go in now?'

I looked back over the seat towards Mark. 'You ready?'

'As I'll ever be.'

The door to the block was heavy, metal and secured with a key-pad entry system. Maksym bent down and entered five numbers. There was a pause and then a click and he pulled the door open.

'How do you kno—'

'It is 03522. It is always the postal code of the place where the blocks are. Never changed from when the secret police needed to get into everywhere.'

'So what's the point in having it?'

Maksym shrugged. 'It makes people think they are safe.' As he traversed the narrow lobby and pressed the button for the elevator he added, 'People are strange.'

*

Bodhan Ravansenko's apartment was on the sixth floor. The lift doors haltingly stumbled backwards on grime filled tracks to reveal a corridor-cum-balcony, partially open to the elements and with a numbered sign that indicated apartments 1-120 were to the right and 121-242 to the left.

'Jesus, how many people live here?' Mark asked.

'In the whole of Troieshchyna,' Maksym said, 'maybe a quarter million.'

I turned left, led us down to apartment 192 and knocked on the door. Then Mark and I stood to one side. We knew Ravansenko was single and I wanted the six-foot-six tall, wide as an oak, broad fore-headed thug of a man that was Maksym Ponomarenko to be the only thing he saw when he answered my knock.

What I hadn't figured on was no answer.

We waited. Maksym looked down at me, shrugged and stepped away. Pulling out his phone he called his friend. A short exchange later and he came back to stand in front of the door. Lowering his voice, he said, 'My colleague say he only watch man enter block. He did not follow up to apartment, but he say no one has left through main door.'

'Are there other ways in and out? There has to be. The place is massive,' Mark whispered.

'Maybe, but we got here only five minutes after he did. He does not know he is followed. No reason to run.' Maksym thumped the front door again as if to punctuate his sentence.

This time his knock was answered. The noise of a chain and a bolt being slid back pre-empted the door opening inwards. For a big man, Maksym moved quickly. He thrust his hand under the chin of Ravansenko, gripping his throat tightly enough to lift him up on to tip-toes, but not hard enough to snap the neck of the scrawny-looking, thirty-four year old Deputy of IT Security. He pushed him back down the hallway as Mark and I bundled in behind him and shut the apartment door.

The short hallway had three doors off it. One on each side of the hallway, both closed. The third, open, at the end opposite the front door and the only lit area, afforded a glimpse of a kitchen bench. By the time Maksym, his throttled cargo, Mark and I were through and into the space, I could appreciate that the apartment designers had actually delivered a practical living area. It was small, but functional. The living-kitchen-dining-room offered all you could want, in a '1984' communist-ruled, utopian empire kind of way.

To the right hand side of the kitchen was a dining room table that had been converted into a computer workstation. While Maksym held Ravansenko against the far wall, Mark sat down in front of the PC.

'The USB isn't here, Luke,' he said, pressing the power button on what to me looked like a computer from the 1990s.

I moved towards Ravansenko, then stopped and considered what I had seen Rachel do when she was after information.

'Sit him down, please.'

Maksym moved to the living room couch, with the ragdoll of a man still in his grip. He threw him into the seat with a force that almost toppled the whole thing.

'Thanks,' I said and then nodded for Maksym to stand behind the couch. between it and the hallway, just in case our host decided to run for it.

I lifted one of the kitchen stools and sat down in front of the pale faced, but red-necked man. The outline of Maksym's hand was clearly visible where it had pressed hard on Ravansenko's throat. His eyes were wide with fear and now that he wasn't being choked, I expected him to start shouting, screaming, objecting to the intrusion, demanding to know why we were here, swearing and protesting his innocence. Instead, I got silence.

'Bodhan, we know what you did. We know you took a third set of data from the bank servers. We have you on camera and we know you downloaded it onto a USB drive. Where is it?'

He didn't look away, didn't adjust his position, didn't speak.

I inclined my head towards Maksym. 'Give me the drive now, or I will have my large friend here strip search you whilst holding you upside down.'

Maksym reached out and placed his left hand on Ravansenko's head. It was like he'd administered an electric shock. The smaller man's face looked even more aghast and his body jerked, as much as it could what with his head being held by a hand almost bigger than his skull. Still, though, he said nothing. I shrugged and stood up. Maksym adjusted his grip to under Ravansenko's armpits and lifted him.

One thing I did know from my days in the military was how to properly search someone. Unlike the movies, and the colloquialism, you don't 'pat down' a suspect. You get in close and roll the material of their clothes. Turn out the pockets, make them take off their shoes, get your hands into the natural cavities of the body; armpits, backs of knees, groin. I wasn't actually going to strip search him, nor was I going to be taking it to the extremes of internal cavities, I doubted even Ravansenko was likely to put a USB drive there, but when I had finished, I still had no USB.

'How are you getting on,' I said over my shoulder to Mark, while Maksym plonked the still frightened Bodhan back on the couch. The big man took up his position again, blocking any likely escape route.

'Believe it or not, this PC has still got a dial-up modem.'

I turned around. 'Seriously?' I tried to think of the last time I had used a PC that wasn't permanently connected to a broadband network.

'Yep.' Mark nodded. 'Bad news is the operating system is so old that every transmission of data is completely transparent.'

'Why's that bad?'

'Because our friend here hasn't transmitted any large amounts of data onto any third parties. If he had, in the last year or two, I'd

know it by now. This system is clean. Well, apart from the usual …
and some more unusual sites.'

I walked round to stand behind Mark and observe what he was
pointing at. The browser history listed rows of web addresses. No
doubt the sites themselves would be in Cyrillic, but the addresses
were all in English. I moved an empty mug aside from the desk so
I could see the screen better. Ravansenko's most visited site was at
the top of the list, Youngrussiannaturists.ua, closely followed by
all the big hitters of the porn world. Various sites that catered for
Asians, teens, twins, and occasionally twin Asian teens, plus a raft
of other usual suspects. Further down there were a couple I hadn't
expected. Transandtinytits.ua followed closely in the ranks of vis-
its over the last 30 days by, hotmen.ua. It seemed Bodhan might
be a little conflicted. Rachel had taught me to use every means at
my disposal in trying to get a source to open up with information.
Ravansenko was just that to me now. A source. However, the fact
he hadn't said anything was confusing me a little. The threat of
Maksym and the fear of potential violence being visited upon him
hadn't budged him. Perhaps the exploration of his sexual prefer-
ences might.

I looked back up from the computer screen and saw two men
in the hall. The closer of them was a mere step or two away from
the doorway behind Maksym. I registered the high-leg boots, jeans,
tight t-shirt over a thin but muscled torso and the short-cropped
jacket. A tattoo on the side of the man's neck showed a black N
with a thick line through the middle of it and the skinhead haircut
completed the look, but all of my shock at this sudden apparition
paled when he raised a pistol in his right hand. The gun began to
level out towards the back of Maksym's head. The muzzle less than
two feet from its intended target. It couldn't miss. My hand was
still next to the empty mug that I had moved earlier. I grabbed and
threw it in a single motion. At the same time I yelled, 'MAKSYM!'

The skinhead looked to me and saw the mug inbound to his
head. He half-twisted and the porcelain smashed harmlessly
against the door frame, but the movement of his head and the
readjusting of his gun hand to swing around to me had taken a
fraction of a second. It wasn't much, but it was enough. Maksym

really was quick for a big man. He swivelled at the waist and threw his left hand backwards in a vicious clubbing motion. The back of his fist connected solidly with the skinhead's left temple and the force of the blow cannoned the man's head into the same spot on the doorframe that the mug had just impacted. I doubted the inside of the skinhead's skull had fared much better than the mug. He dropped straight down in a folded heap. The second man, still in the hallway, tried to bring his own gun up, but Maksym closed the distance to him in one stride and punched him with a straight, full force, right hand. From where I stood it looked like the man's face had imploded. If anything, this second skinhead went down more rapidly than the first. It was like gravity had increased a hundredfold.

Maksym bent down and retrieved both guns. Looking past him I could see one of the doors, halfway up the hall, was open. The corner of a bed was visible. I started to walk forward but Maksym held up his hand for me to stay back. He put one of the retrieved pistols in his waist band and brought the other up into the aim. Then he very quietly, quickly and with a high-degree of professionalism cleared first the bedroom, then he opened the still closed door to the bathroom and ensured it held no more surprises either.

'It is clear,' he said, walking back towards the kitchen.

'Are you alright?'

'Yes, of course. Not a scratch,' he said and smiled broadly.

'Thank you,' I said.

'No. I do not think you need thank me. I think more the other way. He would have killed me if not for you.' Maksym gave the first skinhead a kick in the ribs as he passed. There was a muted grunt from the floor. 'I am the one who owes you. Thank you, Luke.'

I shook my head and told him to forget it.

He came back into the room and stood next to the couch. 'You want me to kill this?' He asked pointing to Ravansenko.

It had all happened so rapidly that Ravansenko hadn't moved from his position on the couch. Only as Maksym pointed to him did he attempt to sit forward. Mark, Maksym and I made towards him, but he held his hands up in surrender.

'No. No. Stop. I don't want trouble. Don't hit me.'

'Now you talk?' I said. Stealing data and ripping off clients was one thing, but this pathetic shit had known there were armed men in his apartment. He'd played us along knowing, or at least hoping that they would rescue him. I felt like asking Maksym to hit him like he'd hit the second skinhead. I felt like doing it myself. Instead I took a breath. 'Where's the USB?'

'They have it,' he said, twisting around to view the human carnage in his hallway. 'Him,' he added, pointing to the second skinhead.

Mark moved forward and I wondered if he was about to lay into Ravansenko. I considered that I would only half-heartedly try to stop him. Instead, he walked past him and knelt next to the second of the skinheads. The USB drive was in the first pocket he searched.

I was relieved we had the drive back, but the whole point of following Ravansenko home was so we could find out where he sent the data on to. To find out he handed it off to a bunch of skinheads was not going to help Pat Harris catch any bigger fish.

I sat back down on the stool and Maksym placed his hands onto Ravansenko's shoulders, forcing him down into the soft fabric of the couch.

'Who are they?' I asked, trying to sound like I was still contemplating having Maksym smash Ravansenko's brains all over the apartment.

'Please, you have to help me, they'll kill me if I tell you.'

I kept the cynical edge in my tone, 'That's not my concern. Who are they?'

It was Maksym who answered, 'They belong to Patriot of Ukraine. Fascist scum.'

The look on Ravansenko's face told me the answer was right. 'How do you know?' I asked.

'The tattoos on their necks.'

'How do a bunch of fascists turn a profit from skimmed credit card data? I wouldn't have thought they'd be sophisticated enough.' I asked it more to myself than to anyone in the room, but Ravansenko took it as a cue.

'They sell it to a Romanian gang.'

'What?'

'They sell the data to a Romanian gang, who sell it on to the Russian Mafia.'

'And just how the hell do you know that?' Mark asked, before I could.

'You have to get me out of here. Please. Then I tell you.'

'Tell me what you know or I swear to God, I will have my friend hit you like he hit them.' I had tried to make it sound as threatening as I could. I wasn't sure I had managed it, but Ravansenko's expression crumbled. As did his resolve to hold out.

'They come here to get the data. They bring their laptop with them. I do all the uploading for them. I know where the data goes.'

'Oh for fuck's sake,' Mark said. 'Where's this bloody laptop?'

Ravansenko pointed back up the hallway. 'They took it with them when you first knocked on door. They hide in bedroom.'

Mark was back in a few seconds with the retrieved laptop. 'How do you connect to the net?'

Ravansenko pointed to a drawer in the kitchen.

'Very nice,' Mark said, in appreciation of the small box he found. 'A portable 3G hotspot. I've seen these in the trade magazines, but I didn't know they were commercially available yet.'

'They buy them from Russian military supplies,' Ravansenko offered. 'Now will you help me?'

'Show us the data paths first,' I said as Mark set up the laptop and network hotspot on the dining room table.

It took less than five minutes for Mark to find what he needed. Five minutes more to plant the malware into the remote server location and one more minute to set up a cleaning routine that would hide all trace of where we had come from.

'That's it. As soon as this routine runs all the data on their servers will be wiped. They'll have no way to trace us and we'll have access to them anytime we want, so if they decide to try again we'll be re—'

I looked up. 'What's wrong, Mark?'

'There's another series of network storage sectors on this server.'

'Okay,' I said, not sure what he meant.

'Credit cards are identifiable, Luke. It's something Steve and Paul have taught me over the last few months. You can ID a card's issuing authority based on the first digits of the number sequence. Steve seems to know most of them on the planet at will. I don't, but I do know our own cards and a few other UK banks.'

'And?'

'And there's a whole folder of UK card data sequestered away in a partitioned sector of this server.'

I moved to stand beside him and out of the corner of my eye watched Maksym checking on the two skinheads in the hallway. They'd both regained consciousness, but the second man he hit was as far from properly conscious as you could get whilst still having your eyes open. I figured he would have had less concussion if he'd been run over by a bus. Regardless of their woozy state, Maksym had tied their hands and legs and gagged them for good measure.

I turned back to Mark. 'What does that mean?'

'It means that as well as skimming all the Ukrainian cards, at some point these Romanians have skimmed, or acquired somehow, a whole bunch of UK cards.'

'Weren't we going to delete all the data anyway? Can't you just delete this too?'

'I can … but I could also try and do a trace back to see where it came from first. See if we could identify a source in the UK.'

'How long will it take. These lads,' I said nodding in the direction of the hallway, 'are meant to be somewhere at some point and if they don't turn up, someone is going to come looking for them. I'd rather we weren't here when they do.'

'Fair enough. It'll take about five minutes to run Paul's tracking algorithm on it. If there's an identifiable source then we'll find it.'

'Then what?' I asked, still not sure what we would achieve.

'Then, if it turns out the source is in the UK we can hand it over to the civilian police and they can arrest the bastards.'

I laughed. 'Ahh … Mark Donoghue, of the RAF Police. I guess you can take the man out of the cops but …'

'Exactly.'

It took less than five minutes. When he was finished we let the other software routines run and the servers virtually disintegrated.

'Time to go,' I said to Maksym.

Ravansenko, who had sat immobile on the couch since showing Mark how to access the Romanian server, said, 'Please, Mr Frankland, please you have to help me. I have helped you. Please can you ask the bank, please. They will come and—'

'Be quiet,' Maksym said, cutting him off before taking me to one side and speaking quietly. 'What do you want to do with him?'

I had been putting off thinking about what would happen to the former Deputy IT Security Manager. The addition of former to his title was the easy part. I was always meant to fire him. The initial plan was to destroy the data and fire him from the bank. With Pat learning that Interpol weren't interested we'd doubted handing him over to the Ukrainian Police was even feasible, but now? Now, if I left him here, a bunch of skinheads would likely kill him within a day.

'I don't think the bank is equipped for a witness protection program,' I said.

'If you like, I can help. I have friends who might be able to get him out of Kiev. Get him to somewhere far away? Would you want me to try?'

'Definitely.'

Maksym switched to Ukrainian and offered Ravansenko a way out. Although I couldn't speak a word of the language, the expression on the man's face told me the offer had been generously and quickly accepted.

'He has fifteen minutes to pack what he can carry. My colleague outside will come and get him. But now, I take you to the airport, yes?'

*

The trip back to Boryspil International was uneventful and passed quietly. On arrival, Maksym alighted and shook my hand.

'You said I had no need to thank you. My girls would disagree. I will be in your debt.'

I shook his massive outstretched hand and Mark and I headed back to London and a date with the Metropolitan Police.

12

He tried to pull the straps on his body armour tighter. It was no use. The boron carbide plates of the Improved Outer Tactical Vest were as tight as they could possibly go. Figuring the new name of the armour sucked, he'd have preferred a Perfect Bullet Proof Suit, he was at least reassured by the reports of its performance. Not that it would help against an Improvised Explosive Device. Another bad choice of a name. Nothing much improvised when you were being supplied military grade explosives by a nation state just over the border. The Taliban IEDs were Invariably Extremely Deadly.

IEDs were not his concern when he was tucked up inside Firebase Phoenix, but that was all going to change in five minutes. He had been specifically invited to a scheduled Shura. The village heads of the settlements closest to the Pech River Road Project, a major engineering program designed to boost the local infrastructure and economy, wanted an update. So far the initiative had been working well enough, but the constant incursions by the Taliban were slowing progress considerably. If the work wasn't going to be constantly delayed and disrupted they, the US forces, had to get the locals on side. Accepting invitations for meals and talks was a massive part of that. Social interaction, trust, looking the local leaders in the eye and dealing with them on a personal level was the true meaning of 'hearts and minds'. The problem was, to win hearts and minds you had to shake hands, and you couldn't do that from within a firebase.

Dan hadn't been invited by name, but the local chiefs wanted the current commander of Phoenix, Captain Steve Mendoza, of Bravo Company, 1st Battalion, to share the latest intelligence on the tribes to the north-east. The groupings there, subtly different from their 'near-cousins' in the lower Korengal Valley, were up to something. No one knew if they were about to throw in their lot with the Taliban or come in alongside the National Afghan Forces loyal to President Karzai. It would be an insult if the Company's actual intelligence officer didn't come and deliver the briefing. So Dan was going outside the wire, for a trip in a Humvee to downtown Armageddon.

**

The noise of the engine was like a demonic Harpy. The high-pitched, intense wail vibrated through every part of his body in contact with one of the vehicle's surfaces. Feet, buttocks and back transmitted the jolts and jarring shudders of every bump and hump of the dirt track. He bowed his head forward to keep the rear of his helmet off the side wall of the Hummer. Ten minutes down the line and so far so good. The engine screamed a little more as it went through the gears and the vehicle slowed. Dan leant into the man next to him as they turned off to the right. The Humvee slowed more. Then stopped. Time to walk.

Strength-sapping was what Dan had been told about the terrain between the drop off point and the villages. It hadn't come close. The darkness of the pre-dawn was turned green by night vision goggles, but there was nothing to be done about the temperature. In the summer, Afghanistan could make hell seem cold, but in the grip of winter, hell froze over.

The ground was rock hard, sometimes covered in a foot of snow, sometimes swept by the wind to reveal rutted sand-coloured tracks beneath. Snow also lay on the small terraces of barren fields.

Slivers of soil, that in the summer provided meagre crops for the families of the Korengal. Dan was amazed at how some of their houses seemed to cling perilously to the mountain sides. Further up, the snow-capped peaks provided a spectacular backdrop, but the bitter wind coming over them and dropping into the valley was harsh. The water in the ditches and irrigation canals froze solid most days and every night. Yet, despite the air showing every puff of his breath in an icy mist, and being able to hear and feel the crunch of snow under his feet, Dan was sweating.

He carried 60lbs of standard gear, plus his M4 assault rifle and as much extra ammunition as he could manage. Within 500 yards of negotiating dirt tracks, frozen ditches, rutted mud and rocky outcrops, he felt like he'd sat in a bath. His clothes were drenched and sheets of sweat poured down his face. The freezing wind ripped into the moisture and turned everything instantly cold.

Staff Sergeant Morrie Lieberman, 1st Squad's leader, dropped back every so often to check in with him and with Private Mercer and Corporal Krakowiak. Dan figured they'd been assigned by Lieberman to look after him. True, he was well used to coming under fire now, almost every night in the confines of the base, but patrolling these tracks; that was going to be different. He guessed Mercy and Kracker, as they were called by all in the platoon, were to make sure 'Captain Dan', would not flake out when the first rounds came in.

Captain Dan. He smiled to himself. He'd been so pleased when he'd finally been promoted and could leave Lieutenant Dan and all its *Forrest Gump* connotations behind. He realised with a little start that his mind had wandered. He refocussed on the back of Mercy's head and watched him climb over a small collection of boulders that looked as if they had just popped up fresh in the middle of the path. The night vision was beginning to bloom around the edges with the merest hint of the sunrise that was beginning to colour the sky. Dan took the head-rig off and paused before stepping through the rocks.

'Hey Kracker,' he called and held out the goggles. Kracker closed up the gap and stowed the NVGs in Dan's pack. Then Dan reciprocated. By the time that was done Mercy was about twenty yards ahead on the track. Dan placed his feet carefully in the small gaps between the strange little rock shapes. The spaces were flat and sandy with snow caught in and around the bottom edges of the boulders. He moved slowly, careful not to twist an ankle. Once through, he waited for Kracker, then both hustled to catch-up. The path was narrow so they jogged along in single file. Not too close together. His training at Benning had hammered that into him on so many occasions. Keep your distance. Don't become isolated, don't bunch up.

His knees and legs were already hurting. He'd not say or do anything to draw attention and he sure as heck wasn't going to be falling out of the patrol anytime soon, but it didn't change the fact he could feel the effort in his thighs and calves. Fitness had never been a concern of his. He'd always liked training in the gym and running, but Fort Benning had taken his inherent fitness to new levels. The life of an infantry soldier was one of hauling loads and fighting. He'd had to meet the same tough physical standards just to be considered for attachment to the 173rd in Italy. He began to consider if he'd have tried as hard knowing where he was going to end up … But the answer was simple. Of course he would have. He'd never not tried to win. Never given up on anyth— The thought hung, half-formed. He had given up on one thing. He saw Luke in his mind's eye and strangely, instead of sadness, felt a smile on his frozen lips. It surprised him. Not smiling at the memory, but that those thoughts could occur halfway up the side of a valley in Afghanistan. He looked ahead, then a glance behind, then back up the slope before looking to his left and peering down to the valley floor. He realised this is what one of the instructors at Fort Benning had meant.

Master Sergeant Williams, with his salt and pepper hair and rumbling, sonorous voice had called them together during a field-exercise. 'You'll not concentrate for hours and hours at a time. Can't be done. You need to get into a routine. The Routine.' He'd pulled out a pack of smokes and told them to take a squat on the sandbagged revetments. 'I've patrolled the streets of Kuwait, dirt-poor villages in Haiti, been shot at in Baghdad and blown up in Kabul. Nothing changes. Routine is always the same. Part of my mind searches for the person trying to kill me and the other part of my mind thinks random thoughts. Keeps you sane, finding the zone. Patrolling is about being alert. But not constantly on edge, not like a hair-trigger. You do that and you'll be wearing a straight-jacket before you get back to base, let alone back home. Hell, you're not gonna to come back home if you're wound like a coiled spring. So walk and watch. Keep your peripheral vision sharp, glance left and right and up ahead and just behind. Then do it all again. And think random thoughts.'

Dan realised he'd forgotten about the Master Sergeant's words until just then. Now he'd found his zone, without being conscious of it. He was, however, conscious of the strain in his calves.

The land had been rising gently, but now there was a distinct step-up in the elevation change. The track, such as it was, snaked and twisted before flattening out again. It was like a series of terraces, each one rising until, at the top, they would come to the village. There they'd meet all the head men of the area, brief them, eat whatever lunch was offered, and make their way back out. A rendezvous with the Humvees and back to Phoenix in good time for whatever evening activities the Taliban had planned.

By now the sky had turned from black to deep grey. There was just enough light to pick out features in the middle-distance. He glanced up at the higher ridges, with their rock faces and dimpled holes. A glacial valley. Ice had long ago hued out caves, holes and indentations from the bedrock. Like some mysterious ice-age hand had understood that the Afghans in the ages to come, would require firing positions and scraped depressions for snipers, along with hidden nooks and crannies for weapons caches.

He glanced behind and could see the remainder of 1st Squad trailing in his wake. To their rear was the Platoon command team including the Platoon leader, Lieutenant Cotter, accompanied by Captain Mendoza and some of his Company command team.

A distance behind them 2nd Squad trekked along and at the foot of the latest series of ridges, he could make out the staggered line of 3rd Squad. Between 2nd and 3rd came the weapons squad. All in all, forty-seven US soldiers, Dan included, to get Mendoza, his

Master Sergeant and Dan himself to have a sit-down lunch with the next-door neighbours. It was crazy.

When he'd first arrived in-country and watched the futility of the patrols going out, the constant firefights around Phoenix and the even scarier attacks being directed at Outpost Restrepo up on Table Rock, he'd wondered, why bother?

The Army used helicopters for resupply and most other tasks they could. Most of the daily foot patrols were being engaged in firefights and never achieving half their objectives, so why not scrap them? Use the helicopters to drop the patrols directly into the villages. He'd even mentioned it to the Battalion Commander, Lieutenant Colonel McGinnis, when he'd come out to Phoenix for a briefing. Dan had been surprised by the answer he had received.

'I totally agree with you Captain, seems like a plan,' McGinnis had said.

Before Dan had a chance to respond, the Lieutenant Colonel continued, 'Thing is. We're here to make the locals believe we're a better bet than the Taliban. Difficult to do that if we can't be seen walking into their villages. Sends entirely the wrong message.'

Dan understood, but McGinnis, an out and out, born and bred warrior wasn't done. 'Also, we have a task to secure this area for the population and to meet and defeat the Taliban and any others who want to try to make this place a safe haven for terrorists again. We do that by mounting fighting patrols. You're attached to the infantry now, Captain Stückl. We are designed for a single purpose. We close with and kill the enemies of America. We do it often and we do it well and we do it on the ground.'

His impromptu speech hadn't been accompanied by a halo of light or a rendition of *The Star Spangled Banner*, nor a shout of 'Hoo-Ya', but the smiles on the infantry officers standing behind the Battalion Commander had been proof enough. Dan figured they were all a little crazy. Here and now, months after that first briefing, he figured he was too.

He glanced up and down and up ahead again. Staff Sergeant Lieberman appeared just to the side of the track. Dan saw him say a few words to Mercy. A smile and a pat on the back for the youngest soldier in the squad, Dan wasn't even sure the kid was shaving on a daily basis. After the brief exchange, the kid seemed to walk taller. Lieberman was a good leader. Dan was impressed. He himself smiled as the Staff Sergeant approached.

'You taken a drink yet, Sir?'

'Yes, Staff, that I have,' Dan said and tapped the top of his water bottle.

'Good, Sir. Pleased to hear it. I know y'all been keeping fit in the outside gym on base, but this is going to be different fer ya.'

'Roger that.'

'This ole ground ain't no treadmill,' he chuckled and fell in beside Dan, kicking a dislodged snow-covered rock aside.

Dan said quietly, 'I'm good Staff. I really appreciate you looking out for me, but I'm okay. No need to be making the trip up and down the line for me. You'll be travelling twice the distance you should be.'

Equally quietly, Lieberman said, 'I appreciate that, Sir and I am sure yer good fer yer word, but it ain't you I come to check on. I'd be looking out for my boys anyways. You jus' happen to be another couple of steps further on.'

They walked together, side by side, Lieberman just off the edge of the rutted track. Each man glanced ahead, then left into the chasm of the valley, then back over their shoulders where Kracker plodded along. The terrain was growing increasingly rugged and Dan could feel the hammer of his heart beats. His breath, like Lieberman's, coming in rapid white puffs of condensation. The sun struggled higher and the sky lightened to a dull, overcast. Heavy clouds threatened snow. Topping another rise and moving around the latest spur of the valley, the first of the outlying smaller villages came into view. One track cut through two rows of houses. Not houses like Dan or Staff Sergeant Lieberman had grown up in. These were tall boxes of sand coloured blocks. One row above the central track, one just below. Both appeared to grow, in some gravity-defying way, straight out of the mountainside.

Children's voices, laughing and happily squealing came from around the corner of the sandy brick house to Dan's front.

'Gotta go, Sir,' Lieberman said and hustled forward to take up his slot second from the front of 1st Squad.

Dan kept walking and soon the six little boys responsible for the laughing came into view. They were frantically running around in a circle. Just little kids playing catch, oblivious to the snaking stream of soldiers making their way through their early morning playground. That was a good sign and a bad one. Good that they were still in their village, not cleared out by Taliban about to launch an ambush. Bad that such young children thought foot patrols of heavily armed men were nothing extraordinary.

They stopped running in circles when Lieberman threw a handful of wrapped candy across to them. It turned their game into a ground scrum with accompanying high-pitched squeals.

A door opened in one of the houses up ahead. A figure appeared in the shadows. Dan felt his adrenaline kick-in and watched Lieberman and the soldiers close to him raise their weapons into the aim. Corporal Torres, on point, also had his weapon coming up, the muzzle traversing the open doorway. Dan reacted slower but his M4 rifle was also trained on the darkness, the open door, the figure in the shadows. He felt his heart beat increase. He saw the shake in his arm.

A veiled woman stepped out and glanced towards the noisy children. Without seeing her face, Dan understood. The nod of her head, the glance across to the soldiers, the raised hand in greeting. A mother come out to see why the children had screamed louder than usual. A mother acknowledging the gift of candy and the soldiers who gave it. No Taliban.

The rifles lowered and the squad continued to move through the village. Once round the next spur, Dan saw Staff Sergeant Lieberman crouched at the corner of the last house. Beyond him a wide open stretch of terrain about 50 yards long, before the ground once more afforded a modicum of natural cover. In the middle of the 50 yards was a fragile looking wall that was just there, in the middle of nowhere. Mercy was kneeling next to it, hunkering down for all the cover it could afford him. It was a strange place to put a wall. It looked, like so much of this country, unkempt, ramshackle. Yet the wall had probably stood here since the British Empire troops had passed by in their bright red tunics. It had probably survived the onslaught of the Russians and served the Mujahedeen defenders. Now it was witness to the full might of the US Army and had become a stopping place in the middle of a sniper's paradise.

Lieberman held out a hand and halted Dan. 'Okay, Sir. You'll dash to the wall as soon as Mercy makes his move. Hold there until I tell Kracker to make his run, then you move to the cover where Corporal Torres is now. We have you and Mercy, then you and Kracker running together, clear?'

'Clear.'

'Don't stop. Speed is the key. Ready.'

Dan crouched and put his foot forward, like a sprinter. 'Ready.'

'Three, two, one …'

13

'GO, GO, GO.' The Enforcer battering ram, pillar-box red and weighing sixteen kilograms, swung back in the police constable's hands and smashed in the bottom right of the front door. A crashing, splintering of wood and a bang as the remnants of the door cannoned off the interior wall was accompanied by a cacophony of shouts.

'ARMED POLICE, ARMED POLICE, ARMED POLICE!'

The eight blue-clad officers, their Heckler and Koch MP5 submachine guns providing covering arcs of fire to one another, snaked quickly through the shattered doorway. Four, in two pairs, entered the rooms off the hallway, whilst the other four Specialist Firearms Officers alighted the stairs. More shouts of, 'Armed Police' sounded throughout the three-storey terrace house. These were followed in turn with staggered shouts of 'Clear, Clear!' as each room was found to be empty. Not that big a surprise at 3:30 am.

I was impressed. The tactical entry had been swift and from my vantage point, on the far side of the street next to the CO19 support vehicles, it seemed flawless. I was also reminded that these guys, and the one woman on the team, did this professionally and unlike myself and Maksym were not likely to be caught out by someone hiding in a bedroom. In fact, after only a few minutes, it turned out that one of the bedrooms was the only occupied room in the house.

Lights in other bedrooms in other houses along Guilford Street were coming on. This northern salient of Holborn, caught between the pincers of Clerkenwell and St Pancras was not used to such a disturbance at such a time of the morning. This was a fashionable area of WC1 where terraced townhouses would set their owners back half a million pounds at least. Faces appeared behind the twitch of curtains, an occasional front door opened a sliver. The disturbed residents quickly retreated inside once they saw the armed police officers streaming out of their neighbour's house.

It was a far cry from what I had been expecting. When Mark and I had returned from Kiev, armed with the information about the London end of the credit card scams, we'd met up with Paul and Steve. It took the three of them about ten minutes to locate the main server that was sending the stolen card information to Kiev and from there, onward to the Romanians.

They'd briefed me and I'd briefed Pat Harris. He'd brought in William Carmichael, the head of Bateleur's physical security, who had contacts in the Met Police. From arriving back in London, to the Met having warrants issued, took less than twelve hours. They asked if Paul would tag along with their arrest team. As soon as they secured the house they wanted Paul to secure any data on the computers inside. It was his algorithm that had tracked down the systems that we knew had, at some point, forwarded the data to Kiev. The police knew that there was a chance the data would be rigged with an in-built self-destruct capability. They were also aware that to disable any coded protection was beyond their skills, and if they lost the data, then they lost all the evidence. Paul was delighted to help, but I was his boss and I couldn't let my most junior team member head out on a police raid without making sure he was okay. So here I was.

It was simply that I had expected *here* to be somewhere in the depths of South Harrow, or Tower Hamlets, not next door to Bloomsbury. That surprise paled when two unarmed constables brought out the only occupant of the house. I didn't know who or what I'd expected, but I suppose my unconscious bias had presumed it would be a bunch of twenty-to-thirty-something males from the former Eastern Bloc. What I got was one old man who looked about ninety, wearing pyjamas, a heavy dressing gown and grey slippers. Despite his age, the officers had handcuffed him and held a firm grip on both his elbows. He was escorted to a waiting patrol car and helped in to the back seat. One of the police put his hand on the old man's head in the way I'd seen on so many cop shows. I wondered if lots of people used to hit their heads on the door sills before that became a thing.

Superintendent Sara Matthews, the Silver Commander on the raid, tapped my shoulder.

'You ready?'

'Yes,' I said, wondering if I actually was. While Paul headed in to the house to secure the evidence, I followed Superintendent Matthews to her car and took a ride to Holborn Police Station.

I'd baulked at the offer initially, but Pat Harris was determined that we should be seen to be actually doing something concrete in the fight against cybercrime. The offer for me to sit in and monitor the interviews of whoever was arrested in the house on Guilford Street was exactly the sort of thing he wanted. Superintendent Matthews had reassured me a little, when she said that I'd be watching from a video suite next to the interview room. I was only there to assist the detectives who, by their own admission, had a limited grasp on how computer crime manifested itself in the real world. She'd ended her pitch by saying I was the nearest they had to an expert witness. Pat had said yes before I could object.

**

The scene playing out on the screen in front of me was strangely familiar, yet I'd never been near a police interview in my life. The physical surroundings of the room where the old man sat and the preliminaries, setting up of tape recorders and the like, was exactly as I'd seen on so many TV police dramas. The Detective Sergeant next to me, Ben Squire, leant forward and turned up the volume on the monitor in time to hear the lead detective start proceedings.

'The time is 7:15 am on Wednesday the 14th of January 2009. I am Detective Inspector Jack Wood, also present is,' Wood paused and the Detective Sergeant next to him said, 'Detective Sergeant Annie Rice.'

'And,' Wood said and waited. No one spoke. 'State your name and date of birth for the tape.'

The old man smiled, then spoke with a voice that was full and strong. 'Thomas Elijah Solomon, 29th of February 1928.'

'The 29th?' Rice asked.

'Yeah. I'm a leap year babe. Means I'm only twenty. Looking good on it, ain't I?' Solomon patted the back of his fingers under the deep jowls of his cheeks and chin.

Rice and Wood smiled wryly at the old man.

Wood pointed to the solicitor sitting next to Solomon. 'And ...'

'David Probert, legal counsel for Mr Solomon.'

Wood took a sip of water from a plastic cup before continuing, 'Thomas—'

'Tom, call me Tom, me old mum only used to call me Thomas when I was in trouble.'

I had to admire the old fella's guile. I also realised that close up, he was a lot stronger looking than the frail old man I had assumed when I'd seen him led from the house in his dressing gown. He might have been in his eighties, but Tom was a vibrant old rogue.

Wood duly obliged him. 'Tom, I have to remind you that you remain under caution and that you do not have to say anything, but it may harm your defence if you do not mention when questioned something which you later rely on in court. Anything you do say may be given in evidence. Do you understand these rights?'

'Yeah. It ain't my first dance around the floor, son.'

Wood ignored the rebuff.

'You are the owner of 115 Guilford Street, London, WC2.'

'Yes.'

'Do you live there on your own?'

'On occasion. I 'ave friends over sometimes.'

'But you are the only permanent resident?'

'Yeah, I guess so.'

'And is all the m—'

Solomon turned to Probert who cut Detective Inspector Wood off in mid-sentence.

'Detective Inspector, my client has a statement that he'd like to make before we go any further. I believe it will save you an awful lot of time.'

I could feel DS Squire next to me almost bristle with annoyance. Under his breath he said, 'That didn't take long.'

'What do you mean?' I asked.

Squire inclined his head towards the monitor. 'Defence 101. Listen and learn why this is a bollocks of a job.'

I turned my attention back to the screen. Probert was handing over a sheet of paper.

'My client has had a number of friends, associates, colleagues and loose acquaintances staying within his house for years. He likes to help out those less fortunate visitors to London, who cannot afford the astronomical rents in the capital. So he lets them stay with him, rent free. They get a leg up and once they have secured a job and their own place, they move on.'

'What has that go—'

Probert cut Wood off again. 'Over the years, a number of these acquaintances and friends have left belongings behind and Mr Solomon has looked after them, until they come back to retrieve their possessions.'

I suddenly knew what DS Squire had meant. Probert, in his mid to late-fifties, a lithe but officious looking man and apparently not a freely provided lawyer of the court, but a highly paid private counsel, was still talking.

'Mr Solomon is willing to cooperate fully with you, but on the understanding that none of the computer equipment within his home belongs to him, nor is he familiar with any of its operations, programs or data stored within it. It is simply there, in his house, waiting for a friend to pick it up. The details of that friend are as written on the sheet of paper I have just handed to you.'

DS Rice picked the paper off the table like it was contaminated. She read aloud, 'Mohammed Ivanov. From Sofia, Bulgaria. Came to London in January 2008. Left in April 2008. Has not been in touch with Mr Solomon, despite repeated attempts to get him to come and remove his computers.' She set the paper down and looked sideways to her DI.

Wood's body language betrayed him. I was surprised. I had expected a decisive back and forth and the detective to win the day. That's how the TV shows went. Instead, even before Wood opened his mouth again, I knew he'd lost.

'So, Tom, your story is that the two massively powerful machines in your basement with their high-speed Internet connections and multiple redundancies, are nothing to do with you and that you are merely looking after them for a friend.'

Solomon grinned as he answered, 'Precisely. That internetty thing? I don't pay for that. All done by me ol' mate, Mo. Remote like. Direct debit I fink. I'm sure you can check.'

'And Mo, that is Mohammed Ivanov, is it?'

'Yeah, Mo. Nice guy. Shame is, I fink old Ivanov as a name is a bit like Smiff here like. Bit common. 'At's why I ain't had much luck tracking him dain.'

'Of course you haven't.' Wood said. 'Perhaps we will have more luck.'

'Perhaps you will … Course, not much to be done anyways, is there?'

Wood let the question hang in the air.

Solomon continued, 'I mean, I guess what with all your armed police and search teams in my 'ouse, you must fink there's somefink valuable on those machines. Mustn't you. Fing is, don't matter.'

I was confused at the blatant front of the old man. Surely the defence that the machines weren't his would be laughed out of court and anyway, it was the data that was key to this. Thousands of stolen credit card details on a machine in his house would see him put away. But I worried I was missing something. It came clear soon enough. Solomon leaned forward and took a breath. When he next spoke, all trace of the heavy Cockney accent was gone. He spoke in the manner of an educated and refined professional.

'Now look Detective Inspector Wood. I don't have any record of ownership for those machines and I don't pay the bills for the network. I may, however, know a few things … that Mo told me.'

'Mo told you. Did he?' Wood's voice was heavy with resignation.

'Yes. That and the fact that I like to keep abreast of current affairs. I know, for example, that if someone had stolen a whole mass of data that could be valuable to some third parties, then the thing to do would be to store that actual, illegal data on a server that exists in another place entirely. Lost in a myriad on ones and noughts somewhere in the middle of Texas or Arizona, or better still, China, Egypt, the Dominican Republic or maybe Venezuela. perhaps even Ukraine.

'Because if one did that, then the Metropolitan Police wouldn't have any jurisdiction over that data. The transfer of the valuable information would occur over networks owned by everybody and nobody. Like a pirate on the high seas. International waters of data and information flow. Again, not something the Met are going to be able to say belongs to their patch.

'And finally, if the illegal data was taken in the first place by means of electronic skimmers fitted to cash machines, allegedly, or lifted off compromised websites, then there wouldn't be so much as a physical credit card anywhere to be found. All in all, Mo would effectively be as clean as a whistle, even if you did find him.'

Solomon sat back in his chair and Wood and Rice suspended the interview. I turned to DS Squire. 'What are they doing?'

'I imagine they're going to wait for your boy, Paul, is it?'

I nodded.

'For him to come back from the house and tell us what physical data is on the machines. If the old man is right and none of it is actually in London, then in less than forty-eight hours, I presume Mr Solomon will walk.'

'But surely that's impo—' I stopped because the reality was that yes, it was entirely possible. Paul's code had found the systems that had, at some point in the past, forwarded UK card information to Kiev, but if there was no further data left on them, and if any illegal data that he could find was stored in another country, then what crime had been committed in the UK? 'Son of a b—'

'My thoughts exactly,' said Squire. 'This bullshit is why cyber fraud is so hard for us to do anything about and why we need guys like you to come and help us more and more. We don't have the measure of this. It's like international drug cartels, but without the drugs being landed on shore. How the hell do we arrest a string of data that is somewhere in the ether?'

I shook my head slowly as I didn't have an answer. 'What was with the list of countries he gave?'

Squire half-smiled. 'That was him being a cocky bastard.'

I frowned in response.

'Non-extradition countries. Even if we found someone to blame, we couldn't go after them if they're in those places.'

I sighed. 'What a list to know by heart.'

'Most of them haven't signed up to the Budapest Convention on Cybercrime either.'

'Ukraine have,' I said, finally hitting on a subject I was familiar with.

'True,' Squire agreed. 'But good luck trying to get a conviction through their law courts.'

Having seen the squalor and dereliction of the Troieshchyna housing estate, I had to think his assessment was accurate.

'You know Solomon's house is just round the corner from the Charles Dickens Museum?' Squire said.

I hadn't, so I shook my head, still lost in thought.

'Dickens had Fagan and the Artful Dodger train Oliver Twist in and around Bloomsbury and Gray's Inn. All the streets round where old man Solomon's house is. Fashionable place even back then, but the old Peelers had it a lot easier in those days.'

'Did they?' I asked, still distracted and hoping that Paul would be able to retrieve something incriminating off the servers.

'Yeah, I think so. Damn sight easier to transport someone to Australia for seven years penal servitude when they've picked a pocket or two and still have the stuff in their possession. But now-adays, well … you hardly need a fence when you're stealing a string of numbers off a magnetic strip and sending it across networks in neat little packets of data.'

I looked at the screen and the old man in the next door room. He was a digital fence for the modern era. He was untouchable.

14

The Shura was dragging on and Dan was becoming increasingly worried. The signals intelligence teams who regularly intercepted Taliban communications, were indicating that the chatter on the net was increasing. Something was moving in the Korengal Valley and the longer Bravo Company were delayed here, in what was more and more a waste of time briefing for men whom Dan didn't trust as far as he could throw, the more chance of running into trouble on the way home.

Eventually, at almost noon, Captain Mendoza stood up, shook the hands of all and made an exit. The trek back down the valley would be made in bright sun, albeit the temperatures were still barely above freezing, but the sky had cleared and visibility was good. In the Korengal, that worked both ways.

Mendoza's command team waited for Bravo Company to shake itself out of perimeter protection, which it had mounted throughout the Shura, and back into a patrol orientation. The three rifle squads and the heavy weapon squad reformed themselves and headed back down to the rendezvous point with the Humvees. The only difference was 1st Squad, with Dan in tow, would be bringing up the rear.

An hour after leaving, and with the return dash across sniper alley done, they entered the village where the kids had been playing in the morning. It was quiet, but Dan wasn't concerned. He checked his watch. Almost one-thirty in the afternoon and the children would be down at the district school. Tacit proof that not having the Taliban in charge was a good thing, for not only the village boys, but the girls too, were getting an education.

He glanced behind to see Kracker casually looking up to the houses above the track. Dan was still looking at him when the right hand side of the Corporal's body disappeared in a ball of grey and black and sand and rocks. The sound came a fraction of a second later. A sharp, massively loud crack, with a rumbling echo. The force of the explosion knocked Dan off his feet. He twisted onto his side, deafened. Looking down the length of his body and past his feet, he stared towards Kracker. One leg, half a torso and a head with no jaw stared lifelessly back at him.

Dan twisted again to look forward. Another swirling cloud of dust was rising up at the head of the track, where it left the far end of the village. In between he could see the remnants of 1st Squad running and ducking for cover. He rolled onto his back and raised his head to look down at his legs. They were still there. Intact. So were his arms. He shook his head but still could hear nothing. His body felt sore, and when he focused on his chest he saw fragments of rocks and metal shards peppering his body armour. He dived his hands in between it and his combat jacket. Pulling his hands out quickly and turning them over, close to his face, he saw no blood. Again he thrust his hands in and checked, lower down. Again there were no tell-tale signs he was wounded. The armour had done exactly what it was meant to, stupid name or not.

He sat up and saw a puff of dust next to his left leg. Another appeared. And another. He felt the frown on his face deepening as he tried to figure out what he was looking at. Then, in ears still muffled, he heard the intensely sharp crack of what he knew was a rifle round passing extremely close to his head. It was like a light coming on. He knew what the puffs of dirt were. Incoming fire. He checked to his right hand side. No puffs. He rolled that way and crawled towards the nearest house. He felt an intense pain in his lower leg. Like a hot poker being put through his calf. He crawled faster. The stock of his M4 clubbed him in the face as he leopard-crawled across snow and sand. The alcove of the door was less than a body-length away. The sounds of rifle fire, rocket launchers and the shouts of his comrades began to reassert themselves in his ears. He raised himself up to take the last step into cover.

The force of the round hitting his chest knocked him sideways. He spun backwards and tried to catch a breath, one hand grabbed the side of the doorway and then what felt like a hammer blow hit him in the head. Darkness folded in around him and he felt himself falling. His last thought was not profound. He wondered if the Taliban gave kids candy.

15

Pat Harris slapped me on the back. 'Cheer up, Luke. You did as well as could be expected and the National High Tech Crime Unit is delighted.'

'But the old man walked away scot-free,' I said.

'True, but his operation is shut down and we did a good thing. The Ukrainian Bank is back in reasonable standing, our credibility with the Met Police is top notch and the bank liaison teams are doing a great job. All in all, you've done marvellously. I'm very pleased. Now, drink?'

He pointed me towards the long buffet table that was weighed down with drinks and finger-food of all descriptions. The room was packed with bank employees, most of whom I didn't know, but my team, as the main reason for the gathering, were of course all here. This was Pat's way of thanking us and raising our kudos, and his, with the top leadership.

I couldn't shake the feeling that we could have done better, but when Paul had found no data on the servers in Tom Solomon's house, there wasn't much left that we could do. We'd left a couple of tell-tale software trackers in place, but we fully expected the actual machines to be replaced wholesale by the gangs Solomon was working with in short order. It would make sense that they wouldn't trust anything the police had been forensically examining. Paul said he had put in a failsafe, but it would be of no use to the police.

I picked up a glass, poured another gin and looked for the tonic. The two small glass bottles in sight were empty. To my left a voice said, 'Looking for this?'

I turned to see one of the hired barmen for the function. He was tall, broad-shouldered with a blonde buzz-cut, a lantern jaw, a diamond-stud earring and a passing resemblance to actor Jason Statham. He held a small tonic bottle in a large outstretched hand.

'Liam?' I said, my hand only half way towards the bottle.

He grinned. 'Hello, Luke, how've you been?'

'I'm g—good.' I hesitated and glanced around, too quickly. I told myself to take a breath. Calm myself. I reached to take the offered tonic.

He didn't let go. Not instantly. He held eye contact with me for a moment too long and I felt a surge of adrenaline course through me. His little finger brushed against my hand. Leaning in fractionally, he said, almost in a whisper, 'Long time no see.' Then he released the bottle and straightened up.

I had flushed red, but Liam and I were isolated at the table and no one in the room would have seen the exchange. Not yet.

I poured the tonic and could see a slight tremor in my hand. I took another calming breath. 'Yeah, it's been a while. Five years? Out in Qatar?'

The former paratrooper smiled. 'Five and a bit. You look as if you've done alright,' he said, looking me up and down before glancing around the room.

'You too,' I replied and instantly regretted it. He was a hired barman at a bank function. Unless he owned the hire company, which I doubted. Liam was many things, but I couldn't see him as entrepreneurial.

'Yeah, I've done really well,' he said sarcastically, pointing up and down his own body, uniformed as it was in black trousers, white shirt and black bow tie.

My eyes lingered on his torso. Some things hadn't changed. 'Are you living locally?' I asked and wasn't sure why I had.

'Fairly.'

I paused, considering options. The thought of Dan, holding me in his arms in a bed in the Lake District flashed through my mind. That was gone and my life had been richer for it and much, much poorer for the loss.

Since then, the truth was, I'd been lonely. Perhaps ...

Liam cut off my thoughts before I could formulate a plan. As if sensing my internal dilemma he said, 'When you're bored with all of this, come find me. We,' he said, indicating his colleagues behind the buffet table, 'are only booked until nine. After we clear up I could do with something proper to eat and drink in surroundings more ... amenable. Join me? If you want to?'

**

Liam Travistock had looked much the same when I first saw him, five years before. Same buzz-cut hair, same jaw, same physique, but the desert combats and the Parachute Regiment's maroon beret had suited him better than black trousers and a now, open-necked, white shirt. He'd also rolled his sleeves up and I could see the Gothic font of "ENGLAND" on his right forearm and the smiling death head, with dog tags twisted around it on his left. I knew, from our shared time in the middle east, that he also had a full rendition of the Para's cap badge, motto and the III for the 3rd Battalion, tattooed on his upper left pec.

I inclined my head to his forearm. 'Got any more since last I saw you?

'A few,' he said, pointing his thumb over his shoulder. 'A big one on my back.' He raised his left leg. 'A smaller one on my calf. You might get to see them if you're lucky.' He grinned and stared me in the eye.

I felt the stirrings of emotions that I hadn't felt for a while. But emotion wasn't the right word. Passion, perhaps. Need, certainly. If I went home with Liam, or more likely, invited him to come home with me, it would be passion and need. Rough passion if I recalled accurately our last meeting five years ago. Very rough, frantic and physical. Raw, animalistic even. Everything I had needed, stuck in the middle of a war that I had known, even then, was illegitimate. Now, with each passing year and each "new" revelation by some lying quisling of a politician, the public was let into a little more of how the situation had been massaged for some greater political gambit to be played out. Weapons of Mass Delusion. I still detested the deceit of those who were meant to be our political "Masters". I considered all of them to be no better than something I would scrape off my shoe. I'd seen the intelligence, I knew the truth.

I'd left the forces, as had Liam but the likes of Dan, still serving and still doing the bidding of idiots, made me agitated. At least being an intelligence officer, wherever Dan was, he'd be out of harm's way. Like I did, every day, I wondered what he was doing. I suddenly realised that all this time, Liam had still been talking. I refocussed.

'... so I was out. I'm okay now like. Well, I—.' He hesitated and an expression I couldn't read clouded his face for a moment. Then it was gone and he kept speaking. 'You look like you've fallen on your feet. You must be making a ton of cash.'

I glanced again at his forearms and his flat stomach, the white fabric of his shirt taught against his body. I picked up my drink. Three quarters of a high-ball glass full of gin and a splash of tonic.

I downed it in one. 'Let's go.'

**

I woke early.

Liam slept soundlessly on his back, the sheets and duvet kicked off him. I checked the alarm clock and considered calling in sick. I could have legitimately claimed that I'd fallen onto a path littered with jagged rocks and on my way down, scraped my back against a series of sharp railings. I had the bruises and scratches to prove it.

I let my gaze slowly wander the length of the man next to me. Then I gave a sigh and swung my legs out of the bed. I had to go into work. I could always re-visit this later.

By the time I had showered and dressed, Liam was awake, propped up in the bed, leaning back against all the pillows.

'Comfortable?' I asked.

'Yes, thank you.'

'I have to go. Help yourself to breakfast, feel free to stay as long as you like. In fact ...' I paused and smiled at him.

'Y..eeee..ss?' he said, drawing the word out in a playful tease.

'I wouldn't be disappointed if you were still here when I got back.'

'Ahh I see. Am I to be your plaything?'

'Ha! You a plaything? You weren't the one who was being thrown about like a ragdoll all night.'

'Perhaps ...'

He gave me the same youthful, teasing grin that had attracted me the first time we met, in the forces compound in Qatar. I glanced around my apartment's bedroom. The floor-to-ceiling window looking out over London. The fixtures specifically designed and tastefully applied. The furniture, my furniture, high-end modern mixed with beautifully appointed antique pieces. The framed limited edition prints of original 19th century Vanity Fair cartoons, hanging next to the reproduction of Rhinebeck's panorama of London. A long, long way from the dust and heat and tackiness of the Qatar Club.

'Perhaps all sorts of things,' I said. 'But for now, I've got to go. See you later?'

'I have a corporate bar function to go to tonight, but I'll give you a call afterwards?'

It hadn't been a deflection. He had work to go to, it was as straightforward as that. I leant down and kissed him. I was tempted to climb back into bed, but I had to go to work. 'Yes. Call me. And here,' I threw him the spare set of electronic keys that allowed access into the apartment complex. 'I'll tell the concierge that I have a friend who might come and go for a while, shall I?'

In reply I got another grin. He might not be Dan's intellectual equal and I knew, even then, he would never move my heart as Dan had, but he certainly worked on other parts of me without effort.

**

When the lift doors opened into the server farm and what was now called the Bateleur Cyber Intelligence HQ, I was rather surprised to see Pat standing next to my desk. I checked my watch. Not yet 7:45 am, so I wasn't late, but he was most definitely early.

'Pat, what's wrong?'

'Nothing, not a thing. In fact, everything is great. After last night's little soiree the CEO took me to one side. We're finally on his radar and he wants you and I to brief him on the potential cyber threats for the bank's next acquisition.'

I was aware Bateleur was still pursuing all possibilities of buying banks in emerging markets, especially as what was now being called the Great Financial Crisis bit harder and harder into our competitors.

'Great, what's the plan?'

'The Chinese Government want us to open a data centre. If it's successful, after three years they'll give us a full banking licence for China.'

'And the CEO wants to do this?' I asked, knowing that neither Pat nor the CEO knew what I knew about China and its state-sponsored cyber espionage efforts against organisations like ours, but still, they weren't idiots.

'Very much so.'

I stifled the groan I wanted to make. 'Where are we putting this new centre?'

'In Shanghai.'

16

'You're one lucky sonofabitch, Sir.'

Dan shrugged himself up in the bed and gave a casual flick of his hand in reply to Staff Sergeant Lieberman's less than formal, left-handed salute and greeting. 'How are you Morrie?'

Lieberman raised the sling on his right arm a little. 'I'll be okay, Sir. Through and through. No bones, just a bit of flesh.'

'Ha! Just a flesh wound,' Dan said and laughed.

Lieberman frowned.

'Not a fan of Monty Python?'

Morrie shook his head.

'Never mind.'

'And you, Sir. Your thick skull okay?'

Dan traced the scar that the 7.62 round had cut high on his left temple. His fingers tracked the narrow furrow that continued to the top of his ear. 'Yeah. I should write a letter of thanks to the helmet manufacturer. Did you see what was left of it?'

'Sure did. Bit like my arm. Round went through and through, took all the force and stopped your brains coating the inside of it. Everything else okay?'

'Not too bad, considering.'

'How's your chest?' Lieberman asked.

'Body armour stopped the bullet cold. I look like I've been trampled by a herd of elephants, but that beats dead. The sorest is the calf, even though the docs reckon it was likely a ricochet. Not much real damage and if it had been a straight shot they say it would have ripped the whole muscle away. As it is, I'll be back up and about in three or four weeks. What about you?'

'Yeah, me too. A month, maybe a little more. Back to light duties in a bit less.'

Dan paused as Morrie settled himself into the seat next to the bed. 'How's the rest of the squad?'

The senior non-commissioned officer, a veteran Dan knew of Panama, Desert Storm, Kosovo, Iraq, twice since 2003, and now on his second tour of Afghanistan, sighed and looked shaken.

'Kracker and Torres are being repatriated tomorrow. They'll be overnighted at Dover before being sent on. Torres' family requested Arlington. Kracker's want him to be laid down in his hometown.'

'Where was that?'

'Minnesota. Place called Winona.'

He waited as the big Staff Sergeant swallowed hard. Dan felt immensely sad at the losses, but these had been Lieberman's boys. He had trained them and nurtured them, looked out for them at home and in battle. Dan reckoned he was feeling their loss as much as any parent would feel the loss of their kids.

'Sergeant Mason will probably lose his right arm, but they want to wait until the head injury stabilises first before they airlift him to Ramstein and send him through to Landstuhl. Wong's already there, with gunshot wounds to both lower legs. Fletch' has a dislocated shoulder, so he's in the next ward down from here. He'll be okay. As will Sergeant Peck. Minor shrapnel in his shoulder and throat. Probably up and about in a day or two. Townsend will take a bit longer. His left knee isn't looking great. Probably have to go back Stateside to get it sorted out.'

It was a disaster. Not one of the squad had come out of the firefight intact. Yet he also knew they'd been damned lucky that any of them had made it out at all. The ambush had been well laid.

As good a piece of work as anything the US Army could have put together. He guessed it was what happened when you had local insurgents who'd been fighting for decades. Dan realised Morrie hadn't mentioned the most junior of the squad, Private Mercer. He had to ask, but dreaded the answer. 'And Mercy?'

Morrie laughed out loud. 'Ha. Mercy! You don't know?'

'Know what?' Dan asked, smiling in accompaniment to Lieberman's laugh and relieved that Mercy was obviously okay.

'That happy-go-lucky kid who I doubted would make PFC in the future, turns out he's a hero.'

Dan laughed too. 'A hero? How come?'

'Not a scratch on him. He was ahead of you so felt the blast from the IED that got Kracker and saw the one that got Torres up ahead. Everyone else, me included was scrambling for cover, ducking, diving and going down to incoming rounds and rocket propelled grenades. He waited till the smoke cleared, by which time most of us had been hit, but he hadn't. He figured almost every house in the village had insurgents inside, laying down a complete cross-field of fire, so he ran to the nearest one, put a grenade through, kicked the door in and sprayed them. Went door to door, killed nine, wounded four. The rest were beginning to bug-out before 2nd Squad had made it back into the village. By that time Mercy had already hauled me and Sergeant Mason to cover. He went back and grabbed you out of the doorway you'd gone down in.'

Dan couldn't figure out what to say. Mercy, not even twenty years old. The baby of the squad. A nice, polite kid and now, a killing machine. Who'd have thought?

'Captain Mendoza called in the air support and as usual the rest of the Taliban melted away, but the firefight was already won. Mendoza's recommending Mercy for the Silver Star. Might even get upgraded.'

'No way,' Dan said. 'A Medal of Honor?'

'Maybe not that high, but could be a DSC. He saved seven of us.' Lieberman said, with a grin that was backed by personal pride in how one of his boys had so fantastically come of age.

A nurse came into the room and approached Dan's bed. 'Staff Sergeant Lieberman, you are meant to be resting, as is Captain Stückl. Go on, get.'

'Yes, Ma'am,' Lieberman drawled in a good natured way.

'Don't you Ma'am me, or next time I take your temperature I'll be asking you to bend over.'

17

I gazed out at the lights of the city and leant back in my chair.

The discussions about the Shanghai data centre had been off and on for nearly a month. I couldn't tell the bank's executives about Chinese Government cyber operations, because the knowledge I had about the People's Liberation Army's cyber effort against the UK was still highly classified. I certainly couldn't recount the fact that I had helped spirit away a Chinese defector or what had subsequently happened, but I could make my feelings known about what would "likely" happen to every piece of data that went through any centre in Shanghai.

The conversations with Pat, the CEO, the COO and the rest of the board members of the bank had been worthwhile, and it appeared that I had stopped them doing something nonsensical, but as soon as the bank's Group Chairman, Sir Anthony Marius, got involved, then it was obvious we were going to be going ahead. Marius appointed a new man, Dickie Lessen, to be the lead on the project. Dickie was overweight, sported a permanent sheen of sweat on his round red face and, in my immediate and lasting opinion, had a most appropriate first name.

Finishing off the remnants of the Chenin Blanc, I waited for the last notes of Eva Cassidy's *Time is a Healer* to fade into the night. Her *Songbird* album didn't have a single bad track on it, even if most of them made me pine for Dan. Liam was working a late bar and I was contemplating the fact that the speed of the bank's decisions were, in equal measure, both impressive and frightening. They'd completed the acquisition of the Rural and Municipal Bank of China in the time it would have taken the Ministry of Defence to draft the first memo about the possibility of looking into things.

Part of the multi-million dollar deal was that a data centre for Bateleur China, must be situated in the Shanghai CBD. I had given up trying to tell Pat and anyone else who would listen, that it would probably be slower to hand over the bank's data to the Chinese Government than the speed with which they would rip it out of the communication lines running through the centre.

No one cared and so, as the soprano top notes of Cassidy opened the haunting, *I Know You By Heart*, I looked back down at my laptop screen and the half-finished letter of resignation. My main concern was having to tell both Mark Donoghue and Rachel Kennedy, that having recruited them, I was quitting. They knew the truth, so I was hopeful they'd see I was doing the right thing. I wasn't going to be surprised if they followed me out the door. It also meant I wouldn't get to attend a conference in Tampa, Florida that I'd been asked to speak at over Easter. Apparently my name was beginning to be known in the world of cyber. If that was the case, then I should be okay getting another job. The Oil and Gas sector seemed very interested in me from the casual approaches I'd had after speaking at conferences and I'd already had a couple of more formal contacts through an online network I'd recently joined called LinkedIn. Perhaps I'd reply to the next one.

I put the laptop down and rose to get another glass of wine as my Blackberry began to vibrate on the kitchen counter. I checked the wall clock, 9:45 pm. Perhaps Liam had finished early. The phone's screen didn't show the usual number recognition.

'Hello?'

'Luke?'

'Who's this?'

'My name is Eugene. We have a mutual friend in Rob Curzon. I worked with him. As did you.'

I said nothing. Waiting. When I'd been in the UK MoD's Joint Operations Centre for Coordinated Security, Rob Curzon had been a liaison officer on my team. He worked at the Government Communications Headquarters in Cheltenham. Known to most as GCHQ.

'I was wondering if I could meet you, in person?' Eugene said.

'For?'

'Better discussed in person.'

I was intrigued. 'Okay. When?'

'I was rather hoping, now.'

I re-checked the clock. 'Seriously?'

'Yes.'

'Where?'

'I'm across the street, in the Upper Deck.'

I was familiar with the restaurant, situated as its name implied on the top floor of a nearby hotel.

'How will I know you? I assume you won't be wearing a red carnation or carrying an umbrella and a copy of *The Times*.'

He laughed. 'No. Not quite. I'm alone at a table for two. I had a white wine ordered for you and a dessert of the Chef's speciality, a raspberry soufflé in its own individual pot. I'm sure you won't be able to miss me.'

The line went dead. I stared down at the phone for a moment and wondered if I should ignore it, but I couldn't. GCHQ didn't hold meetings at this time of night, or any other time, for the fun of it. Something was happening and my curiosity wouldn't have let me ignore it. I went into the bedroom, put on shoes and a splash of musk from my favourite perfumer in St James, before grabbing my coat from the hallway rack. As I was leaving the apartment I heard Eva's voice start on the opening lines of *People Get Ready, There's a Train a-Coming*.

**

The soufflé was exceptional and the wine was outstanding. All in all, regardless of what Eugene wanted, I was quite glad I'd made the two-minute walk across the road. I wiped my mouth on the starched linen napkin.

'Go on then, what do you want?'

'We'd like you to shut up about the Chinese data centre being a bad idea and embrace it as a done deal.'

I wasn't shocked they knew the internal machinations of the bank. GCHQ had fingers and ears in all sorts of places. 'Well that's easy and you didn't need to buy me dessert to get me to do that. I'm putting in my resignation tomorrow and that will be that. They can do as they please.'

Eugene, like all the men who worked in clandestine intelligence, was as non-descript and bland of expression as if he'd been painted exclusively in grey tones, but even he failed to hide the surprised look on his face. 'No!' He said, a little too forcibly.

I sat back. 'Yes. I'm not going to be wor—'

'No,' he repeated at a more considered level. 'We don't need you to quit. We need you to take a stance that says, yes, the place may be at the whims of the Chinese, but you will go along with the bank and do your best to secure things.'

'But you know as well as I do, there won't be any securing it. The communication lines in and out of the place will be laid by the Chinese authorities and our networks riddled with Chinese state-sponsored espionage activity. They will not have to tap the lines as they will be routed through Chinese Government exchanges. Any voice or data sent over them will be hoovered up by the Chinese PLA Cyber Units. It's not stoppable. You, of all people, Cheltenham I mean, know that.'

'Well of course we do. But that's exactly the reason we want you in there.'

I was confused. I reached for the wine glass and took another drink.

Eugene said, 'Those communication landlines. You're correct. They'll come into your bank's data centre and then they will scurry away and into the PLA main analysis centres. Unfettered access, completely un-securable.'

I set the glass down. 'I know.'

'But that works two ways.'

Pausing, I contemplated what he had said. Then I felt the smile spreading across my face. It was genius. With one small, yet notable, problem. 'You can't possibly mean you want me to help you bug a UK commercial entity?'

'Of course not,' Eugene said. 'That would be illegal on so many levels. You and I would end up in the highest courts of the land. But ... we would like you to take a special device out to site and place it inside a foreign government's communication infrastructure. That wouldn't be illegal.'

'And why can't you?'

'Sorry?'

'Why can't you place it?'

'How many years do you think it would take GCHQ to gain access to Chinese PLA data lines running back unfiltered into their own analysis centres? Short of sending a team out to downtown Beijing or Shanghai and digging up the road, that's not feasible. You're about to have it handed to you on a plate.'

'But won't they sniff it out as soon as it is placed?'

'Nope. We aren't planting anything active. We're just going to flow up their lines and hoover up everything and anything we can access. Do to them what they've been doing to us for years.'

'But, you could send active software in?'

'Yes. Of course we could. With direct access like this we could send an infection throughout their networks, but better to keep the communication lines up and running than kill them off. It could be an active intelligence source for years.'

'Source protection,' I said, more as an observation.

'Always,' Eugene said. 'However, it's a little problematic. All the servers, PCs and everything else anyone supplies into that data centre will be checked and checked again before they're fitted. The Chinese are a lot of things, but stupid is not one of them. They'll strip every item down to its component parts.'

'If that's the case, then how do you get your kit in?' I asked, knowing that the answer was going to be obvious and the reason I was being treated to a soufflé.

'You'll have to go out there and fit the device yourself. Once they've commissioned everything, it'll be virtually undetectable.'

'I'm not an electronics engineer,' I said.

'We know. But we'll show you how.' He lifted the half-full bottle of white out of the cooler. 'So, will you do it?'

I moved my glass over. 'I couldn't think of many things that would give me greater pleasure.'

**

Liam had been a paratrooper. As far as the world was concerned, and he agreed, he'd been an elite soldier. A ferocious fighter. He still was. Trouble breaking out in a bar was no bother to him. Feet, hands, head, teeth. All of them were fair weapons to employ when a proper barney was going down. Fight like your life depended on it. Nowadays, with knives and guns on the streets, it could well be the truth. He was scared of almost no one. Almost no one.

Two men were the exception. One was a thug and gangster. The other was Liam himself.

The years immediately after the army had been tough. On his return from Helmand Province he'd been on leave for a few weeks. Winding down, chilling. Spending time with friends. Having a laugh. He'd never once admitted his sexual orientation. The fling with Luke in Qatar was typical. Brief, illicit, rough. Since he'd joined up, the odd one-night stand or swift blow-job or hand-shandy from another closeted soldier was how it worked. But when on leave, he could indulge himself a bit more. He decided to visit a couple of civilian mates, down in Camden and Soho.

At chucking out time from the legendary gay pub, the Admiral Duncan, he'd walked into Old Compton Street. On the corner of Dean Street, he'd given both of his friends farewell pecks on the cheek before he headed to Leicester Square Tube Station. He'd not gone five feet before a couple of pricks who'd seen the goodbye embraces, called him, 'A fucking queer'.

Something snapped deep down inside Liam. Perhaps it was the tension of the previous months in Helmand. Perhaps it was a lifetime of hiding. He'd never know. Nor, he knew, would he ever be able to remember what he had done that night. The doctors and psychologists had called it a reactive aggression trigger within his amygdala and an inability for that part of his brain to communicate with the control centres of his frontal lobes. He'd laughed out loud at the abbreviation of the condition known as intermittent explosive disorder. He was an IED, all by himself.

The army had trained him to be an elite fighting man. When he used those skills on the streets of London, they didn't want to know. He was sentenced to nine months prison and was released in five and a half. He'd been dishonourably discharged from the army on the day of his sentencing. No lump-sum in payoff. No pension. He was cast aside as an irrelevant embarrassment.

As well as no money, he obviously had no job, no immediate prospects of one and the added complication of no home. His father, an ex-para himself, initially stood by him. He'd gone to the court case every day, until the revelation that his son was gay. Then he disowned him.

Liam had needed money and he'd earned it in any way he could. Now things were different. Now he had a steady job, his own place and a developing relationship with Luke. But the past had a way of finding him out. As it had tonight.

An hour before he was due to come home, a casual "hello" from a punter, stopped him cold. Liam recognised the voice. He turned with a Scotch bottle in his hand. Dreading who he would see. Knowing that his feet, hands, head and teeth were useless, for the threat this man posed was not violent and even if Liam let loose his inner rage, more would turn up. And the next ones wouldn't say hello. If he punched and kicked and head-butted this messenger, the next ones showing up would just kill him. So he smiled and poured the man a drink.

His mistake hadn't been saying no to the offer. His mistake had been mentioning he was in a relationship. That his life had moved on for the better. His mistake was desperately trying to back-peddle. Trying not to mention Luke's name. By the time the man walked away, Liam felt like his stomach had been ripped out. The anger and pain and massive waves of regret were like the blackest of clouds enveloping him.

He made it home after three and crawled into bed beside the already sleeping Luke.

18

Shanghai, 10th June 2009

The bank liaison officer was obviously a member of the Chinese Ministry for State Security. She was as petite as she was polite and I supposed sexy, if you were into small Asian women. Or into women at all as a gender. I had no doubt she'd been assigned to me, the head of the bank's cyber intelligence division, in order to use every charm she had to compromise me. In every meaning of the word. I had chuckled when I'd first met her. Someone hadn't done their homework properly.

Nevertheless, she introduced herself using impeccable, accent-less English and her Westernised name, Sharon. She was to be my go-to person for anything I needed. A walk into town to get a coffee? Sharon would happily go with me to help and translate and watch and monitor and generally report back any and everything I did. It was a minor irritation, but nothing I was too bothered about and nothing I hadn't expected.

The one place she wasn't coming to was the British Consulate General's offices in the Shanghai Centre. The Consul General had laid on welcome drinks for the Bateleur team who had arrived to finish the setup on the Data Centre.

Again, the bank had accelerated the development of an asset much faster than anything the Ministry of Defence or any other UK Government department could have managed. It meant the fit out of the building, completed by a local Shanghai firm working under the direction of both the bank and the Chinese Central Commerce Committee, and no doubt with a fair amount of hidden input from Sharon's employers, had been finished in a few months, rather than the year it would have taken in England. Another example of what human ingenuity is capable of if you throw enough bodies at it. As for me, I'd been preparing too. Every week I had practiced and every week I had become better and better at what I was going to have to do. Now I could do it blindfolded and in under two minutes. Which was just as well.

The preceding months had passed quickly. Liam and I were still involved, although he was falling deeper for me than I ever could for him and it was beginning to worry me. I didn't want to hurt him, but I knew I would. Ultimately, I felt nothing much for him other than the physical. My heart and head were still firmly wedded to Dan. Wherever he was. However, the issue of breaking up with Liam could wait. For now, I had one job and that was to hit back at the Chinese Government's cyber capability. To do that, I needed Eugene from GCHQ's little bug. To get it meant going for a drink. I found that chore completely within my skill set.

**

'No Ferrero Rocher?' Rachel Kennedy quipped as we entered the British Consulate within the impressive high rise complex of the Shanghai Centre.

'I think they're only for ambassadors.' A woman said from behind me.

Rachel blushed. That was something that didn't happen often, but as I turned I understood.

'Hello. I'm Margaret Carr. Welcome to Shanghai.' The greeting was accompanied by an outstretched hand held with poise and grace. It matched the voice and the rest of the speaker.

I recognised her from the pre-briefing material Rachel, myself and the rest of the Bateleur team had been given and also from

121

the portrait that hung in the entrance foyer of the Consulate. This was Her Britannic Majesty's Consul General in Shanghai.

I shook the offered hand. 'I'm Luke Frankland, Miss Carr. It's a pleasure. This is Rachel Kennedy.'

Rachel apologised as she shook Carr's hand.

'Please, Margaret is fine and no need to apologise. I could open a confectioners when I get back to London with the amount of those damned sweets I have been gifted over the years,' Carr said with a warm smile. 'I wouldn't mind, but I don't even like them. I would much have preferred the advertising agencies had used any other product to be the *choice at ambassador's parties.*'

'What would your go-to gift of choice be?' Rachel asked.

'Diamonds? Pimm's perhaps?' Carr laughed and held out an arm by way of invitation to walk into the main room. It was already busy with the Bateleur people, Consulate civil servants and local British business types, amidst an array of waiting staff who were circulating with finger food and drinks. Rachel turned and Carr walked beside her.

They hadn't gone two steps before Dickie Lessen hurried from the main reception space and intercepted them. He was, as usual, badly stuffed into a suit and his face glistened with sweat. The folds of fat on his neck meant he had loosened his collar so his tie had slipped down and the knot sat askew. I thought, not for the first time, that he was a pair of round spectacles and a school cap away from being a middle-aged Billy Bunter.

'Ah, Consul General Carr, I'm Bateleur's lead executive here in Shanghai. It is such a great honour to meet you.' He thrust out a hand at the same time as giving a strange little bob of his head. Like the two actions had been attached by some invisible thread. His outstretched arm also forced a gap between Carr and Rachel, into which Lessen squeezed himself. Had he screamed, *'Oh look at me, I'm important,'* he couldn't have been more obnoxiously transparent.

Rachel glanced back to me and rolled her eyes.

Carr stopped in her tracks and reared backwards, although she shook his hand, more I thought due to a surprised, automatic reaction. 'Oh. Yes. Well it's good to meet you, Mister?'

'Lessen. Dickie Lessen. Please let me introduce you to some of my top staff.' He stepped alongside her, put his hand on her elbow and guided her into her own Consulate.

Rachel lingered. 'I counted about five breaches of standard protocol there. What a dick.'

'He is that,' I agreed. 'Keep an eye on him, discreetly. Maybe rescue the good Consul from him if you get the chance?'

She nodded and walked into the room. As I made to follow I noticed Eugene standing inside a small ante-room, just off the main foyer.

'Evening, Luke. All set?' He asked.

'As I shall ever be, Eugene. Do I take it now?'

'When you're leaving.' He inclined his head towards another side door.

'Any problems getting it here?' I asked.

'No. None. That's what diplomatic bags are for, mate.'

**

I had to admit, the new data centre was a marvel. On the top floor of the building, the eighth, it was bright, open and light. Walls of glass, rows of servers mounted on raised platforms, air-conditioned, thermally-sensitive environments automatically adjusted. Smart energy use, mostly powered by solar cells mounted on the roof. Chinese panels of course, but I had noted the German solar inverters, which had surprised me. I expected it all to be 'Made in China'. I suspected the German kit had been thoroughly reverse engineered by the Chinese for future exploitation.

The modern high-tech layout of the centre was great for the staff who would be working here full time, but not brilliant for what I needed to do during my brief stay. My team and I were simply here for a month to commission the building and put in place what were supposedly robust, but in practice were superfluous, computer network defence measures. External firewalls and digital tripwires designed to catch external intrusions. Our threats in this place were not going to be coming from external sources, they were being built into the fabric of the centre by the Chinese Government and there was nothing I could do about it. However,

I was no longer concerned by any of that. All I had to do was get Eugene's smart-chip mounted inside a server rack without anyone, including my own team, knowing about it.

I'd never be back in Shanghai, but Mark and Rachel, Steve, Paul and no doubt others would come and go. They could not know anything about the planted device. They needed full and plausible deniability. Almost. I did need Rachel to do me a favour, but she knew better than to ask why.

The day had gone well, we'd made progress, and Sharon hadn't left my side once. Then again, I hadn't expected her to. I'd been well briefed on what to expect. I checked my watch. Five minutes to five. We'd knock off at five-thirty.

'Sharon?'

She looked up from whatever clandestine, Machiavellian machinations she was involved in. Or perhaps she was doing exactly what it looked like; reading the English-language Shanghai Daily.

'Yes, Luke.'

'I think everything is coming together well. I'd like to take the team out to a good restaurant this evening?'

'That sounds great,' she said, folding the newspaper closed and smoothing it out on the desk top.

'Do you think you could recommend one? Traditional Chinese, but perhaps with a Western twist? Reflective of what we are now in Bateleur,' I said and even managed to make it sound convincing to my own ears.

She beamed. 'Oh, yes. I know exactly the place,' she said. Then her face dropped a little.

'What's wrong?'

'I might have to check if we can get in. You see there is a large, eh, event happening.'

'What type of event?'

Sharon physically squirmed and looked exceedingly uncomfortable. 'It is a great shame to have to tell you of it.'

I was perplexed. 'Pardon?'

'In Shanghai, this week. There is a, series of events. Venues are hosting parties and music and performances. They are all centred near to the restaurant I was thinking of.'

'Sounds great,' I said. 'Why is that a problem?'

Again the uncomfortable expression, the hesitation. 'It is the first of this type we have ever had in Shanghai. The first in China I think. It is called, pride.' She uttered the last word like it was poison on her tongue.

I almost fell off my seat. 'Pride? In Shanghai? As in Gay Pride?' I couldn't hide the incredulity in my voice. Sharon mistook it far too easily for something else.

'I know. It brings shame on our city. These … these unnatural people. I am sorry for you to have to be here.'

'But why is the government not simply stopping it?' Again my tone was incredulous and once more Sharon mistook me.

'Because they changed the law. Stopped it being a mental disorder. Now these people surface.'

I felt the first flush of annoyance. 'A mental disorder?'

'Yes, until 2001. Now we have to treat them as normal.'

I bit my lip. The Chinese had changed their laws in 2001. I remembered reading that the Olympics were usually awarded about six or seven years before the actual summer in which they were to take place. It was a good bet therefore that the Chinese had been awarded the 2008 Games in 2001. The games they had hosted in Beijing only last year. I doubted it was all coincidence. I was much more inclined to believe that the monetary benefits of an Olympics would have made all sorts of pressures come to bear from Western nations. It was a shame that those pressures hadn't done much in changing Sharon's attitude.

I felt like I had in the back of Maksym's taxi in Kiev. Not that Maksym, as it had transpired, had actually thought that way, but his language was pejorative and the culture that bred it was wrong. Now, here with Sharon it was so much worse. This woman thought that homosexuality was a mental disorder. So had her nation's government, until less than a decade ago and I was sure their actual attitudes hadn't changed that much.

I wanted to argue and remonstrate about how wrong they were, how wrong she was. I wanted to grab her by the shoulders and shake some sense into her. I wanted to stand up and say, you know what, you are wrong. There is nothing defective with me or the people like me. I wanted to do it all and I did none of it. And what was worse, I knew I wouldn't. Not now and not while I worked for the bank. For the truth was that the vast majority of those I had met since coming to work in the confines of Canary Wharf held the same attitude as Sharon. The only difference was that they wouldn't voice it as openly as she had because of the supposed tolerance of UK society. Perhaps Sharon was the more honest.

Inner frustrations at my inability to stand up and be counted fuelled my desire to at least get my part of the GCHQ job done. I refocussed. I knew what I needed to do and I had to do it now. 'I see,' I said, weakly. 'I'm sure you'll be able to find another restaurant, even if not the one you first thought of?'

She looked up and forced a smile. 'Yes. Of course.'

'Great. Well, let's call everyone together and tell them where and when to meet?'

'Oh, yes,' she said, a little more enthused. Her voice, quiet and polite, carried throughout the open-plan working areas on the server suite floor. The Chinese technical staff began to walk over to my desk.

I waved to Rachel. 'Can you get the guys from inside the server racks, Rach?'

'Sure,' she said and went into the server farm itself. Now it was all about timing.

The server rack spaces emptied and Rachel appeared at the door.

'Is that everyone, Rach?' I asked as the thirty staff members congregated around the front of my desk. I stepped to one side to see Rachel at the server farm door.

'I'll just check,' she said and went back into the server farm racks. She would walk to the far wall. To the point on that wall where the rearmost 'break glass to activate' fire alarm box was mounted. She would check left and right as she went. The internal CCTV cameras would track her movements and record them onto tape. A tape that I was certain would be checked to ensure there had been no anomalies within the server room. A check that would most definitely be carried out after what I needed to do was completed. But that was for the future. For now, I merely knew that

Rachel was about to stumble and put her hand out. It was all about timing.

On the activation of a fire alarm within the server room a backup, instant surge generator kicked in. It was isolated and protected but due to its instantaneous ability to take on a supply load, it was incredibly expensive. We had only one fitted within each Bateleur server location and even then the total cost was staggering. The transition of electrical load was triggered on the first ring of the alarm but the power from that single generator only went to stabilise the servers and ensure the internal fire suppression system was active. The other backup generators, that supplied emergency lighting, fire door activation and other ancillary systems, were much less responsive. On the activation of an alarm the standard electricity supply shut down and the backups came online, but they could take up to two minutes to fully take on the load. Until then, things were confused, and dark.

I was still standing to the side of my desk. Sharon was standing to my left. All the staff, bar Rachel, were in the area between my desk and the next line of workstations. The harsh ringing of the internal fire alarm sounded and the lights went out. Sharon let out a small, involuntary yelp. A few more gasps and mixed Chinese and English exclamations accompanied the pitch blackness. It was all about timing. I had already started to count inside my head. One, one thousand, two, one thousand, three.

'Okay everyone,' I called. 'Quiet!' The alarm was loud and I needed to raise my voice. 'Sharon, translate and tell everyone to remain calm. No one is to move. The lights will come back on in a moment and then we shall evacuate via the stairs. Until then they are to remain still and quiet.' There was no response from next to me. 'Sharon!' I said it as a command.

'Yes. Yes, Luke, certainly,' she answered and began to translate. It was all about timing. Sixteen, seventeen, eighteen, go.

The layout of the eighth floor of the Bateleur Data Centre was exactly as per the plans we had sent over months before and exactly as Eugene and his guys had replicated in an old aircraft hangar in Middlesex. I'd spent days walking through it, so that now, in total darkness, I slid my heel back to contact against the right front leg of my desk, then I stepped two steps sideways and half-turned right. I walked forward five steps, turned left, two more, turned right. Fifteen more steps. Sharon was still talking. I assumed she was telling everyone what I had said. No one was to panic. The lights would be on in a moment. Stay calm. Be quiet.

Thirty, thirty-one, thirty-two.

Thank God we had a policy of no mobile phones or other electronic devices within the suite whilst we were commissioning it – no danger of screen light or some little LED torches being turned on. Two more steps, then forward to the door of the server farm, whose electronic locks had instantly deactivated with the fire alarm. Pull it open, step up two steps. Forward, left, left again, Five steps forward. Kneel down.

Forty-five, forty-six, forty-seven.

Pull the server box forward. Slide the front panel to the left, and lift it off. Reach inside, feel the integrated chip mounted half-way back on the printed circuit board. One thumb width to the left an unused port on the board. Reach with my left hand into my pocket. Retrieve the micro bug with its ten little metal legs that Eugene had given to me at the consulate party. Orientate it.

Fifty-six, fifty-seven, fifty-eight.

Plug it in. Slide the cover back into place. Fuck. Missed its seating. Calm. Breathe. Count.

Sixty-eight, sixty-nine, seventy.

Re-seat the cover. Slide it on. Drop it down. Slide it right. Push the box back into place. Stand.

Ninety, ninety-one, ninety-two.

Walk the opposite route. Step down out of the server farm carefully. Walk quickly, but quietly in the utter blackness.

The emergency lighting flicked on. The green haze and white surrounds of the emergency evacuation signs dimly illuminated the space. The staff were still congregated in front of my desk. Rachel was appearing at the door to the server farm. Sharon turned to her right and looked at where I had been standing when the lights went off.

I smiled down at her.

19

London, 30th June 2009

Liam walked into Plough Yard, just off Shoreditch High Street at ten minutes after midnight. The 'Yard', little more than a narrow, confined lane was dimly lit by the glare of the city's lights less than a stone's throw from it.

'You're late.' The voice came from the shadows of a doorway on his left, set back from the road.

'I had to work,' Liam answered, turning towards the man he knew as Vasile Constă.

'Are you ready?'

Liam couldn't see the man's features, but he heard the edge to his voice. He checked behind. Two of Vasile's men stood in the opposite doorway to their boss.

'It might be a little while longer,' Liam said and cursed internally at the weakness he had heard in his own voice.

'I think not,' Vasile said stepping out of the shadows. 'We have account. We have conversation, we have web history. We have arrangements all recorded online, yes?'

Liam didn't speak, but gave a terse nod of his head.

'You have been seen with him in public? The people at his apartment reception. You have done as I told you? You have talked to them, they will remember you, yes?'

Again, Liam said nothing. Vasile barked at him, 'Yes?'

'Yes. Yes, it is all done.'

'Then no more delays.' Vasile raised his hand and indicated for Liam to come closer.

He didn't get a chance to move before the punch that landed on the nape of his neck dropped him to his knees. He toppled forward and only his outstretched hands, impacting harshly on the roadway, stopped him face planting into the broken cobblestones of the lane's footpath. It would have been better if he had continued to fall, as on all fours there was little he could do to defend against the kick aimed at his head.

**

He came to in blackness. His first reaction was to raise his hands and shield himself from more blows, but he was alone. The pounding in his head told him that he was at least alive, although it also told him he'd have one hell of a headache from the punches and kicks he'd received. Gingerly he felt his nose. Not the first time he'd had it broken, probably wouldn't be the last. He managed a grin as his fingers touched the bridge. Sore, certainly, but at least it felt straight enough. Small wins. He didn't fancy having to go to a casualty department to get it reset.

The raw throbbing pain of his right eye and the sharp, needle-like jabs of soreness on his lower lip told him that in the morning light, he would look exactly like he should. Someone who had been beaten-up, but not severely. This was a reminder. Nothing more. A simple message.

Shame they couldn't have just told me, he thought as his eyes adjusted and he realised he was lying in the doorway that the original voice, Vasile's, had come from. Concealed from anyone using the lane as a cut though, Liam's unconscious form would only have been disturbed by someone trying to use the door to the small commercial premises beyond and that was unlikely on a Saturday night. He took out his phone and saw it was 3:22 am, Sunday morning. Anyone passing by would have thought him just another homeless guy sleeping rough. At least it was a dry and warm night. He rolled out of the doorway and got unsteadily to his feet. In the half-light of the city glow he saw the trails of blood down his shirt. He'd have to walk back to Luke's apartment, but no one on the streets at this time would give him a second glance.

More small wins. Luke wasn't due back from China until Friday evening, by which time, hopefully, the majority of the bruising should have abated. Liam could always pass it off as a brawl at one of the clubs or pubs he worked. He smoothed his hands down the dried blood stains and noticed a crumpled page from a notebook had been shoved into his shirt's breast pocket. Retrieving it he stepped further into the laneway to catch the dim streetlights.

NO MORE DELAYS
YOU HAVE TWO WEEKS - LAST CHANCE
FOR BOTH OF YOU – REMEMBER NICO

The last words hit him as hard as the first punch had. Liam reached out a hand and slumped back against the doorway. He liked, perhaps it was more than liked, Luke. As he considered this, he knew with a strange certainty it was more than liked. That's why he had been so resolute to avoid and delay Vasile's demands. He'd done his best and managed to keep the Romanian at arm's length, but even if it was love, all his efforts were at an end. He'd do what Vasile wanted, for there was no way on earth that Liam would allow what had happened to Nico to happen to himself. Or Luke. He slid to the ground and hugged his knees, screwing his eyes tight shut, trying not to think of a night, long ago, in a warehouse that echoed to screams.

**

'Well?' Kelly Martin asked.

'It's up and running.'

'Access all areas then?' Eugene's boss chuckled to herself. 'How long before we make inroads to their organisational structures?'

'Not long,' Eugene said. 'I mean in relative terms. If we didn't have her to analyse the data, then probably years. With her, I figure a month, maybe two.'

'And she is being fully cooperative?'

'Of course. Why wouldn't she be?'

'I know her insights have been invaluable for our defensive cyber operations these last few years, but this is the first time we're putting her to work actively against her former colleagues. It is always a big step.'

Eugene considered the premise. He hadn't given it too much thought, but Kelly Martin, the newly appointed head of GCHQ was making a valid point. He paused and considered his last few interactions with the analysis team in Cheltenham responsible for Chinese cyber. 'No. I can't say I've noticed any drop off in her performance. If anything she's more motivated. She knows this operation will have a massive impact.' This time the pause was on the other end of the line. Eugene waited for what felt like a full minute. 'Ma'am? You still there?'

'Yes. Sorry Eugene, I was just thinking about how things play out in our world. Seems ironic that the minister who we had to hide her from isn't even in parliament now.'

Eugene didn't reply with more than an agreeable 'Mmm.'

He knew Kelly, the first woman ever to be appointed head of GCHQ, was an exceptional intelligence operator. He also knew she had been shielded by her predecessor from certain operations. Just a select few missions that had been so far off the books as to be one hundred percent deniable.

Eugene had been the lead crypto-analyst on one of them. He and the other team members had been hand-picked. Three from Cheltenham and one from the Secret Intelligence Service, or MI6 as the public still referred to them. All four men had their own reasons to see it through. A simple bugging and surveillance exercise, nothing spectacular other than who it was run against.

To monitor members of foreign governments was well within GCHQ's remit. To monitor members of the UK parliament had occasionally been authorised by the sitting Prime Minister. But to run an operation against both the incumbent Home and Foreign

Secretaries of Her Majesty's Government without any top-cover by members of the cabinet or Joint Intelligence Committee was bordering on treason. It was certainly illegal for an MI6 operator to act on UK soil, so Andy Gibson, the man assigned to the team by SIS's director, Sir Colin Hope, was more exposed than any of them, but Eugene recalled, Gibson had probably been the most motivated of them all to get the job done.

As operations went, it had been remarkably easy. The Home Secretary, Duncan Stephenson and the Foreign Secretary, Mary South, had been having an affair for months. Both of them were married with families living in their respective constituencies, so they used South's London apartment, paid for on parliamentary expenses, as their preferred rendezvous. It was simple to get audio and imagery and then systematically leak it to the tabloids. It cost them their Ministerial roles and in South's case it cost her a very expensive divorce. The stress of it, and Eugene knew, the pressure exerted by an increasingly shaky Prime Minister, led her to resign her seat. The subsequent by-election had been won by the opposition, further increasing the pressure on a Labour government that was reeling from more and more scandals as their long tenure in office continued. As for Stephenson, he was reduced to being a non-influential backbencher and would never stand a chance of bidding for his party's leadership, a thing he looked to have been destined for.

It had been a sweet revenge for the chaos those two ministers had tried to bring down on an otherwise stellar intelligence coup. Even more sweet that South had suffered the most. Cheltenham and MI6 were certain that she had ordered the death of a defector and had been willing to sacrifice the asset's mother and brother as well. What they'd never worked out was why. They also had no proof. Or at least none that a UK court would respect, but they knew. As certain as the sun rose, they knew. Mary South had given the orders and Mary South had been prepared to see two innocents shipped back to a Chinese regime that would have killed them as soon as they'd touched down.

So Sir Colin had instigated a counter-plan. A subterfuge that needed complete secrecy to work and for alternative identities to be manufactured. Easy enough for his organisation. He'd been planning on playing a long game, but circumstances had changed rapidly in the middle of a domestic incident that no one could have foreseen, and he'd reacted accordingly. All in all, it had gone well. The last stroke was to bring down South and Stephenson. It had taken a while, but they'd done it. Eugene's only regret, one shared with Andy Gibson, was that they hadn't been able to tell Luke Frankland. After all, he had been the one who had made contact with the defector in the first place.

'When are you back in GCHQ?' Kelly asked, interrupting the kaleidoscope of memories and images that had flashed through Eugene's mind.

'Next Monday.'

'Okay. I'll make some time in my schedule. I'd like you to drop in and brief me first-hand.'

'Certainly, Ma'am.'

'And bring Lily as well, please. I'd like to hear her take on the developing penetration ops.'

20

London, 3rd July 2009

I arrived back into my apartment just after 9:00 pm. Considering the flight from Shanghai had been nearly fourteen hours I was feeling fairly refreshed. The BA business class flat beds were a godsend in combatting jetlag and the frequent upgrades to First Class even more so.

The apartment was empty, but that was no surprise. Liam had texted to say he'd be working and would be home after midnight. I dropped my gear in the bedroom, grabbed a shower and then made my way, wrapped in a dressing gown, back into the lounge. Ripping the seal off the duty free carrier bag I lifted out a box of King Edward cigars and a one-litre bottle of Tanqueray No. Ten. The bar cabinetry I had installed halfway along the main kitchen wall was petite but well appointed. On the top shelf were cut glass Waterford Crystal tumblers, a cigar cutter, a heavy lead crystal ashtray and a retro Dunhill table lighter. Underneath was a small fridge stocked with, among other things, a six-pack of tonic mixers. Once I had made a drink to my liking, heavy on the gin, light on the tonic, I cracked open the balcony door and took a seat. The cigar smoke wafted around me, filling my nostrils and mixing with the warm air of a summer night.

The cockpit lights of a Lufthansa Cityline Embraer E-190 seemed within reach as the aircraft passed by on final approach into London City Airport. I raised my glass in unseen salute to the pilot and drained the contents in a single hit. After another couple of the same I felt more inclined to listen to some music over and above the background hum of the city. I allowed the half-finished cigar to die in the ashtray and came back in from the balcony. My iPod was hooked into the stereo system and I chose Lionel Richie's *Can't Slow Down* album. Eight tracks of perfection, but I thumbed the selector wheel to number four; *Stuck on You*.

Dan had been into heavy metal and punk, yet he'd listened to my music and adapted. A little at least. I had introduced him to genres that the good old boys from his part of Nebraska wouldn't have given the time of day to. He had always said that Richie's *Stuck on You* summed up exactly how he felt about me.

I sank into the armchair and poured another drink. The clear, smooth gin slipped into the glass as easily as Lionel's clear and smooth lyrics wrapped me in memories. I felt the familiar tug of longing and regret. The black dread that sat at the back of my mind began to overtake me. It was pathetic. I should have been over him by now. Moved on. I'd had no word, not one, since that awful October night nearly four years ago. Four years. It should have made everything easier. Less hurtful. It hadn't. Not in any way did I feel ready to let my need for him go. None of the sensible arguments that I shouted and yelled inside my head stopped my heart tearing itself into pieces each and every day. Thoughts of Dan were the first to occur to me in the mornings and the last at night, they invaded my dreams or more usually, kept me awake. I was tired of it, but I could no more change the way I felt than I could …

I stared at the glass in my hand. Than I could stop drinking? No. That wasn't true. I didn't need to drink. I liked it. Sure. The taste, the relaxation that came from a good strong G&T, but I didn't need it. I could stop if I wanted to. I would stop, but just for now, it helped me sleep, took the edge off the broiling thoughts of missed opportunity and parallel lives not lived. Allowed me a modicum of peace. But I didn't need it. As much as I didn't need

Liam. He was a passing interest. A way to distract myself and take the edge off whatever loneliness I felt without Dan, but I didn't need him. In fact, I didn't want him. I drained my glass again as the rhythmic drumbeat intro of *Love Will Find a Way* played.

Jesus, it was as if Lionel had written it for me. I concentrated on the words and it was like a flashgun going off in my head. The lyrics were a wake-up call. I could use the gin to take the edge off, and would do for as long as I wanted, but I couldn't drag Liam along for the same reasons. It was so obvious that he felt more for me than I ever could for him and that would only get worse if I let it continue. It was time for me to find my own way and let him go. Reaching for the Tanqueray I poured a double, or perhaps it was closer to a triple. It was heavy-handed whatever the measure. I'd let Liam down as gently as I could. It wasn't like he'd be homeless. He had his own place, although not as comfortable as mine, but his small flat in Whitechapel was functional. He had a job, money and he'd been doing okay before me. He'd do okay after me. Probably a lot better and it was the right thing to do. Let him go before it became overly complicated.

Tomorrow then. A Saturday. We usually spent the weekend mornings in a slow unfurling of ourselves. I'd probably miss those if I missed anything. Although it had never replaced the weekend mornings that Dan and I had enjoyed, but I doubted anything would. Still, even with Liam it was a pleasant way to begin the day, and he needed the mornings to be relaxed if he'd worked late the night before, so I'd give him that. We'd make aggressive love tonight and in the morning, after breakfast, I'd tell him we were done. I might never get Dan back, but I was through making do.

**

I woke early and slipped out of bed, allowing Liam to sleep on. He had surprised me by not wanting to make love on his return home. Said he was tired, but I got the idea something was wrong, though I didn't pursue it. I also noticed he had faded bruising on his face, but it wasn't the first time he'd been caught up in a bar brawl when he was working. I figured his potentially distant mood would make the break-up go easier.

After a rapid shower I got dressed and headed down to the deli on the corner. Five minutes to get there, five more to wait for two takeaway coffees and a collection of pastries and five minutes back. I expected to find Liam still in bed, but as I came through the apartment door he was dressed and in the living room, gazing out of the windows over the city. He didn't turn as I entered. Whatever grump he was in was of no concern. Breakfast first, I reminded myself.

'Morning, Liam. You're up early. Not like you after a late night,' I said, forcing myself to be upbeat as I arranged the pastries on a platter.

He gave a shrug in reply, lifted one of the coffee cups and took a long drink. In some strange way it reminded me of how I liked to drink my first proper drink of the day. Like a comfort and a kicker all in one. The difference was my face would have been relaxed by the action. His looked anything but.

'What's the matter?'

He set the cup down and mumbled, 'Nothing.'

I felt a swell of annoyance. He had no clue that I was going to break up with him, but the last thing I needed was for him to be in a mood before I had the conversation. I turned away to get two side plates, still determined to have breakfast first.

'I want fifty thousand pounds or I'm going to out you to the bank.'

My hand was reaching up to the plates as he said it and I froze in mid-reach. The gloss doors of the kitchen cabinets provided a blurred and distorted reflection of him, standing on the opposite side of the kitchen bench. I realised my arm was still up in the air. Slowly lowering it, I stayed facing away from him. 'What?'

'You heard. I want fifty thousand or I out you.'

His voice was weak and unconvincing. I knew Liam. I may not have loved him, but I knew him. He was anything but weak. Physically it was what had attracted me to him back in Qatar. Two lonely souls grasping for one another in the heat of a desert. He had been then and still was rugged and strong. His voice was deep and most definitely masculine and yet, in this … in this what exactly, extortion? Threat? He sounded like a lost teenager. His weakness was pathetic, but the words he had used, the threat he had made slammed into me. Not like a punch, leaving me debilitated, but like a crashing shock of water. I rarely, if ever, lost my temper. My father had once told me that my fuse was as long as the Humber Bridge, and even now I felt no anger, but I did feel something. A clarity I had never known before. My family knew I was gay. They were the only people that mattered. My former employers in the military had known and not cared. Why should I care if the bank found out that I was gay? Pat Harris was delighted with my work. He might be surprised at my sexual orientation, but as sure as hell he wasn't going to fire me for it. That would have been illegal in the first instance and after Ukraine, I was his golden child. He was already pushing me to be a key-note speaker at international conferences, flying the flag for Bateleur. So I liked men, so what? I turned to face Liam and calmly said, 'Fuck off.'

The profanity made him straighten up. 'Didn't you hear wh—'

'Yes I heard you and the answer is the same. Fuck off. I don't have fifty grand in change and even if I did, the bank won't give a toss that I'm gay.'

'They'll care you used a prostitute.'

It caught me off guard. I felt a deep frown furrow my brow. 'What? I've never used a prostitute in my life?'

Liam walked to the dining room table. I hadn't noticed my laptop was open on it. He picked it up and carried it back to the kitchen bench. The screen showed some sort of chat room or community forum.

'And what's that meant to be?'

He pointed to an open chat window. 'That's your account. On Gaydar dot com. You've been chatting to people in here.'

If I had learnt anything from being in cyber security, it was that setting up an account in someone's name was easy. Even easier if you had direct access to their laptop. It made me hesitate a little. The bank wouldn't be pleased that a corporate machine had been accessing some gay dating site, but Liam would need a lot more than that for it to be a major issue.

'So?' I asked, feeling more belligerent, less patient.

'This is the commercial side.'

'For what? Gay men in business?' I was genuinely confused by what he meant, but a little alarm bell went off in my head.

'Well, yes, I suppose. Just not the businesses you're thinking of.'

It dawned on me. 'You mean rent boys?'

He nodded.

'Oh do fuck off Liam. You think by going to the bank and telling them I have been using a chatroom they'd fire me? There's no proof whatsoever I have been with any man from on here, no money exchanged no smoking gun. Get your stuff and get out.'

Rather than walk away he reached again for the laptop and opened up a new browser window. A profile page appeared. He expanded part of the screen. It showed a user called ParaIII. The account had been active for over four years. Total comments numbered into the thousands. Instinctively, I knew what was going to happen, but as if in slow motion Liam's finger traced across the touch pad of the laptop and clicked on the full profile link. It opened to show a muscled and tattooed man, wearing only a pair of jeans, leaning against a five-rail fence in a rural setting. The photo looked a few years old, but there was no mistaking it was Liam.

'You have an account on here,' he said, opening a chatroom history transcript. 'I made it for you. You've been talking to me online for months. Your concierge and the rest of the apartment's reception team know me. They'll happily back up the fact I've been coming in and out of here.' He paused and allowed me time to process what he was telling me.

Use of paid sex workers was a dismissible offence. I'd been told that during William Carmichael's rapid brief to me before my trip to South African, albeit he had meant female prostitutes, but I had no doubt a male rent boy would be viewed in a worse light by the homophobic culture of Canary Wharf. Still though, there was a massive piece of the jigsaw missing.

Liam's hand traced across the touchpad again, opening more chatroom history pages. His profile. Years of profile history. Chats with other users who sported a variety of cringe worthy usernames themed on terrible gay innuendo and puns. As he opened each transcript I saw the conversation threads. Starting off with innocent greetings before moving to transaction details, short negotiations, confirmation of money amounts, meeting places. I wondered why Liam had paid these men for sex and then, like a large penny dropping slowly I focussed on the text in front of me and realised the truth.

'You're the prostitute?'

He didn't reply. I looked up from the screen expecting to see a defiant, hostile face staring back at me, but instead Liam's features looked like he was on the verge of crying.

'What the fuck is going on?' I asked, but the words carried no venom. I was confused and somehow, in a way that I couldn't understand, I felt protective of him. This rent boy trying to extort money from me with some elaborate con that might have been going on from our first meeting, yet I couldn't muster any anger or resentment, not with the way he looked.

'Liam, talk to me?'

He didn't respond and I began to ask again, but stopped. Once more, Rachel's example of how to interrogate subjects leapt into my mind. Leave the silence between questions. Let them soak it up. Let them have time. Look at them and wait. So I did. After a minute Liam's intensely sad eyes came up to meet mine.

'We have to pay, Luke. We have to pay or they'll kill us.'

21

London, 4th July 2009

I lifted the lion's head and rapped it on the still new looking door of 115 Guilford Street. The bright red paint and brass knocker had all, no doubt, been paid for by the compensation department of the Metropolitan Police. It took no time for the octogenarian to answer. Even less for him to look at me and Liam and dismiss us out of hand.

'Whatever the fuck you're selling, I don't want it.'

The door started to close. 'I think you'll want to listen to me, Tom.' The use of his name slowed the door's motion slightly, but his main response was to lift his left hand and raise his middle finger. Liam pushed the door open and lifted Tom back inside the hallway. I followed. It was much gentler than Maksym had been in the Ukraine, but the effect was the same. I closed the door behind me.

Liam held Tom against the hallway wall, a hand clamped over his mouth. I leant down next to the old man's long earlobe. 'You're going to want to listen to what I have to say. Otherwise your old friend Mohammed from Bulgaria is going to be very pissed off. Is there anyone else in the house?'

Tom's eyes widened at mention of Mo the Bulgarian. Even if the man from Sofia didn't exist, Tom was certainly paying me all the attention I wanted.

'Is there anyone else in the house?' I repeated.

Liam slackened his grip a little. Not enough for Tom to make a noise but it allowed a shake of the head. For good effect Liam added, 'If you're lying, I'll break every bone in your body before I kill you. Is there anyone here?'

Another shake. Liam took his hand away completely.

I expected a shaky, tremulous voice. Panic perhaps. Tom was eighty-one years of age and had just had his home invaded in the middle of the day by two much younger and much fitter men. One of whom, with his buzz-cut hair, tattooed forearm, boots, jeans and tight-fitting black t-shirt looked like a proper thug. I'd stuck with my usual suit and tie so probably wasn't as intimidating, but regardless, I'd expected a bit of fear from Tom. Instead I got the same calm strength as I'd seen at the police station. With a few more profanities than either DI Wood or DS Rice had received.

'Who the fuck are you and what the fuck do you want?'

'My name is Luke and I want a cup of tea. Where's the kitchen?'

He pointed back up the hallway. Liam took a firm grip on Tom's arm and walked him into the bright and airy room. I was impressed, there was an actual AGA stove. The rest of the kitchen was equally tasteful and, most definitely, expensively equipped.

'Sit,' Liam said before producing two plastic tie-wraps from his pocket and binding Tom's wrists. 'I'll check out the rest of the house, make sure he's not lying,' he said and headed out the door.

I lifted a Le Creuset kettle, resplendent with an actual whistle in the spout and filled it with water.

'Who are you?' Tom asked from his chair at the table.

'All in good time, Tom. All in good time.' I opened three cupboards before I found the mugs. Another two to track down sugar, tea bags and an unlooked for bonus of a full pack of ginger nut biscuits. By the time Liam was back I'd retrieved the milk from the fridge and spoons from a cutlery drawer that had contained another unlooked for bonus.

Liam came back into the kitchen and gave me a discrete nod. The house was clear and the basement was full of PCs again. Then he looked down at the table.

'Wow! Where did you find that?' he asked, pointing at the Browning 9mm high-power handgun on the table.

'In with the knives, forks and spoons. Seems our Tom here is full of surprises. He had ginger nuts as well,' I said, pointing to the biscuits.

'Nice. Have you checked it?' Liam asked

'Of course, but, just for your sake.' I lifted the handgun, pressed the magazine release, removed the loaded magazine, set it on the table, pulled the slide back, tilted the weapon to show Liam it was clear, released the slide forward, refitted the magazine, pointed the muzzle at the ground and fired off the action. 'It's simple muscle memory,' I said. All through the pistol drills Tom had sat quietly in the chair. The whistle of the kettle prompted Liam to lift it off the stove.

'Tea?' I asked Tom.

He nodded, but also held up his bound wrists. I lifted the Browning again, pulled back the slide and chambered a round. I swapped the gun into my left hand and levelled it across the table. 'Sure. I can't see why not.'

Liam cut the ties off Tom's wrists.

'See, this is much more civilised, isn't it?' I said and toasted him with my mug.

Tom put milk into his tea and took a sip. There wasn't so much as the smallest tremor in his hands. I was, once more, struck by the gall of the man. Nothing phased him. But perhaps I could change that. I had to hope I could, otherwise this was a wasted journey.

'Right then, Tom. I need some information,' I began.

'You ain't police,' he interrupted. 'Police don't go pointing guns at people. Not in this country at least. 'And you ain't any of the European gangs, not with your posh voice and his England tattoo. That means I don't know who you are. So go fuck yourself for your information.'

'Well done. You're right. I'm not police, but I was involved with their little visit to you back in January. Got to watch your less than productive interview. It was one of my guys who found nothing of note on the PCs in your basement. It was also us who left the software trackers on those machines, but then you did what we knew you would and got rid of them entirely. Probably just dumped in a skip somewhere. Am I right?'

No answer, save for a small smirk of a smile.

'Thing is, you see. I'm not that technical, but the people who work for me are. One in particular was really annoyed at not being able to pin anything on you, so he left another failsafe in place. One that could cope even if you ditched your hardware. Only problem was, to do it, he had to sort of break the law. He needed to infect a couple of UK-based communication companies, so that as and when you guys turned everything back on, he could infect you again.'

Tom tried to hide his reaction, but whilst the old fellow had bravado, he wasn't the best poker player in the world. He had a tell. I paused to see if he was going to speak, but he managed to stifle the need.

'I say sort of, like that was an option. That's the problem with the law, isn't it. You either break it or you don't. Not really a middle ground. My guy's software would flag up if you were trying to rip off our credit card systems again, but it would be of no use in a court. I was okay with that. You know? Just wanted to look out for my own backyard as it were. You get that, don't you, Tom? Looking out for your own self interests?'

I took a sip of tea and watched him over the rim of the mug. The smallest frown adding to the heavy wrinkles that came with his age, told me he was calculating if what I was saying was true. I knew he'd believe me. Not because I was a good liar, but because what I was telling him was true.

After the initial raid on his house, Paul had indeed left trackers and managed to position a failsafe that would be persistent and invasive if hardware was swapped in or out. It was nowhere near as effective as the physical bug Cheltenham had given me to plant into the Chinese servers, but it did what we needed it to do. Sitting dormant since January, it had quietly monitored and waited. If Tom's colleagues tried to go after Bateleur systems again, we'd be able to destroy him from the inside out. Also true was that the mechanisms we had used were illegal under UK law. I had wanted a pre-emptive and destructive capability, not justice.

Eventually he said, 'Go on.'

'We have access to your systems. I could destroy them if I wanted, but you'd just come back, again and again. However, that access also allows me to plant things. Add records. Make transactions. Create false accounts. Not exactly stealing your identity like in the movies, rather it would make your friends in Eastern Europe think you had ripped them off to the tune of a good few hundreds of thousands of pounds.'

The colour drained from Tom's face. It was the most significant emotional response I had seen on the old man since I'd first laid eyes on him. So dramatic that I hesitated and almost asked if he was okay. Instead, I pressed home the advantage. 'You know what the Ukrainians and Romanians and the rest of their ilk are like when it comes to being ripped off. It won't be a quick death. They'll take their time over you.' I lifted my mug and took another sip of tea. Waiting. Letting him consider his options. I wondered how long it would take. Mere seconds was the answer.

'What do you want?'

'Information. That's all.'

'On what?'

'Ever heard of a guy called Vasile Constă?'

I expected diversion tactics, denial, lies and obfuscation. Tom surprised me again.

'Of course I have.'

'Is he connected to your contacts in Ukraine or Romania?'

'Not really. He's an old school gangster based down in Whitechapel. Runs protection, bit of pimping, massage parlours, escorts, that sort of thing. Likes to do knife work on his people if they misbehave. Fucking animal in that regard I've heard.'

I glanced up at Liam. He'd told me of Vasile's handiwork on a former associate who hadn't paid what was owed and how Liam and others had been forced to watch whilst the man had been, quite literally, cut to ribbons. 'What did you mean, not really?' I asked.

'His manor extends up as far as Hackney. Includes Spitalfields and Shoreditch. We have some businesses interests down in Shoreditch.'

'Isn't that a problem?'

'How'd you mean, a problem?'

'Aren't gangs territorial? Don't you all have your own areas?'

Tom laughed. 'You watch too much *Sopranos*, son. It's not like New Jersey. This is London. Anyone can run anything anywhere, so long as they don't interfere with each other.'

'And Vasile doesn't interfere?'

'Nah. I told you, he's old school, down in the weeds money. Hustles and hookers.'

'And your business interests don't cross over?'

'Nah. We don't do that sort of low-level crap. Why risk getting your hands dirty when you can lift ten times as much money in a single night sitting in your living room, on a computer, wearing a dressing gown …'

I had worried that this was a long shot. Romanian gangs had infiltrated all aspects of UK criminal exploits and although Tom was my only, tenuous at best, link with them, it had been unlikely he actually worked with Vasile. I had missed the rest of what he had said. 'Sorry. Say again?'

The old man stopped talking and his head went back a little, tilted to one side. He had a quizzical look on his face. 'Say again?'

'Yes. I missed what you said after dressing gown. Say it again.'

'I know, but you said, say again.'

'So?'

He twisted to look at Liam who was standing behind him, then he came back to face me.

He nodded at the gun in my hand. 'And you know your way around a Browning. Are you military?'

'No. Well, not anymore.'

'But you were?'

'Yes. No secret in that,' I said, getting a little defensive about his question, which in itself surprised me. 'So what?'

'And him?' he asked pointing over his shoulder to Liam.

'Yes, him too. He was a Para and I was Air Force. So?'

Tom unbuttoned the sleeve of his shirt and rolled up the cuff. On his inner arm was a faded tattoo; a six-digit serial number. I was stunned. I'd obviously heard of tattoos like that, but never seen one in real life.

'I got this in Auschwitz in 1942. Later they made us march out of there and I ended up in Bergen-Belsen. The Brits found us. A few months after that I was flown to England as a refugee. The British medics had looked after us, got us fit to travel. The Royal Air Force flew us in Dakotas to England. Gave us soup and bread when we arrived. And lumpy custard. I'd never tasted anything so good.' He smiled at the memory. I looked up at Liam, who shrugged back at me. He had no clue either why the old man was reminiscing. I wasn't sure what to say, so said nothing.

'I'd wanted to join up myself when I got a bit older, but the typhus and other shit I'd had in the camps didn't let me. Made me deaf in one ear. That and I was as thin as a rake and sounded like I was German, which was a fact, 'cos I was.'

I knew he was a thief, but his story was compelling. I tried to imagine how tough conditions would have been in England for a teenage German boy who had just survived the camps. I had no reason to, but I said, 'I'm sorry, Tom.'

'Not your fault, was it? Anyways, I was lucky, weren't I. Family in Hackney took me in. They was Jewish too like, but the old fella was hard as nails. Taught me to stand up for myself. Be a man and all that sort of stuff.' He paused and I could see his memories of his family were warm ones. 'Owe them everything I do.'

'Your adopted family?'

'Yes. Them, of course, but I meant the Army and the Air Force. Liberating the camp when they did, flying me to England. If it hadn't been for them, I'd be dead. No question.' He stopped and reached for his tea. I waited, not sure what to say or do. A quick look at Liam got another shrug in reply.

Tom set his mug down on the table and placed his hands flat on the surface. 'So you were Air Force?'

'Yeah.'

'And now you do what?'

'Work for a bank. Cyber security.'

He nodded. 'Makes sense. And you and him are partners?' he asked, pointing over his shoulder again at Liam.

I felt the flush of colour in my cheeks.

'I'll take that as a yes then,' Tom said and laughed. 'Listen, boys, what's your names and what do you want with Vasile? Wouldn't imagine he's in your usual social circles.'

I knew all the rules of interview and interrogation. I was meant to keep the upper hand, control the flow of information. Perhaps it was having heard Tom's story or seeing the faded ink on his inner arm, but whatever the reason, I told him the truth.

'I'm Luke. This is Liam, He got into a bit of bother when he came back from a tour of Afghanistan. Ended up out of the army.'

Liam sat down at the table. 'The judge didn't value the army as much as you do. Sent me down for a few months for beating up a couple of low-life scum. Army weren't too keen on the publicity it stirred up so that was that. Career over. No pay out, no pension.'

'How's Vasile come into the frame?' Tom asked, and I was distinctly aware he was now running the conversation. I didn't mind.

Liam hesitated, so I continued. 'That can be the problem with suddenly having to leave the military. You lose everything. He was living rough, doing what he needed to get by …' I left the sentence hanging, but Tom's sage-like nod of the head told me he understood. Liam looked down at the table. Yet again Solomon surprised me as he reached out and patted Liam's hand.

'S'okay son. We all have to do what we need to survive. No shame in it. But I suppose that's where Vasile comes into it? Got you out of the gutter and working for him?'

Liam nodded.

'And now?'

I brought Tom up to date. Vasile had run into Liam again and wanted him back running the rent-boy scam. Had a client he wanted to blackmail, but when Liam had tried to say no he'd let slip that he was in a relationship. From there it hadn't taken long for Vasile to simply adjust his plan. He wanted Liam to extort cash from me. Lots of it.

By the time I'd finished, Tom was rubbing his chin and looking annoyed.

'He's a right bastard that Vasile. I ain't had nothing directly to do with him, but like I say, I heard he can be a handful. Thing is, I do know a lot of Romanians. One of my best and oldest friends was a proper Romani. You know? Gypsy through and through. We was on that same Dakota flight into Britain. He had one of these,' he pointed down at his tattoo. 'Only his had a Z in front of the number. Me and him had some times together when we was younger. All his boys went into the family business, if you know what I mean,' he tapped the side of his nose and laughed.

'Is that how you got connected with the Ukrainians and the cyber fencing?' I asked, not meaning it to be a continuation of any search for information. I was genuinely curious.

'Ah, that'd be telling. I mean, allegedly, if I was to do that sort of thing, it might have been handy.' Another laugh. 'Anyway, when does Vasile want his money?'

Liam took the question. 'Ten days at the latest.'

'And was your plan to come here and if Vasile was connected to me, use the threat of fucking me up to fuck him up?'

The question was specifically directed at me. There was little point in trying to lie. 'Pretty much. I knew it was thin, but we had nothing else.'

'You didn't think of going to your pals in the Met?'

'Not an option. I'd be okay, but if we went to the cops then Vasile would just get his guys to kill Liam at some point. We need to fight force with real force.'

Despite it probably being cold by now, Tom drained the last of his tea. Setting the mug down on the table he looked between Liam and I a couple of times.

'I haven't done favours or good turns for many people, but I always made sure I tried to do the right thing for any military guys I met. You know, not roll them on a Friday night, or nick their wallet or their watch, that type of thing. And here you two are. Both forces, and him a war hero no less.'

'Hardly a hero,' Liam offered.

'You say that, but you went and done your bit. And you, from the Air Force to cyber in a bank. That's a journey. Tell me something, you said your team were good. How good are they? How good are you?'

I didn't get a chance to answer before Liam said, 'He's one of the top ten cyber intel guys in the world. He'd not tell you himself, far too modest, but he's paid a fortune and the amount of times he's being asked to go and speak at conferences and write articles. That's why Vasile thinks he can nail him for the money. Destroy him if he doesn't pay, 'cos he has a lot to lose.'

It was said with an intensity I hadn't expected. All I could do was offer a small shrug. I still didn't take compliments easily.

'And your technical team,' Tom continued. 'Can they really do the stuff you said?'

'Yeah. They can,' I answered. 'Why do you ask, Tom. Where's this heading?'

'I don't like bullies and thugs. Never have. Understandable I suppose, seeing the company I was forced to keep as a boy. Vasile's always been a bit of a rough edge, but we've ignored him 'cos he ain't rubbed us up the wrong way. Maybe we should change that?'

'It's like you said, Tom, my only knowledge about gangs is from the TV, but won't doing something against him cause a rift on the streets.'

'More than a rift. It'd start an all-out war if my lads were to single him out for no reason, but that won't be the case. Not if your team can do what you say they can.'

'Ah! I see.'

'And anyway, I'm not getting any younger. My old mate died a few years ago and hardly got to enjoy any of the money he'd made. I was thinking of hanging up my boots, passing it all on to a couple of his lads and bowing out. They have the tech skills and me and their old man taught them the street smarts. Maybe I'll make this my last hurrah.

'Always fancied seeing Cuba. You can go there on holidays now. Maybe I'll go see Jerusalem as well. Never been in all my years. Probably should go take a look. What do you reckon?'

'I imagine it would be impressive and Cuba sounds good,' Liam agreed.

'No. Not the holiday, son. Fucking up Vasile so he doesn't come near you again?'

'Oh! Well, yeah, that sounds good too,' Liam said with a sheepish grin. 'What do you need us to do?'

'I imagine you'd like to jump up and down on his head, but sadly this is one of those times when you'll have to sit it out. Unless you're into cyber fraud?'

'Not me,' Liam said.

'Well then, Luke, can your crew actually take down systems from the inside out?'

'Yes. Easily,' I answered, never having thought of Rachel, Mark, Steve and Paul as a crew before.

'What about changing things so hard evidence was left?'

'Like a trail of breadcrumbs?' I asked, thinking back to what Steve and Paul had done against the Ukrainian bank servers.

'Yeah, but not coming back to me, obviously. Do you think, if I got a way in for you, they could make it look like Vasile was trying to rip my guys off?'

'If you get me a way in I can make it more than look like it. I can move the money to be in whatever account you want.'

'A reverse?' Tom offered.

'A what?'

'A reverse. It's what we used to call it when you picked a pocket and planted it into someone else's. Handy skill if the law or the mark thought they'd seen you do the first lift.' He gave a broad grin and added, 'Allegedly, of course.'

'Of course. Allegedly. But yeah, if that's what it is, we could do a reverse and plant any amount of cash in any account. Like I got told while I was watching your police interview, picking a packet or two is easier than pockets.'

Tom gave me a wink and patted Liam's hand again. 'Well then boys, we might be in business … In fact, now I think about it, I might have a role for you to play after all Liam. You up for it?'

'Absolutely, what do you need?'

22

Afghanistan, 8th July 2009

Dan threw his kit bag into the corner of the hooch and sat on the sad-looking camp bed. He subconsciously drew his hand over the faded scar on his head before picking up his rifle and stripping it down to clean.

It was disorientating. Less than forty-eight hours earlier he'd sat in a round-circle meeting in a conversion camp in Nebraska. Now he was back in the Korengal. He seriously wondered which of the two experiences was worse for his mental state. Although the conversion therapy didn't come with the threat of being shot, maimed or killed, so he supposed it was technically safer. For him at least. The emotions of the two days spent back in that place had made him seriously consider shooting Shirlene.

Dan had been granted a compassionate 7-day pass to go home because the new baby, Lilly-Anne, had been diagnosed with bacterial meningitis. Shirlene had been visiting her folks up in Stanton, Nebraska so the baby had been rushed to Faith Regional. It had taken him an agonising thirty-three hours to get from Korengal to Kabul to Offutt Air Force Base and thence to the bedside of his three month old daughter. By the time he was there, the immediate crisis was over. The antibiotics were working and the baby was recovering well. He was massively relieved and spent hours gazing down at the little bundle in the incubator-cum-crib as she gurgled up at him.

Not the best of circumstances, still, it was a wonderful chance to set eyes on his new daughter for the first time and to get home to a soft bed, clean towels and a decent shower. He'd had down time recovering from the wounds in January, but that had all been spent in-country and mostly at Bagram Airbase Hospital. The usual mid-deployment R&R had come around in April and he'd spent it in Qatar on the Army R2P2 program. Whilst much-needed and especially the couple of deep sea fishing trips out in the Gulf waters, what he'd wanted to do had been swap that R&R for a few days stateside in May, when the baby had been born, but the Army had said, no dice. So to be able to get home and see Lilly-Anne, despite her being in hospital, hooked up to monitors and with in-travenous driplines in her tiny arms, had been a huge boon. Having to put up with Shirlene, less so.

When she wasn't moaning at him she was shooting her mouth off about President Obama. According to her he was the worst thing to have happened to the country. Even worse were the vile comments she would make about the First Lady. Dan ignored it, and Shirlene in general, as best he could, but was thinking seven days compassionate was about as much as he could take. Then to add to his joy, his parents had arrived.

Not enough to come themselves, his father insisted on bringing Pastor Harold to pray for the baby and for Dan's continued journey down the straight and narrow path to God's forgiveness. Dan knew full well that his father's emphasis was on the straight. To have them turn up was annoying enough, but for the ex-con turned preacher to suggest Dan re-join him for a 2-day "refresher" at the conversion therapy camp had been the last thing he wanted to hear. His father and Shirlene turned the suggestion into a de-mand.

'You go, boy. It'll be good for you,' his father had said. 'Make sure you don't slip into any bad ways again. Let the Lord see to your soul, like he saw to your body when he saved your life. He has plans for you son.' He'd repeated it like a mantra for almost a full day. At least he had made reference to the wounds Dan had suffered. Shirlene, her voice shriller and more cutting, hadn't even acknowledged the fact he'd almost been killed.

'You should just do what your daddy is telling you to. I don't need you around here, not now the baby is getting better. Where were you for the birth? Some husband and father you are. You won't even be here when I have to go back down to Georgia and wait for you. And Ryan won't even remember what you look like by the time you get home for good. Leaving me on my own and we were meant to be in Italy like a proper family. You should go and pray for your soul and for forgiveness for what you went and done to me.'

She'd continued for hours, but he'd tuned her out. He'd played with Ryan and told him his little sister would be fine. Then he packed his bag and went with the Pastor. A return to a conversion camp was preferred over Shirlene. The cowardice of his actions and an inability to walk away from his shrew of a wife ate into him, but he knew he couldn't risk a divorce. He'd never win custody of the kids whilst he was in the military. Sitting in the midst of the conversion circle he was as sure as ever that he still loved Luke, but like a lightbulb going off in his head, he was also sure that he would likely never leave Shirlene. He'd boarded the transport to Kabul with a regret borne not from leaving home once more, but of an unobtainable longing.

The actions in cleaning his M4 assault rifle were automatic. He reassembled the weapon and then drew his sidearm. Straightening out the cloth on his cot, he field stripped and cleaned the Beretta M9 pistol. The routine of the mundane was cathartic and allowed his thoughts to drift across a myriad of images and memories. Once the pistol was thoroughly clean he reassembled it, refitted the 15-round magazine and dropped the hammer. The gun sat neatly in his hand, the weight of it somehow comfortingly familiar. He turned the weapon, so that the muzzle pointed up at him. A push of his thumb and the safety would disengage. A double pull on the trigger and that would be that. No more need to worry about anything. He wondered at the men, mostly men, who had done those things and saw only blackness. Did the regret of their actions flood the last micro-seconds between the pull on the trigger and the round smashing into their brain? And what of the darkness? His family and Shirlene spouted that God's love was first and foremost, then family, then the great United States of America. He wasn't so sure. Luke had hated religion and detested the man-made conglomerates each had become. Pastor Harold had been saved by it. Dan's problem wasn't with anyone having faith, it was when they tried to mould that faith to suit their own needs. Hadn't Jesus told all of humanity to love one another? So why did certain people of faith decide that love couldn't be extended to gays or people of opposing faiths, or a frightened girl who wanted to terminate a pregnancy or people whose skin was a different colour? He couldn't accept that.

Staring down the barrel of the gun he felt his thumb against the safety. Push it down, pull back on the trigger. Simple.

The sun was fading quickly behind the mountains and darkness was enveloping him. Taking a deep breath, Dan lifted his thumb off the safety, turned the pistol back around and holstered it. A few moments went by, or it could have been an hour, as Dan sat in silent contemplation, lost in his own thoughts. Eventually the light clicked on, its white intensity scattering the shadows from the room and his mind.

'Ah! I was told you'd made it back. Kid doing okay?'

'Yes Morrie, she sure is,' he answered in as upbeat a tone as he could manage.

'Well, can't imagine you'd choose to be in this shithole, Sir, but it's good to see you.' Staff Sergeant Lieberman handed over a mug of coffee and took the only other seat in the hooch. 'Ten weeks today, we'll all be out of here and you can cuddle that little girl of yours for ever and a day.'

**

I looked out from my new glass-walled office on the 20th floor of Bateleur, London and wondered, yet again, how the heck I was going to raise the matter with Mark.

The office had been a necessity rather than a luxury. I'd had it designed specifically to ensure I wasn't cut off from my team, but it did allow me to take phone calls and conference calls away from the hum of machines and the often spirited debates that tended to erupt between Paul, Steve, Mark and Rachel.

I was beginning to worry again. I'd already wasted a day and a half trying to figure out how I could convince Mark to help me launder a substantial sum of money in order to frame Vasile.

Mark certainly had the skills, but I had no idea if he would bend his moral code to do what I needed. The plan was simple enough. Tom had been in the game long enough to come up with a devious twist in order to solve the problem of Vasile once and for all, but he didn't have the means to pull it off. In return for me providing those means, Tom had all but guaranteed Vasile would forget about any extortion racket. The means I was to supply were an advanced level of technical, forensic and programming skills. The natural choice was Paul, but I didn't feel comfortable coercing the young man into doing it. I was certain he'd have felt obliged to do what his boss told him and that would have been wrong of me.

Conversely, I was sure that Steve and Mark, both possessing the necessary technical abilities, would tell me to sod off if they didn't feel happy helping me. As would Rachel, but she didn't have high-end programming skills. Given my longstanding relationship with Mark, it was an easy choice to make. Easy, but difficult to instigate. Mark was an ex-military cop and I worried he'd be less than pleased that I was asking him to do something like this. My approach needed to be finessed, but the clock was ticking. Vasile wanted his money in eight days. I had to bite the bullet. I got up from my chair just as Rachel walked through the office door. There was never any need to knock or hover, that wasn't my way, so she strolled in and as was her style, got straight to the point.

'We may have a bit of a situation brewing.'

'Go on.'

'Rumours coming out of Egypt.'

'Really? I thought all was well in the land of the pharaohs. Wasn't President Obama's speech in Cairo last month meant to signal a new beginning?'

'Mmm, something like that. Word is the new beginning might well be starting but I suspect no one has told President Mubarak.'

'So what's happening and how does it affect us?'

'It might be nothing but the country head of Bateleur down there is an English guy called Fabian Judd.'

'Why do I recognise that name?' I asked, retaking my seat and waving Rachel into another.

'He was at the first meeting of the Inter-Bank Task Force.'

I paused and thought back to the awkward beginnings of what was now such a valuable information and proactive intelligence resource. 'Tall guy, blonde hair? Looked like he should have been opening the batting for the England First XI?'

Rachel confirmed with a nod of her head. 'Yep. He was the non-technical rep that National Citie sent along. Apparently the Bateleur HR department recruited him to be head of Egyptian Bank Operations about three months ago.'

'And he's in trouble because he doesn't speak Arabic?'

'No, not that at all. Surprisingly, he speaks it fluently. He was picked for the role because he has, in addition to a Politics, Philosophy and Economics degree from Oxford, a Masters in Islamic Studies and History.'

'I'm impressed,' I said and actually was. I recalled him more now and what with his name, Fabian Judd, his appearance of tall, blonde and blue-eyed and an accent that I remembered being "plummy", I wouldn't have guessed him for an Islamic scholar. 'So what is Mr Judd concerned about?'

'Apparently there have been a rising number of labour strikes that have been swiftly put down by the police with the help of the State Security Investigations Service. Ringleaders rounded up and never seen again, mass arrests, beatings, standard stuff.'

'Okay. Nothing Mubarak hasn't been doing for years. What's new this time?'

'There are counter-demos happening now. Probably instigated by the SSIS, again nothing new, but these ones are being staged in front of union buildings and firms that have union members. All straight out of how-to-keep-a-dictator-in-power 101. Problem is, the Union of Textile Workers is one of the largest in the country, one of the most vocal in its condemnation of the Mubarak regime and therefore one of the prime targets for the demonstrators.'

It made sense in a depressingly familiar, non-democratic way. I couldn't imagine the bravery needed to be a voice for liberation and freedom in such a situation. 'And Fabian is reporting this through to us because …?'

'The Textile Union does all of its banking with the Banque de la Société Commerciale d'Egypte.'

'Phew,' I said. 'I thought you were going to say they do all their banking with us.'

'Yeah, well there's the rub. We bought that bank six weeks ago in our continuing merger and acquisitions program.'

'Oh shit!'

**

Rachel and I were standing at the head of the small conference table. The audience of three were Pat Harris, William Carmichael and, for reasons I couldn't grasp as yet, Dickie Lessen.

Rachel finished taking them through the news from Egypt. She had hardly stopped talking before Lessen launched in.

'And why is this any of your concern, Raquel?'

I took over. 'It's Rachel, not Raquel, Dickie. We received the report because my team control the inter-country communications networks. We're also the final gateway to Bateleur London's internal communication servers. All inter-departmental reports come through us and any security reports land on my desk first. Usually, this would also have gone to William, but Fabian hasn't been in post that long and he knows me and Rachel, so he sent it to us because he knew we would flag it up.'

'Well that's all very interesting I'm sure. I was more enquiring about, mmm, let's see if I can make it more straightforward for you …'

I felt a rise of annoyance and a flush of red spreading up my neck. I was about to shoot this supercilious pompous ass down in flames, when I saw the slightest of movements from Pat. The smallest shake of the head. I held my tongue.

'… why should we care that there are demonstrations?'

Rachel and I hadn't expected that we'd need to remind Pat or William, but obviously that wasn't the case with Dickie. Her voice, unlike what mine would have been, remained calm and neutral. 'Because there is precedent in situations like this. In Morocco five years ago, Tunisia a couple of years ago and only last year in the Democratic Republic of the Congo. Government sponsored counter-protests have targeted any assets that were seen to be backing the anti-government movements. That includes financial institutions that might be linked. Various bank officials have been murdered, or their families kidnapped or both. The bank gives in and cuts off all accounts so that the anti-government group is starved of financial resources.'

'Yes, well I am sure that may have happened to some regional tin-pot banks in those countries, but it is hardly going to happen to us at Bateleur,' Dickie said, folding his arms over his belly.

I looked between William and Pat. Both said nothing. I knew I was missing something important, but I couldn't work out what. Rachel looked to me and raised an eyebrow. 'Dickie, the thing is,' I said, fighting to keep the annoyance out of my voice. 'The situation warrants that we keep a very close eye on it. I was coming to brief William because as Head of Physical Security he will need to have a plan in place to get Fabian and his family out of Cairo if things worsen. Pat needs to know because if we do evacuate, then we will also have to assume the bank's premises will be compromised. William will look after the physical side of that too, but my team will have to remotely secure and clear the Cairo server farm.'

Dickie turned in his seat to look at William. 'Is this right?'

'Yes, of course,' the large man said, in his usual gruff tone, yet even in such a short reply I could sense an added frustration.

'Well your job's simple enough. I can't imagine you'd need much of a plan. Can't they just go to the airport and get on a plane?'

Dickie had no clue as to how stupid his question was. I liked people who admitted they didn't know things and asked for help, but the way he had led off by dismissing William's input wouldn't warm him to anyone. I half-expected, or perhaps it was hoped, that William would raise one of his very large fists and thump Dickie in his fat mouth. Sadly, he didn't.

'It's not that easy,' William answered. 'If Bateleur Bank officials are under physical threat, I go out with one of our sub-contracted security teams and escort them to safety. Otherwise there's no guarantee they'd even make it past their front door, let alone to an airport. It's how we do things in cases like this. It's the only way to be sure they are protected.'

'And how much does all that cost?' Dickie asked.

'As much as it takes,' William answered.

Dickie stood up. 'Well let's just be very clear on one thing. That's how you may have done things in the past, but I'm the new sheriff in town. No one does anything or starts writing out blank cheques for some *Boy's Own* rescue adventure without my absolute approval.'

Again, I said nothing, and waited for Pat or William to tell this horrid man to shut up, but they didn't. Dickie stomped out and pulled the door closed behind him. Rachel's face was, I guessed, reflecting the surprise and shock on my own.

'Umm, what just happened?' I asked.

Pat gestured for me and Rachel to sit down. 'I'm sorry you were blindsided. It hasn't been formally announced yet, obviously, or I know you would have been in to my office as mad as a kicked rattlesnake.'

I was still confused. 'Why was Lessen here and what hasn't been announced?'

'There's been a shake-up of the executive management teams. A cabinet reshuffle so to speak. Sir Anthony,' Pat said, referring to the bank's Group Chairman, 'has decided that moving the executives around a bit will be good for their overall management skills. He also decided to reward a few with promotions. Dickie was one of those.'

'Reward for what exactly?' Rachel asked before I could.

'For leading the Shanghai data centre project and opening it early and under budget.'

'But he did nothing on that project other than be a figurehead and a blundering one at that. The nitty-gritty was all your work, Pat,' I said, completely incredulous that Sir Anthony Marius, who

I had always thought of as smart, could have been hoodwinked by someone like Dickie Lessen.

'It's fine, Luke. It isn't anything I wouldn't have expected. You've seen how Dickie is around high-powered people. He ingratiates himself and they're left with an impression.'

'More like a bad aftertaste,' Rachel said under her breath.

Pat shrugged. 'Anyway, it's all due to be announced later this week, but he's already moved into his new office and was talking to William when you phoned for this briefing. He decided to invite himself.'

'But why? What's he been promoted to?' I asked, dreading the answer.

'Global Executive Director of Security. He's now my boss. And Pat's too,' William said.

'And ultimately, yours as well,' Pat added with a sigh. Rachel and I walked back with him to the elevators.

'One bright spot, Luke.'

'Yes?'

'I've been approached by a company asking if we'd be prepared to put forward a paper and a speaker for the Inaugural Cyber Crime, Forensics and something, something Conference.'

'Something, something?' Rachel said. 'Catchy title.'

'Yeah well, you know what these things are like. Title made by committee. Wonder it isn't called Nerds and Ne'er-do-wells.'

'Now that is a catchy title,' I said laughing. 'When and where?'

'End of September. Doha. They were impressed by your presentation at the Tampa Conference over Easter.'

'Sounds okay. Yes, I'd be happy to.'

'Good, because when I found out yesterday that Dickie was going to be promoted in over me and that he'd have control of the budget, I rang the company back and volunteered you. It's all locked in now, so there's nothing he'll be able to do.'

'Oh! Okay. What am I speaking on?'

'They want a forty-five minute address on cyber intelligence acquisition and exploitation.' Pat gave me a wink. 'Piece of cake, as you Brits would say.'

**

When I got back to the 20th floor with Rachel we briefed the rest of the team on the news about Lessen. Amidst groans and complaints, which I would usually have tried to stem, I said nothing. The man was a dick. Plain and simple. I was reminded of how quickly one bad leader could demoralise even the best of teams. I'd seen it in the military and now here it was again.

When we had finally settled back into work mode, I asked Mark to come into the office. I thought direct and honest would be the key. 'I'm in a spot of bother.'

He answered immediately. 'What can I do to help?'

Twenty minutes later he said, 'Of course, you daft sod. Why on earth would you think I wouldn't help you? It'll be fun playing at being a bad guy for a change.'

23

Restaurants, barber's shops, hairdressers, pizza takeaways, and bars. Rivington Street, Shoreditch had them all. There was even a small laundrette at the corner with Shoreditch High Street, a fitting nod to the origins of the term that encompassed what this street was fantastic for. The only shame was the lack of a casino along its narrow length, but I could allow a bit of grace as there was one right across the street to the west and another not two minutes' walk to the south. Rivington Street was a veritable perfect storm for money laundering.

I had known how it worked in theory, but when Tom explained how it actually worked in practise I was stunned. It was way more labour intensive that I had imagined. In Tom's case, there was an additional step to the usual model I was familiar with. His front-end operation was the collection of credit card and bank account details. It turned out, that was relatively straightforward. They used a few well-placed skimmers or compromised a Common Point of Purchase, like in the Ukrainian incident, for the cards. The bank details were obtained using cloned websites and phishing emails.

Then his associates, the exact number of which he was still coy about, but I got the impression there were a lot spread throughout the world, used the stolen information to make cloned cards. From there it was a case of some frantic shopping sprees before the bank or the account holder realised their funds were being drained and put a hold in place.

Worst case, from Tom's perspective, they got to use a cloned card for about half an hour, or perhaps one single purchase. Best case, in his experience, had been three weeks and a total fraud of fifty seven thousand pounds on a single card number. In the end they'd voluntarily ditched it because they feared the next time they used it the authorities would be waiting.

Usually though, his global army of buyers simply made as much as they could in the time available and, given the numbers, even a single transaction for a few pounds, dollars or euros all added up. The majority of purchases were for medium value cash gift cards. Alternatively they'd buy high-value electronics or jewellery that was then sold on eBay for a fraction of the price. In some cases, if they were in the right part of the world, they'd simply make a cash withdrawal through a shop using the cloned card and a signature that they didn't even have to forge. This wasn't stealing credit cards from wallets, this was stealing the data and making a replica card, so they could add their own random squiggle on the back of it if needed.

The gift cards were cashed, the eBay money transferred and through a myriad of secondary accounts and multiple transfer points, all of it ended up in six separate feeder accounts.

Until 2005, that had been how they'd made the majority of their money, but since his old friend had died and the Ukrainians had taken a bigger role, the majority of the income now came from selling stolen credit card data to other entities. The going rate was $25 US for a single card's data. As Tom was explaining that, Mark had given a low whistle.

'There were over fourteen thousand cards compromised in that latest Ukrainian scam alone. That's over a quarter of a million dollars.'

'Three hundred and fifty six thousand, seven hundred dollars to be precise,' Tom said, before adding, 'Allegedly.'

I could do nothing but shake my head.

The bill had been paid in gift cards and untraceable mobile phone wire transfers. Regardless of how it was sourced, spending sprees or reselling, all the income streams ended up in the same feeder accounts and from there, Tom and a few UK-based people lifted it from ATMs, converting it back into cash. Yet, after all of that, technically the money was still dirty. It had been acquired and moved to obscure it, but if Tom used it to buy a car or a house or anything at all, then the Inland Revenue would want to know where he'd gotten it all from. Hence the need for Rivington Street.

**

'Why here?' I asked.

Tom crossed the street and spoke over his shoulder to me, 'London always was the centre of world money and business. Government after government has encouraged new enterprises to start-up. Been that way since the 16th century. Did you know that nowadays you can set up a company in the UK for about twelve quid? Even better, use an assistance company to set up a company and most of them won't bother checking IDs. You have a company and a bank account set up in a false ID and then you're set to go.'

Mark, his copper's head still firmly attached to his shoulders, added, 'Even if an ID was found to be a bit suss, there hasn't been one prosecution brought under that legislation. Not one. Ever.'

'See?' Tom said, his old eyes twinkling with mischief. 'Almost like they want us to be here.'

'Yeah, but why are we here?'

'Ahh,' Tom said and pointed to the end of the street. 'From the laundrette to,' he turned and pointed in the other direction, 'the pub on the corner, there are fifteen cash intensive businesses on this street. Plus a couple of casinos nearby. Me and my colleagues come down here every day and place the cash we've lifted into the tills of these businesses. The extra income is explained away by false receipts or invoices or sometimes, like the laundrette and the casino there's no need for any of that, it just is what it is. Not like you give out receipts for a spin of a washing machine or a roulette wheel. As long as we don't have spikes and troughs and we keep things consistent, then we're good.'

'Placement,' I said. 'This is where you do your placement.'

'Yep.' Tom said. 'C'mon, I'll treat you to lunch.'

**

We ate in a restaurant that was far from full, but the food was good and the wine was excellent.

'This place does about sixteen grand in sales each week. That's legit sales. We boost that to about thirty six. The accountants do their magic and at the far end we clear about a million-one each year.'

'But how can you more than double an income stream without raising suspicions?' I asked, looking about the place.

'Easy. It's London. We added expensive things onto the menu, that we don't actually sell and added more tables than we could ever fill. A cursory inspection by a taxman wouldn't see anything out of the ordinary. Lots of seats, lots of expensive dishes. Hell, I could probably wash even more through this place and it not be a problem.'

'I guess it also helps that all of the prices in all of the Rivington Street restaurants you run are a little inflated, and yet they're all doing well, but the connection between businesses isn't made as they're all registered in different company names?' Mark asked.

'That's right. We're a little hot spot of gastronomic delight,' Tom said with a chuckle. 'And the restaurants are the low end of things. We clean millions more through the bars and nightclubs, but the casinos are the real hard workers.'

'And that's that. You take a cut of the profits and the money is clean and good to go?' I said, thinking that it was no wonder credit card fraud was so prevalent.

'No. Not by a long way. We still need to build in protection,' Tom said. 'If, for whatever reason, this business got bounced and properly investigated, then I don't want my name anywhere near it. That's why it's registered under dummy identities. So we have to shift the dough till it can't be traced back.'

Mark nodded almost appreciatively. This was called layering. I had always imagined it like an electronic version of that old card game, *Follow The Lady*. Money jumped from one account to another, back and forth, in and out of share accounts, investment accounts and back into clean accounts. By the time it arrived at the end of the line, trying to trace it back was virtually impossible.

'That's where things have really changed,' Tom continued. 'Used to be we'd manually move it around the place, but now you get an 18-year-old kid to write five lines of code and the money does all the dancing for you. Also means we can add in a lot more hops.'

'How many are you looking at?' Mark asked.

'Guess?' Tom teased and raised his own glass of wine.

'Ten?'

'Not even close.'

'More than ten? Oh well, I have no idea then,' Mark said.

'We average about forty-five. Quite a lot of it has a final hop through Guangdong Province in China, because of its proximity to Macau.'

I thought back to a windswept Macau and a luxury casino that gave Mont Blanc fountain pens away as a courtesy gift. Millions of dollars could pass through there without turning a single hair on a head.

'And then you get your pay out?' I asked.

'Yeah. I have my regular investments and income, long established and completely legit,' Tom said with a grin. 'I'm well enough set.' He reached for his glass and finished his wine. 'Okay, to work. Did you bring the laptop?'

Mark opened his briefcase, lifted out the PC and turned it on.

'Great, and the software, you find it okay?'

'Yep,' Mark said, opening up a program called CredentialTaker. 'We actually had a copy on our system. I've used it for penetration testing, but this'll be the first time I've ever seen what it can do from the other side. I do need to link it to the reader.'

Tom reached into his jacket pocket and produced a two-inch square piece of plastic. It had a slot running down one side and a recessed button in the top.

'Whoa, that's a lot smaller than I was expecting,' Mark said.

'Technology advances, what can I tell you?' Tom laughed. 'And, Luke, you're coming with me, yes?'

'Yes,' I said.

'Okay. Ready?'

Mark entered a command on the keyboard. A single green light next to the recessed button of the reader lit up.

'Take this and test it out,' Tom said, handing me the reader.

I swiped one of my debit cards through it. Instantly the device wirelessly transmitted the details of the card to the laptop.

'Got them,' Mark said and turned the screen round. Not just the card number but all the details of the card, including my name, the bank sort code and account number, the debit transactions were linked to, and every other piece of data needed to make a clone, captured in the time it took to swipe a magnetic strip. It was impressive … and frightening.

'The software is free to download and you can buy a reader like this from a few websites for less than two hundred bucks. Pair it up with a card printer and some plastic blanks, all of which cost about three hundred and you're in business,' Tom said and patted me on the shoulder as he stood up. 'Your job in cyber is only gonna get tougher young man. Right, let's go.'

**

The meeting place had been set by Vasile and was in the heart of his home manor of Whitechapel. Apparently he liked to hold court in an upmarket coffee shop that nestled in Gunthorpe Street's narrow confines. Diagonally opposite and only a few feet further down the cobbled street was the side door to the equally narrow White Hart Pub.

Tom and I entered through the front door of the pub, above which was a sign proudly boasting that it had been established in 1721. The interior of it was exactly how I imagined an East End boozer. All dark brown woods, lead-light windows and copper memorabilia hanging off every hook.

'Bit of an egotistically gruesome prick is Vasile, ain't he?' Tom said, after I'd ordered him a pint and me a gin and tonic.

'Think the gruesome goes without saying. Liam told me what he'd done to one of his own guys for not paying a debt. But, egotistical?"

'To have his little fiefdom centred here,' Tom said, inclining his head towards the side door.

'I don't follow.'

He twisted on the bar stool and pointed to a painted wooden wall plaque. The picture showed a Victorian-era lady and gent, him with a doctor's bag in hand. The swirling script told the story of Martha Tabram, sometimes known as Martha Turner, prostitute, who had her last drink in this very pub on Bank Holiday Monday, 6th August 1888. Early the next morning she'd been brutally murdered in a building further up the side ally, on what was now Gunthorpe Street. Savagely stabbed thirty-nine times, Martha was widely presumed to be the first of Jack the Ripper's victims.

'Ah! I see what you mean. Wow, I didn't know that was here.'

'Yeah, out that door, past his coffee shop and up a bit. I mean the building she was found in is long gone, but for a guy who has a reputation for knife work to base himself down here, well, either he's an ignorant fuck who doesn't know his history, or an egotistical little prick. I'd go for the second. The Romanians tend to know history. All that Vlad the fucking Impaler stuff.'

'Quite cool though, that the same pub's still here,' I said.

'Yeah, I guess, but it ain't that long ago. Not really.'

I did the math in my head. 'A hundred and twenty-one years next month? That's quite a while.'

'For you youngsters it is. Think about this, dear old Martha only died forty years before I was born. Any Londoner about my age will have known people who knew her.'

He was right and for some reason my thoughts went to Dan. What little time we all had and how fleeting it was.

We sat quietly for a few more minutes and watched the clock tick by. At five to three, Liam walked in the front door and angled towards us. He was in his usual jeans and t-shirt but had a loose fitting jacket on over the top. Tom took out a five centimetre thick envelope from his inside pocket and slipped it into the left hand side pocket of Liam's jacket. The motion was slickly done and because Liam hadn't faltered in his stride, almost impossible to have been seen by anyone in the pub. He continued out through the side door.

Tom got up and followed. I took a slim cigar from my pocket and walked out too, but whereas Tom followed Liam up to the café, I loitered just past the entrance door of the pub, another smoker relegated to stand outside for their habit. My vantage point gave me a clear line of sight to the coffee shop's main window and inside to the faux leather settees and hipster artwork.

The plan was fairly straightforward. Tom knew of Vasile, but had never actually met him and didn't know what he looked like. Whether Vasile was even aware of Tom's existence was a moot point, but he certainly wouldn't have known Tom to see. Vasile knew of me, but didn't know what I looked like. Liam was the lynchpin.

The café was Vasile's home turf, where he felt safe and secure, but it was still a commercial venture, so customers came and went, especially on a summer's day at the height of the London tourist season. I had wondered at that, but Tom said it was good cover for the Romanian, and even better for us. By now, I had no choice, I had to trust the old man.

My phone beeped. Mark's message was short, "Here".

Behind me, on the other side of the White Hart Pub, so only about thirty yards in a straight line, was a burger restaurant. Inside it, Mark had set up the laptop. I checked the reader. The green light was on. I checked my watch. Three o'clock. Showtime.

**

A beautiful young woman was walking down from the far end of Gunthorpe Street. As Liam entered the café, the woman, whose name Tom had told me was Monika, and who was wearing a bright "I 'heart' London" t-shirt, gave a cheery wave and a cry of, '*Huhu!*'

Tom waved back, they embraced and then they too entered the café. I watched on as unobtrusively as I could. At the angle I was standing to it, the broad picture window gave off no reflections and seeing into the interior was like watching a drama on a flat-screen TV. Real life *Eastenders*.

Vasile looked exactly as I had imagined. Thin, wiry, tall, but not as tall as Liam. Rough stubble on his chin and on his head. Dark features and dark clothes. Black jeans, black open-necked shirt. Sleeves rolled up to show blue-ink tattoos on his forearms. More showing on his neck. He sat on a settee next to the far wall of the café and didn't move when Liam entered. Two men, dressed in suits and about the same size and shape as Liam got up from an adjoining table. Not to do anything as overt as frisking Liam, just to assert their presence and to position a chair opposite the settee. Vasile, who finally stood and shook hands, offered Liam to sit.

Tom and Monika meanwhile had entered the café and walked to the counter. The girl was one of the few living relatives Tom had. His Grandfather's youngest brother had been the only other member of Tom's family to have survived the war and technically he'd explained that Monika was his eighteen year old second cousin twice removed, but within the family everyone called her his niece. She and her parents had visited him often over the years and this trip was going to be her last for a while before she started her training as a flight attendant with Lufthansa. The fact she'd been in town was a convenience that had stopped Tom having to involve any of his usual street associates, or worse, trying to do it alone.

One other detail he'd told me about his niece was how, as a little girl, she'd delighted in the game of him picking her pockets and making the objects appear elsewhere. As she grew, she became an accomplished singer and a skier, both of which required prac-tise to excel. In his telling me of her, Tom had been most proud of the fact that throughout the years, she had practised equally hard to perfect the skills he had taught her.

I understood that with them talking German and her in her tourist t-shirt, long brown hair and youthful vibrancy, he with his arm linked through hers and taking on the mantle of a slightly stooping old man, no one in London in July would give them a second look. Tom shuffled to a seat and Monika stayed at the counter, waiting for their order.

Liam and Vasile were in discussions, and then Liam reached into his left hand pocket and took out the five centimetre thick brown envelope. Vasile, so confident that no one would dare stare at him, let alone approach or reproach him, didn't even glance to the other customers or make any effort to hide his actions. Opening the envelope he riffled his thumb across the four hundred, fifty pound notes. A first instalment. £20,000. Liam would explain how it had taken me time to get the full amount and that the rest would be through on Tuesday morning. Just inside the two week deadline. This was a show of good faith. Vasile was prepared to take it, but the deadline still stood. The threat of not paying was made clear. Liam and I both knew that the final instalment would never be final. Vasile would continue to come back again and again and again. The Romanian smiled. Smug bastard. Closing the envelope, he handed it over to one of his men, who put it into the inside pocket of his suit jacket.

Tom, sitting like a stereotypical eighty year old, hunched shoulders and bowed head, was a little bundle in a seat on the far side of the café. Monika, tall and young and obviously thrilled to be a tourist in London still stood at the café counter.

Liam got up from his seat. Vasile stayed in his and gave a dismissive flick of his hand. Liam turned to go, before Vasile must have called him again. The Romanian made a less than subtle gesture that showed where and how he'd cut Liam if the rest of the money didn't come by Tuesday.

Liam exited the café and turned right, walking north to the far end of Gunthorpe Street and disappearing out of sight.

Vasile relaxed back into the settee and lifted a newspaper. Monika took hold of one bottle of water and one takeaway coffee. Tom stood unsteadily, then staggered forward. One of Vasile's men stepped towards him. Monika ran and reached out, calling as she'd been instructed, *'Opa, opa geht es dir gut?'* Which even with my rudimentary German I understood to be, 'Grandpa, Grandpa, are you okay?'

Tom sagged and was stopped from falling by the nearest of Vasile's men. Monika reached them and set the cup and bottle of water on the chair Liam had vacated. Tom, now being held up by

Vasile's security man, went limp. I was quite impressed as the other of Vasile's security guys didn't get involved. He moved away, scanning the room for possible threats, realising that this could be a diversion for an attack on his boss. Shame he wasn't focussed on the real action. Monika hurried to be beside her "Opa" and pointed to the settee. Vasile had no choice but to stand. Opa was set down and seemed to revive. Monika gave him a sip of water. The security guys stayed standing. Vasile sat back down, angling himself to look down the front of Monika's "heart t-shirt" as she bent forward helping her Opa.

Three minutes dragged like a lifetime, but Tom recovered, Monika was gushing in her thanks and hugs were exchanged all round by her to the security man who had stopped Opa falling and for Vasile, who was very happy to have her cling on to him. Then, taking her bottle of water and Opa, she left the café. Out of the door, turn left. Straight past me, through the archway and onto the Whitechapel High Street. I dropped my cigar into the metal can on the wall and re-entered the pub. Monika and Tom came in through the front door and joined me in the small foyer just inside the side door.

Monika handed over the cards from the wallet she'd lifted from Vasile and I swiped each through the reader. She replaced them precisely and then turned away. Back out the front door, back up through the archway, up the cobbled street and into the café. Tom and I peered through the side door's panel of dimpled glass and could just about see what was happening.

She arrived inside the café. Looked about, saw the coffee cup left on the seat. Picked it up. Laughed. Shared a joke. Moved to leave, then turned back. Set the cup down. Held her hands out. Vasile stood and took another long hug from the beautiful young German girl. Then she took her coffee and left. Back down the street, through the archway, into Whitechapel High Street and into the black cab that myself, Mark and her "Opa" Tom were waiting in. We'd meet Liam back at Tom's place.

'Drinks are most certainly on me,' I said.

Tom reached into his inside pocket and took out the brown envelope that he had given to Liam. 'Oh, I'm sure Vasile won't mind making a contribution too.'

24

London, 11th July 2009

Vasile would realise he'd been done out of his twenty grand as soon as he asked his man for it. That might be in an hour, or maybe at the end of the day. Maybe the security guy might panic, think he'd lost it. Know what Vasile would do to him if he found out. Maybe he'd try to replace it without letting his boss know. Or, he'd spot he'd had it stolen and tell Vasile and they'd all be on the look-out for an old German man and his granddaughter. In any case, spot the cash was missing sooner or later, or not at all, Vasile wouldn't have a clue that his wallet had been lifted and replaced within less than a minute.

We were gathered in Tom's basement. Mark had his laptop open and hooked into a monitor. It showed a network of lines and shapes, that looked like a strange take on the London Tube Map crossed with a plumber's plan for complicated pipework. One of the routes, or pipes, displayed was a dotted line between a small square and a large cylinder.

'This,' Mark said, pointing to the square, 'is our laptop, Luke.'

'And this,' Tom said, pointing to the cylinder, 'is one of my main servers. You're into it now and have full access to all of our network.'

It was surreal. Full and unfettered, behind the firewalls ac-cess to a major fraud and money laundering network. I was acutely aware that Mark had software on his laptop that, should he choose to run it, would destroy the whole of Tom's Ukrainian and Roma-nian operations. Thing is, Vasile would still come after Liam. Per-haps even faster if he thought Liam had been connected to the pickpocket scam. Tom would be killed by his Ukrainians for allow-ing us access. Monika would be "uncle-less" and I'd not be able to tell anyone that Mark and I had brought the network down anyway as I'd never be able to admit why we had access in the first place. Apart from which, I owed Tom. And, I had to admit, I liked the old man.

So, instead of taking down a major cyber fraud network, I tapped Mark's shoulder and said, 'Okay, let's do it.'

A series of command lines appeared on the monitor. The code was abbreviated, machine-level commands that made little sense to me, or I imagined Tom, Liam or Monika. They were also scroll-ing up the screen too quickly to read. Mark was well used to work-ing with me, and knew to give a running commentary.

'This replicates an external hack into Tom's mainframe. It's vir-tual of course, and the fact that I am plugged into the actual front end means it will be completely invisible and untraceable. It will look like an almost perfect clandestine entry, once it's discovered.'

'If it's invisible, how will they find it?' Monika asked.

'Oh, the boys whom Tom's told me actually look after this end of things will be able to see the opening I made, but they won't be able to trace where it came from. No way of saying, hang on, Tom, someone plugged into your server. I figure that would be a bad thing to happen.'

Tom shrugged. 'Yeah, I reckon Cuba would be cancelled.'

'From here,' Mark paused as another few lines of code rolled up the screen. 'We should … yep … and … yep. Okay, that's it. Who wants to press the button?'

We all looked to Liam. 'That's it?' he asked.

Mark pursed his lips. 'Yeah. That's it. Hit enter and money will start filtering out of Tom's six feeder accounts, at a rate of $180 a minute. It will bounce a total of 32 times, across four continents and eighteen countries. Although these hops will be traceable. They'll look like a talented amateur has done the work and if Tom's network guys are decent, they'll find the path easily enough. Eventually it will end up in Vasile's account that was connected to this card.' He indicated a string of numbers on screen. 'It's an off-shore account in the British Virgin Islands. I guess he uses it for his own illicit money.'

'And then?' Liam asked.

'And then an alarm will go off on this,' Tom said, walking across to a small monitor set off to one side of the room. 'We have a standing setup that monitors unauthorised or unusual cash flow. Don't ask me how it works,' Tom said, holding up his hands to pre-emptively stop Liam's question.

'Same software we use inside banks to look for fraudulent transactions and automatically block credit cards,' Mark said. 'It's like an early warning tripwire. My only surprise was that you guys have access to it as well and that you use it in the same way we do.'

'Good guys, bad guys. All just a matter of point-of-view,' the old man said laughing. Monika reached over and gave him a hug.

'Once the alarm trips, Tom's associates who look after the net-work will investigate. They'll see the entry point and the hops and it should take them about ten minutes to trace it to the account. At which point,' Mark stopped and held his hand out to Tom.

'They'll call me and ask who the fuck Vasile Constă is.'

'Language,' Monika said.

'Sorry, sweetheart. They'll call and ask me who he is. I'll tell them he's a Bucharest boy, based here, who has been trying to muscle in on a few of our areas. Getting a bit big for his boots. Then I'll ask why and they'll tell me not to worry. Not my concern. That end of things ain't my problem you see.'

'Then what?' Liam asked, his finger still hovering over the key-board.

'Then they'll have about five or six lads get off a plane in Heathrow tomorrow and Vasile will be of no concern to anyone by nightfall,' Tom answered.

'Won't they interrogate him, ask him for the money back, find out he had nothing to do with it?' Liam asked, much more hesitant than I thought he would be, or indeed how I felt.

'No, son,' Tom said. 'The money will have been recovered from his account. The trace will have led straight to him. They'll have asked me my opinion and I'll have told them. There is nothing to answer. You press that button and it's a done deal. And it'll be a clean done deal too. They won't fuck about cutting him.'

'Language,' Monika chirped again.

'Sorry sweetheart. No cutting, just a clean shot to the head and made to disappear.'

I nearly laughed. It could have been due to the tension in the room, or the seriousness of what I was implicated in, but I mostly thought it was because Monika had pulled the old man up for swearing, yet was nonplussed at the prospect of an execution-style shooting and the managed disappearance of a body.

'Luke?' Liam asked.

Initially, I had struggled over where all of this would likely lead to. The story Liam had told me about Vasile's torture of a man called Nico had dispersed most of my reservations. The methodical knife work on Nico's ears, lips and eyelids that had made most of the forced onlookers throw up. Liam had stood resolute, but was terrified that a man could do this to another with such matter-of-fact disdain. Vasile had egged himself on, cheering each slash of his knife like a weird, self-congratulating matador. When Liam told me how Vasile had cut out an eye, I stopped him. I didn't need to hear anymore. Nico's torture and death had helped me decide to launch us on this course of action. That and the fact that, like Tom, but for different reasons, I didn't like bullies. Especially ones who tried to blackmail gay men.

Now, as I was being asked to give Liam the final blessing, I thought of how innocents had died when I'd been in the military, surrendered on an altar of political expediency, and yet men like Vasile, evil in the vilest sense, lived on.

Drawing a deep breath I said, 'Vasile's not going to be a loss to society. What would Nico want?'

Liam pressed enter.

**

It took two days, not one, but only because Vasile got tipped off that serious-minded and very well-connected gangsters were on their way to London to sort him out. He'd run, but not far.

Tom told us not to worry, it was tidied up. He had placed the twenty grand he'd 'lent' Liam for the payoff back into his own laundering systems and as far as he and anyone else was concerned, the little episode had been a minor blip.

As a thank you, the following Friday I invited him and Monika to a meal along with Liam and Mark. By dessert I was reminded how small the world was when I learnt Monika's parents and grandparents owned the guesthouse in the Bavarian Alps where my family and I used to go on holiday.

I was also aware that her being in London at the right time had been a happy coincidence. Fortuitous timing. Exactly the sort of happy timing I would need for my overdue conversation with Liam. In my head we were most definitely over as an item, but I'd not said anything whilst the Vasile situation had been ongoing. The days immediately following it had seemed a bit too soon. I thought it cruel to have seen Liam so relieved at the end of a horrendous experience to then be dumped. I'd have the conversation, probably sooner rather than later, but it could wait for tonight. I was tired, yet surprisingly, I realised, horny. The build-up of tension over the proceeding weeks was quite an aphrodisiac. I squeezed Liam's hand under the table. He squeezed my thigh so hard I thought he would break my leg. I felt the anticipation in other parts too.

**

6:00 am. The morning light struggled weakly through the crack in the curtains and I rolled myself out of bed slowly and gently. Both from a desire not to wake Liam and a need not to strain my arms and shoulders any more than they had been throughout the night's rough sex with him.

The deli wouldn't open for another hour, but I needed the time to figure out what I was going to say, or if I was going to say it at all. I knew I would. I had to. I just didn't know when would be best. I also needed a drink to think properly.

The kettle boiled. I poured the water over the loose tea in the pot and gave it a couple of stirs. Taking a cup down from the shelf I added a splash of milk and three-quarters filled it with the tea. Quietly I lifted a bottle of vodka from the cabinet and topped-up my cup. I didn't need it, it was only a way to give my system a little jolt. A little hair of the dog, as we'd gone through a fair bit of wine at dinner the night before. It really was no different from a double espresso.

I drained my cup and repeated the process just as my Blackberry started vibrating against the dining room table. I got to it before it rang off. It was Rachel's number. That didn't bode well at this time on a Saturday.

'Hello? What's wrong?'

'Egypt. Things got a lot more volatile after yesterday's Friday prayers. Fabian Judd reported barricades on the street outside the bank HQ. Also some instances of sporadic rioting in Cairo. He made a formal request to leave late last night.'

'And?'

'And Dickie Lessen refused.'

**

Pat Harris, William Carmichael and Rachel were already in Pat's office when I arrived. A map of Cairo was on the wall, with red dots placed on various road intersections.

I took a seat. 'Morning, what's the latest?'

William spoke. 'The labour dispute is gaining momentum. It began up in El-Mahalla El-Kubra, north of Cairo, with the Union of Textile Workers, but through social media and a new youth movement, the three biggest unions and the majority of student bodies are now threatening strike action. Yesterday, after Friday prayers, some of the students took the protest to the streets. Pro-government forces did what you'd expect.'

'Smashed heads?' I offered.

'Yep, and the government declared any strike would be illegal.'

'Striking for what?'

'They want Mubarak to raise the wages in state-run industries. It's all kicking off because of the rise in world food prices. They're spiking again, not as bad as 2008, but they're on the way up. It's one of those unseen factors that the media hardly ever reports on, but if you want a pre-cursor for rapid civil disobedience, starve the population. Make kids go hungry. Works like a charm. Meanwhile in the West, we don't even acknowledge a blip in food prices. What's a few pence on a banana or a jump in the cost of your avocado? But in the developing nations? Different story.'

'Luke, I was still in the Ministry of Defence last year,' Rachel added. 'It was barely reported in the British media, but over ten thousand workers rioted in Bangladesh last summer. Pakistan deployed their army to secure food stocks and there were riots in Burkina Faso, Cameroon, Indonesia and a host of other places, including, of course, widespread disorder in Egypt.'

'Mubarak's regime cracked down on it last year, in their normal calm manner.' William said. 'A young boy was shot dead, hundreds of protestors arrested, some tortured, some disappeared. Usual stuff. Now, the protestors have had a year to lick their wounds and try again,'

'Did we have anyone in Egypt last year?'

'Yes,' Pat answered. 'But only a couple of investment bankers working for an investment fund. They left on a commercial flight at the first sign of trouble. Now, with the acquisition of the Banque de la Société Commerciale d'Egypte, we have, to use a phrase from my homeland, skin in the game.'

'And Lessen overruled sending out a team to get Judd and his family?' I asked.

William bristled at the mention of Lessen. 'Yes. But it's more complicated than that. We'll take you through it, but his bottom line is that the press aren't reporting anything untoward and his budget can't afford it,' he said through gritted teeth.

'So if it's not on the BBC it isn't happening?' I said sarcastically. 'And what's with his fixation on budget?'

'The reshuffle that Sir Anthony put into motion also has a few harsh fiscal targets to be met. Lessen is newly promoted and wants to be seen as a bright boy. He's already asked me if I couldn't just pare back all the IT security "things" as he called them,' Pat said with a shake of his head.

'By things, I assume he means me and Rachel, Mark, Steve and Paul?'

'Yeah, probably. I ignored him.'

'So what's the current situation on the ground,' I asked William.

'The bank is in Cairo's CBD and the street it's on, along with a number of surrounding ones, is already barricaded off. Burnt-out cars, oil drums, that sort of thing.'

'And Judd's family?'

'They lived almost fifteen kilometres south of the CBD, in a suburb called Maadi, so they were relatively out of harm's way, but Judd decided to take no chances. He paid for his wife, son and daughter to get out on a BA flight last night.' William checked his watch. 'Well, this morning really. They arrive into Heathrow at nine. My guys will meet them and take them to Mrs Judd's mother's house in Warwick.'

'And Fabian has stayed, because?'

'Initially, because he has twenty local staff, three of whom are trapped inside the bank. He reckoned leaving them would send the wrong message about how Bateleur cared for staff in times of trouble. Ultimately these demonstrations will come to an end and he has to work with his people in the future,' William said.

'Commendable. Shame Dickie Lessen doesn't have the same ethics. Anyway, what's the plan? I presume you want me to get Steve to remotely wipe the Egyptian servers?'

The room went quiet and I couldn't miss the shared looks between Pat, William and Rachel. After a second or two, it was she who spoke.

'Yeah, you see, Luke, that's the problem. You know I've been monitoring all the email messages from Cairo back to us. Fabian dropped off email last night and I started getting good old fax and telex messages. The power was still on in the bank, I guess the government-backed protestors and the security services know we have back-up generators, but we don't have back-up comms lines. The last fax line went down at eleven last night.'

'That's when Fabian rang me,' William said, 'using a satellite phone and requested an extraction. I rang Pat and we took the fall back scenario to Lessen. He completely canned it. Said he wouldn't countenance the destruction of the equipment.'

I sat back in my seat and thought through the situation. The bank's operational IT divisions held a complete triple-redundancy back-up of every bank server worldwide. In the event of a planned withdrawal from a country, they would remotely wipe all the data from the in-country servers and Pat and I would be satisfied that there could be no possible breach of cyber security as the servers were blanked using military-grade disk-wiping technology. Once peace returned, the clean servers were restored using the last back-up and all was well.

If a bank was physically overrun by force with little warning, like in a civil war or most Middle East and African insurgencies over the previous two decades, or if the communication lines that allowed a remote wipe to be instigated by London were out of action, then the local bank manager could press a single button that actively burnt-out every circuit within the local server farms. It was drastic, but absolutely secured the data as there was no way anyone could recover it. It didn't set fire to the server room, it simply passed a high-voltage pulse through each server and fried every circuit and memory board. When peace descended, it was accompanied by the bank's IT division also descending but with a completely new server build as there was no way to restore the original. Once the new hardware was installed, the back-ups were restored and again, all was well. This latter option obviously came with a much higher price tag and Dickie Lessen didn't want to foot the bill. Rachel's assessment of him had been correct. What a dick.

'Mmm, so when you said Fabian had initially declined to leave because of his staff, I presume that now he thinks his presence might somehow deter looters, or more likely, officers from the Egyptian State Security Investigations Service from ripping out all our intact and data-heavy servers?' I asked.

Pat and William nodded.

'Equally commendable, but fundamentally stupid. If he gets in their way they'll put a bullet in him and dump him in the desert.' I said. 'Can you not go over Lessen's head, Pat?'

'The only person over him is Sir Anthony,' Pat said.

'Yes, and?'

'And he's currently sailing around the Mediterranean on a cruise ship that won't dock in Valetta harbour until Tuesday. His wife won't allow him to take his secure Blackberry on holiday. She threw the last one overboard on their cruise last year.'

'So who's deputising for Sir Anthony while he's away?'

Pat shook his head. 'This isn't the military, Luke. We don't have deputy after deputy lining up in the wings. When the Group Chair isn't here the Group Executive Committee members look after their own portfolios. So at present, and until Tuesday, Lessen is his own boss with no one to answer to.'

'For Chr—' I stopped myself. There was no point in arguing against the futility of it.

William said, 'And Fabian Judd is new to the bank, so he's highly unlikely to press that button because we tell him to. He'd be signing his own resignation and would potentially be liable for the bill. I would imagine Dickie would sue him just for fun.'

The options were stark. I'd learnt enough about the Egyptian internal security services, SSIS, from my time working in military intelligence. They, and President Mubarak, were closely linked to the Russians. Having our bank's internal servers physically compromised would be equivalent to giving the SSIS and whoever they shared it with, the same access as Mark had enjoyed within Tom's servers. Only the SSIS wouldn't be so restrained. It would open the whole of our cyber-operations up to potential havoc. It couldn't be allowed to happen.

'When do we leave?' I asked, finally realising why I'd been called in at this time on a Saturday.

'There is only one direct flight a day with BA and it doesn't leave until 8:30 tonight, so we'll probably use EgyptAir. Leaves at two. Can you round up your lads before then?' Pat asked.

'Easily.'

'Thing is, Luke, by the time we get into the city, do what we need to and get back out, we'll probably not have any options for a flight home until tomorrow morning, around this time. So we may have a bit of an edgy night. You'll have to tell whoever you send to be prepared,' William said.

'Whoever I send? You say that like I wouldn't be coming too.'

'Are you?' Pat asked.

'Of course. What on earth made you think I would send my people into harm's way and stay here? Also, regarding the flight, can you give me a few minutes? I might have an alternative, if we're lucky.'

**

'Mac MacLellan.'

Stuart Campbell MacLellan the Third. Mac to all who knew him. His Canadian accent long ago washed over with tones of Texas and an ego so big it would barely fit into his beloved Dallas Cowboy's brand new, 80,000-seater stadium. He was rich, brash and crucially, the last time I had met him, the owner of a Bombardier Challenger 604 business jet.

'Howdy, Mac. It's Luke. From that trip to Hong Kong? I hope you remem—'

'Well I'll be damned. How are you, Luke?'

'I'm good, Mac. Real good. And you?'

'I'm staggered is what I am, Luke. I am one hundred percent staggered. I mean that trip of ours must be what, nearly four years ago and I've moved on to new ventures since then, but I declare to all that's holy, I was absolutely, no word of a lie, thinking about you most of last week. I even called our old mutual buddy Steve to find out if he had a phone number for you.'

He was referring to Steve Jäeger, a man I was convinced was CIA and whose background I had never discovered but had been sure it was both multi-layered and fascinating. 'Well, if anyone could get it for you, Steve could, but no, sadly I haven't spoken to him since back then. We lost touch. I'm glad to hear his name. Is he okay?'

'Sure is. Slippery as usual and still doing whatever the hell it is he does. Did he get in touch? Ask you to call me?'

'No. Not at all. Why did you want to talk, Mac?'

'Well that is just the strangest thing. See, I've been doing a bit of research and blow me if your name didn't keep coming up again and again.'

'Really? Research on what?'

'Cyber-intelligence.'

That stopped me in my tracks. Why on earth would a man like Mac want to know about my world? I barely managed to keep the surprise out of my voice. 'Cyber? Really?'

'Sure and it was you who kinda' started me thinking about it all those years ago. I was intrigued and you know how it is, the more you think about something, the more you notice it. Anyway, fast-forward to this year and I had a bit of a breakthrough. Figured I'd see who the top commercial cyber intelligence guys were and in every list I found, there you were. Luke Frankland, speaking at conferences and writing articles and being interviewed. I thought to myself, wow, I know that kid and look at him now, head of cyber intelligence for a global bank like Bateleur. But, hey, you rang me and if it wasn't Steve who asked you, what's up kid, what do you need?'

I took a breath. 'Got to admit, Mac, it's a call to ask a pretty big favour.'

'Always happy to help a friend in need. What's going down?'

'You still got your Bombardier Challenger 604?'

'Nope. Got rid of that about two years ago.'

I was genuinely surprised. I thought the private jet was one of Mac's most needed props. I needn't have been concerned.

'Upgraded to the 605. Beautiful piece of engineering. Why'd you ask?'

'I know it's a longshot, but I was wondering, are you anywhere near to Europe?'

'Afraid not. I'm sitting in a hotel in Washington DC. You need a lift somewhere?'

I checked my watch. It would be about 2:00 am in DC. 'Oh, I'm sorry Mac. I didn't mean to wake you.'

'Nonsense, you know me, I rarely sleep. What do you need?'

'You were right. It was a lift I needed. Cheeky to ask, I know, but nothing ventured.'

'That is true, that is true and not cheeky at all. Serendipitous is what it is, but unless you can wait until the end of the month, I don't think I can help. End of the month any good?'

'Afraid not, Mac, but hey, thanks anyway. I'll let you go, I'm sure you're as busy as usual.'

'Whoa up there, Luke. Now that I have you, tell me this, are you happy in your job?'

The question caught me cold. A series of images flashed through my head. Rachel, Mark, Steve and Paul all laughing and working together, preventing cyber-attacks. The Inter-Bank Task Force collaborating and becoming truly effective. The Chinese bug. Tom. Pat and William. Dickie Lessen. I ignored the latter. Then another thought struck me. 'Why didn't you contact me through the bank. I'd have been easy to find?'

'Ah, I wanted to contact you privately. Didn't want to raise any flags at your work ... Well, are you?'

'Am I what?'

'Happy, kid. Are you happy in your job? Because I have a new prospect coming up and I think you might be just the person I'm looking for.'

I had no clue what he meant, not that I got a chance to ask as Mac ploughed on.

'Seems to me you are a well-known force in cyber intelligence and more importantly, we have history. Thought you might come work for me. How's that sound?'

I had no clue why Mac would think I would come work for him. Despite him alluding to new prospects, as far as I knew he was still flying high-roller gamblers in and out of Macau and Hong Kong. I was very confused. 'Exactly what are we talking about, Mac.'

'Cyber intelligence, what else d'ya think I'd want you for? Like I said, you got me thinking all those years ago. We have stocks and shares forecasters and financial intel on markets, heck we even have weather forecasters throwing their two cents in if you invest in crops and agriculture, but when I started looking, there weren't no private providers of what you were doing. Got me thinking. Figured out it could be worth a few dollars and you know me, always looking to turn a buck. Took me a while to wrap up my other interests, but like I said, I had a breakthrough this year. What do you say?'

Surprised was a massive understatement. Both at the fact Mac MacLellan would have moved into commercial cyber intelligence and more so that he was trying to head hunt me. 'Eh, I … I'm flattered, Mac. But I don't think I can give you a proper answer at the moment. I'm kind of in the middle of something. What if I text you my email? Can you send me some details?'

'Okay, kid. That's easy. I think you'll like it. It's gonna be a sure-fire success and the best of its kind in the market. You text me now, or I might just fly over there and knock on your door.'

I let slide the fact he hadn't found my phone number, so I doubted he'd find my apartment. 'I will, Mac. I promise. I'll do it straight away.'

'Great. Serendipity you calling me, kid, I tell you. It's going to be fantastic. You'll love it.'

The line went dead and I stared at the phone for a while. Mac-private-jet-MacLellan. More money than anyone I'd ever met. Proud Canadian, cowboy boot wearing adoptee of Texas. Him running a cyber intelligence company? It would be like me running a non-alcoholic bar at a Labour Party fundraiser. Possible, but not likely. Although, the man did have business sense and could indeed turn a buck. I composed a text message with my email and sent it. Couldn't hurt.

I went back into the office. 'No good on the alternative transport arrangements. Guess we'll be on EgyptAir.'

25

Landing at Cairo International at 8:40 pm wasn't ideal, yet it all felt very mundane. Like any normal business trip, except we'd swapped our suits for various versions of jeans, t-shirts and casual jackets. We'd also decided that walking boots and backpacks would replace Oxfords and briefcases. Of course we'd still travelled business class, because although it was technically a self-funded trip, Pat had paid for Steve, Paul, Mark and me on his personal credit card. It was chicken feed to him.

William had paid for himself and his sub-contracted security guys. We all figured that at least Dickie wouldn't be able to fire them for misspending the budget, but Pat figured he'd probably fire them for something or other.

The mundaneness of the trip persisted when we signed for three Nissan X-Trail hire cars. However, as we left the terminal building any idea that things were normal disappeared. On the road adjacent to the terminal, marked with signs attesting to its normal use as a set down and pick-up zone for passengers, were two US-made M113 Bradley Armoured Personnel Carriers, two Russian-made BMP-1 Infantry Fighting Vehicles, a Russian T-62 Main Battle Tank and blocking either end of the road, two US M1

Abrams MBTs. The mix of weapon suppliers a testament to Egypt's chequered history during the Cold War. I was as shocked by the presence of the armour as I was at how easily I had remembered their names. Obviously the equipment recognition training I'd had to do in the military intelligence school had sunk in to places I hadn't realised. There was also a large contingent of troops in various positions of repose, on top of, leaning next to, or lying beside the armour. A few pairs meandered about with their AK-47s slung backwards over their shoulders. Most, even those on patrol, had cigarettes in hand.

'Not the Grenadier Guards, are they?' Mark said behind me.

'Nope. But as they have AKs and we don't, then we should be nice,' I replied.

'Tsk, tsk, Luke. You should know better. They're Maadis. An indigenous version of the AK.'

'Well praise be for geeks like you, who can keep me corrected,' I laughed. 'Anyway, I thought Maadi was where Judd's family lived.'

'It is,' William pitched in. 'It's also the name of the weapons manufacturer.'

'God, I'm surrounded,' I said. 'I've never asked, William, are you ex-military?'

'No. First the Met and then Greater Manchester Police.'

'Oh God! Even worse, two geeky ex-cops,' I said as Mark and William high-fived each other.

'They aren't ex-cops though, are they?' I said, looking at the four sub-contracted security guys whom William had introduced, but whose names I had to admit I'd forgotten. All four were dressed in black or brown cargo pants and heavy outer jackets. I guessed they were all in their late twenties or early thirties and each was broader and taller than the broad and tall William.

They were British and carried themselves like the special forces I had met on operations, but they weren't wiry little guys like most of the SAS I'd encountered.

'No,' William agreed. 'Not ex-cops. Former UK Special Boat Service.'

'And did you rent those so they'd feel at home,' Steve asked, pointing at the three black Nissan X-Trails, sitting on their own in the middle lane of the rental car parking bays. The 4x4s were big and tough looking; black matte paint and heavily tinted windows.

'Kind of,' William agreed. 'Why have guys trained in advanced driving techniques within hostile environments and not give them something worthwhile to play with?'

'Cool,' Paul said, throwing his kit into the nearest car.

We gathered round the vehicles and William rang Rachel, back in London. She and Pat were our eyes and ears as to what was going on in Cairo. They were getting most of their updates via Al Jazeera with occasional snippets from Internet chat forums and an open line to Fabian Judd's satellite phone. The situation on the ground, not good after Friday prayers, had worsened considerably.

We split ourselves between the three cars. William and two of his guys up front. Mark, Steve and another SBS guy in the rear vehicle. Me, Paul and the fourth of William's men in the middle.

'I'm sorry, I can't remember what your name is?' I said as he got behind the wheel.

'Owen. You ready?' He said in a light, but discernible, Welsh accent.

'Sure,' I said, and felt anything but.

**

Bateleur's building in downtown Cairo was a half-hour drive to the southwest of the International Airport. On a good day.

A straight shot down the wide, three-lane highway called El Oroba Street. Join Salah Salem, negotiate a series of impressive looking interchanges, bridges and tunnels, then take a right into the city next to Al-Azhar Park. From there it was ten kilometres, with a couple of last twists and turns around Ezbekiya Gardens. Easy.

Except Al-Azhar Park was next to the Darrash Campus of the Al-Azhar University and the road we'd normally have used was barricaded off. Rachel and Pat were watching live-feed from an Al Jazeera camera crew who were just west of the park. Currently Egyptian Police were using tear gas and water cannon to try to disperse the thousands of angry students currently blockading all the roads around their campus, including the main feeder routes into the city's central business district.

We couldn't go further south and loop back up as another riot was in full swing next to Salah El-Deen Square, in a space bounded by four mosques. According to Rachel, Al Jazeera was reporting that police were desperately trying to prevent any encroachment into the massive 700-year old Sultan Hassan Mosque and its newer, but equally massive neighbour, the 100-year old Al-Rifa'i Mosque. In an alternative narrative, the Internet chatrooms were suggesting protestors belonging to the Union of Metal Workers were taking shelter within the two 500-year old mosques on the other side of the square. All reports agreed that police had fired live rounds and bodies were visible in the side streets. Regardless, we wouldn't be driving through in three Nissans. I'd only have considered it if we could have borrowed the tanks I'd seen at the airport.

Going even further south, looping up alongside the eastern bank of the Nile and coming into the city from that direction was also out as rioters were in El Tahrir Square. This, the historical heart of protests within Cairo, was the main scene of disturbances between government forces, members of various unions, led by the Textile Workers, and the majority of the city's students.

The last option, heading north and coming in from there was what we'd planned to do before we left London, but now Pat had told us that all roads from the north were blocked by government forces. They and various irregular paramilitary units loyal to the regime were preventing any more protestors coming in from El-Mahalla El-Kubra, north of Cairo. This traditional heartland of the Textile and Agricultural Unions was where all the disturbances had started.

Plan B, which had been Plan E in reality, was to get as far as we could and then go on foot. It was now promoted to Plan A and made ever more complicated by unconfirmed reports of rioting spreading further out from the city centre. We decided we would have to err on the side of caution. It meant more walking and a longer transit time in and out, but it would ultimately be safer.

We ditched the cars in a darkened stretch of grassland behind the Arab Contractors Medical Centre. I had no clue who the Arab

Contractors were, but if their medical and sporting facilities were anything to go by, they had a few quid.

'They're a football team,' Paul said, pointing across the large parkland towards a football stadium.

'Ah, I thought they were actual contractors.'

'They are. One of the biggest in the Middle East.'

I wasn't quite sure why I should have been, but I was surprised that it had been Owen who answered.

'Really?'

'Yep. Huge. Build all sorts. Right, let's go,' he said, closing the car door and shouldering his backpack. 'Try to stay close to me and if I duck down you duck down. If I stand still, you stand still and if I run, try to keep up.'

**

The sounds of a city in turmoil stretched out through the night. Sirens pierced the constant thump of helicopter rotors overhead. Sporadic cameos, lifted on the eddies of a light breeze tore through the humidity and showcased pinpricks of misery. The traumatised cry of a woman, the crashing whoosh of a Molotov cocktail. The crump of a plastic baton round or, thankfully rarely, the sharp crack of live ammunition. Their reverberations strangely amplified as they bounced off heavy clouds hanging in an almost moonless sky. We had been fortunate, through no planning of our own. It was a simple quirk of the calendar. The waning crescent moon barely cast any light through the rare breaks in the clouds.

Adding to the natural cover of a dark night, Owen and his comrades threaded us through claustrophobic residential streets, whose buildings crowded the narrow roads and footpaths, peering down on our passing like nosey neighbours. There were no street lights and every window of the close-packed homes or low-level apartment blocks was cloistered. The residents collectively desperate to hide themselves from the fear and destruction sweeping the city. For our part, we too stuck to the shadows. Fastidiously avoiding every police station, hospital, mosque or commercial strip that might have any form of external lighting. Nine dark-clothed ghouls on a stop-start, clandestine, seven kilometre route march into a city that was tearing itself apart. It wasn't the Saturday night I had envisioned.

Two and a half hours after ditching the cars, we arrived without incident at Mohammed Roushdy, the street that housed the former headquarters of the Banque de la Société Commerciale d'Egypte. In the reflected light of burning oil drums, set within a barricade of burnt-out cars at the west end of the road, I was able to pick out the Bateleur Eagle, mounted over the building's main entrance.

The bank, a six-storey, sand coloured rectangular construction was styled after a Parisian apartment block, complete with faux shuttered windows and metal balustrade balconies. It looked strangely at odds, yet at the same time somehow comfortably in partnership with, the two-storey, ramparted and arched, medieval looking mosque that butted up alongside it. Lights atop the mosque's minaret added no real illumination to the street and we sheltered in the doorway of an electrical retailers, waiting for the signal from William to cross the road. Despite the burning oil drums, the barricades appeared to be devoid of people, but the darkness would work in the favour of any government security forces as well as it worked for us.

I moved to William's side. 'What's the hold-up?'

'We have a problem. All cell phone coverage dropped out about two streets back. I think the government is using mobile phone jammers.'

'Makes sense. That'd stop the rioters communicating between sites, disrupt their coordination. So can we backtrack until we get coverage?' I asked.

'I was going to, but Ryan insisted on doing it for us,' William said, referring to the leader of the ex-SBS guys. 'He'll call London and they'll call Fabian in the bank. Even when we had full coverage I couldn't get him on his satellite phone. So we'll do it by relay.'

'How will we find out if Ryan's got through?' I asked, checking all around me again. When I faced back towards the eagle atop the main entrance, the door under its claws swung inward.

'I think we just did,' William said.

**

The bank had standby power generators and what I thought had been faux French shutters on the windows were actually real, heavy duty, early 20th century oak. It meant we could have the lights on and, of course, had the ability to boil a kettle. Only in the midst of riots and a need to completely wipe a bank's server farm before making a hazardous seven kilometre escape through dark and potentially violent streets, could the requirement for a cup of tea have been any more British.

Fabian Judd was as I had remembered him. Although where I pictured him in my mind's eye wearing the all-white of the English cricket team, he was in fact dressed in an almost mirror image of me. Boots, jeans, dark jumper. His blonde hair slightly flattened against his head and his eyes looking heavy with fatigue.

'How long have you been up?' I asked.

He checked his watch. 'Eh … since four on Friday morning.'

I checked my own. It had taken us an hour to get through the airport, buy our requisite temporary visas, clear immigration and pick up the rental cars. Twenty minutes to get to the Contractors area to dump them, and two and a half hours to walk in. Then the usual faffing about before Paul, Steve and Mark were able to start running the scripts against the servers. Still, I'd been surprised to realise it was already 1:10 am.

'Fabian, you need to get some sleep, mate. We won't be leaving for a couple of hours at least. Get your head down. Tell your staff to do the same,' I said, looking across to the three Egyptians sitting in what would usually have been a customer waiting area. Two women, Tahiya and Mona, sat with their male colleague, Hossam. They all looked as knackered as Fabian.

'Yes, good idea.' He stood to go, then turned back. 'Thank you.'

'No need to thank me. Anyway, all I'm about to do is wake you in a few hours and make you walk a bloody long way. Thank me when we get to Heathrow. Oh, one thing; I need to know where your people live. Can you get me their addresses?'

'Yes, certainly.'

He was back a few minutes later. I took the piece of paper, left Fabian to get some sleep and trudged up the four flights of stairs to the server rooms and IT suites. Despite the bank having back-up generators, they didn't power the lifts.

Paul, Steve and Mark sat beside one another at a long line of monitors and laptops. I'd initially only wanted to take Mark or Steve with me, but all three had said that for any hope of getting the back-ups completed and the servers wiped in as short a time as possible, all three of them would need to be here. They could work simultaneously on the server farm, dividing and conquering the task. It meant they'd need six backup disks instead of two, as the complete data set of the whole server farm would be split into three separate partitions, but apparently, that wasn't a concern. I had, as usual, trusted their technical skills to get the job done.

To facilitate this splitting of the backups, we had each carried in three, two terabyte hard drives in our backpacks. We'd added in a safety factor of having a full set of spares. Not that the drives failed much, but it wasn't unknown and this wouldn't have been the time to be caught short. We could hardly nip out to a hardware store, and anyway, they weren't exactly big items to carry.

The drives, barely fifteen centimetres long by ten wide and about three deep still fascinated me. I was never technical, but I could recall when a 40 megabyte hard drive had been a major piece of hardware and terabytes were almost science fiction. Now, with three drives currently in use, the nine spare drives sat in a stack barely thirty centimetres high. Going by what Mark had once told me, I could have stored the complete Library of Congress on just eight of them. With less gravitas, I could have filled all nine with enough full length movies to watch non-stop, twenty-four hours a day, seven days a week for just over a year. Alternatively, Steve had told me once that a single two terabyte drive was the equivalent of almost two million of the small, hard-cased floppy drives I had used when I'd been in school. That meant there was the equivalent of almost eighteen million floppy disks sitting on the desk. I guessed that stack would be considerably higher and we'd have been here till past dawn swapping those in and out for a backup.

Surrounded by the low whirr of server fans and the hum of electricity I was struck with a clarity of thought like I'd never had before. The protection of digital data was a hard task and the use of dedicated intelligence resources, like me and my team were only going to become increasingly important. Vital even. Barriers and blocks in the form of both digital and physical impediments were of course essential, but if criminals got behind the defences, as it seemed criminals in every crime arena always did, then with drive size knowing no limits, the amounts of data that could be stolen in a short time was frankly staggering.

If intelligence didn't lead the fight, to deter and prevent illegal access before it happened, then every defence in the world would, eventually, be breached. We had known the truth of this in the military and we certainly knew it in banking, but there was very little out there in the rest of the world. Maybe Mac MacLellan had stumbled on to a seriously good idea. Business decisions made by intelligence-driven cyber security. It was an intriguing prospect.

I was roused from my thoughts by Steve shouting, 'Luke?'

'Sorry, miles away. How goes it?'

'Good. The backups are more than a quarter way through. Then it's a case of setting the sanitisation scripts running. We should be finished by,' he glanced up at the large wall clock, 'say, two-thirty, three at the latest.'

'Nice work. I'm off to see William and his boys. We need to work out how we can get the local staff home safely.'

Leaving the server room I ducked into the nearest toilets. As well as the hard drives, I'd also carried in a small flask in my back-pack. It was only in case I needed a bit of a pick me up. I'd known it was going to turn into a long day and even longer night, so I simply wanted something to keep me sharp. I hadn't been sure that I'd have had access to a kettle, or tea, or coffee. This was just a little banker, to make sure I had a fall back. No big deal.

**

I met William back downstairs. 'Okay, what do you need?'

He pointed to the line of teller machines arrayed behind the long front desk of the ground floor banking centre. 'Unplug the machines and the screens, then follow my guys down two floors into the basement. We put all the portable, valuable and attractive stuff in the vault. Once we're done here, we'll go floor by floor. If it's portable, then we move it.'

'Okay,' I said with a trace of hesitancy.

'I know it sounds daft, but if looters break into our buildings, like we had back in Iraq in '03, then they nick anything that is bright, shiny and simple to steal. If it's secured behind a vault door, then they don't. Fabian and his guys moved all the staff PCs and printers from the office spaces, but they didn't consider dismantling the teller desks. Truth is, if we don't then any looter will, only they'll likely do it with a hatchet.'

'Fair enough,' I said and unplugged the first screen.

**

The last of the equipment we could shift, two flat screen TVs from the bank staff's lunch room, were secured in the vault, just as Paul came down the stairs to find me.

'Problems?' I asked.

'Nope, all done. Just coming to tell you we've finished the back-ups and wiped the servers. Steve says we're set to go.'

I checked my watch. 2:50 am. 'Good work,' I said, watching William spin the lock on the vault door. The three of us headed for the stairs back to the ground floor.

'Here,' Paul said, handing me three hard drives. 'They're clean and unused. Steve, Mark and I will carry the actual backups.' He paused. 'Are you okay?'

'Sure, why not?' I asked.

'Umm, no it's nothing. You just look a little flushed.'

'No, I'm good,' I said. 'I guess, running up and down stairs for the last hour carting all and sundry has me a bit puffed. I'm not as fit as I used to be. Or as young as you, it appears, sadly.'

I wandered over to where Fabian still slept and gave him a shake. 'Time to go.'

We met the rest inside the entrance foyer. As the phone networks were still down, or being jammed, Ryan and another of his colleagues were going to go a couple of blocks distant to try to phone London for the latest update. Before he left, like a strange parody of the worst family outing, Ryan cast himself in the role of "Dad", and advised us that now was the time to make a final visit to the toilet.

Most of us, like wayward children who hadn't considered the consequences, trooped off down the corridor. I went, and when in the cubicle, took the opportunity to almost finish off the last of my flask. It was easier to drink the majority of it and reduce the extra weight. That was common sense.

As if to undo all our good work, when I got back to the foyer, William was handing out small bottles of water from the open door of a large vending machine. 'Might as well take it with us. Probably only get looted once we leave,' he said, handing me over a couple.

I looked about me. All the Brits were suitably dressed for this. But Tahiya, Mona and Hossam were wearing their usual business attire, albeit after almost two days trapped inside the bank, it was looking decidedly crumbled. Tahiya, who was in her early twenties, wore a light blue hijab, a blue blouse, black trousers and flat shoes. Hossam, a small man in his early sixties still wore his conservative dark blue business suit, but had long ago discarded the tie. He'd buttoned his jacket and turned up the collar to better hide his white shirt. Mona, one of Fabian's supervisors, was in her mid-thirties and although she wore no scarf, she had on a dark blue blouse and an almost ankle-length black skirt. Crucially, she also had flat shoes. I was immediately grateful for the modest fashions worn by the majority of Egyptian women as I had no clue how Mona or Tahiya would have coped with a seven kilometre hike in the type of heels Abby Becker had worn to my initial interview.

There was a soft double knock on the bank's main door. Fabian opened it and the two ex-SBS guys stepped inside.

'The TV networks are reporting a shaky calm throughout much of the city,' Ryan said in a tone that gave no impression he and his mate had sprinted two hundred metres there and back again to make a call in the middle of a city that was falling apart. I was impressed.

'However,' he continued, 'they're also saying that tomorrow would usually mark the start of seven days of commemorations and celebrations for the anniversary of the 1952 revolution. Given the atmosphere in the city they reckon things could really kick off. As for the immediate vicinity, it's clear. If we're going, now's the time.'

We snaked out the door, crossed the street as fast as each of us could and waited in the shadows whilst William secured the main door of the bank. Then we followed Ryan into the dark of eastern Cairo. I realised for the first time that there were now thirteen of us. Would that be unlucky?

**

To avoid the numerous university campuses, hospitals or police stations meant a winding pathway back through the narrowest streets we could find. It had worked on the way in and as we transitioned through downtown, into Al Muski and then El-Gamaleya everything looked on track. The halfway point marked the part of the inward journey that had freaked me out the most. We'd had to navigate our way through the southern reaches of the Northern Cemetery; part of the famous Islamic-era Necropolis of Cairo, or more usually called, the City of the Dead. It had, over the previous century, seen people know as 'tomb-dwellers' move in to the tombs and mausoleums. Although numbers had reduced in the previous decades, there were still plenty of tomb-dwellers living inside its boundaries. On the way into the city it had been eerily quiet and much like I had imagined walking through a massive, ancient cemetery on a moonless night would have been. This time, it was different.

There were people on some of the avenues and pathways that intersected the tombs and mausoleums. I couldn't see them, but we could all hear them. Low voices in the dark. A clink of a bottle on glass. The strike of a match, but no accompanying illumination as the tight avenues obscured a direct view.

Ryan stopped us and we gathered in close.

'We need to split into smaller groups.' he whispered. 'The idea is to stay out of sight, undetected. We can't do that as well in here if there's a long line of us. The city wards were easy because the streets were deserted, but that's obviously not the case in here.'

It made sense and even if we hadn't agreed, I doubted any of the Bateleur people, me included, fancied leading us a merry dance through this place.

'So, same split we had in the cars coming in. Except I'll take Mona, Hossam and Tahiya.'

I was getting more impressed by these SBS guys all the time. I wasn't even aware he'd spoken to the local staff inside the bank, yet here he was knowing their names. I still couldn't recall half the names of his team. Although I was about to get a reminder.

'Karl, you go with Neil. Owen, you take your original guys and Fabian. Three minute separation between us and we meet back at the cars. Questions?' There were none, so Ryan moved off with his charges in tow.

The rest of us stood in silence, waiting for the first three minutes to tick by. It was pitch black at ground level, but the weak moonlight leant the sky enough illumination to provide a contrast. It allowed the profiles of the tombs and monuments to be just visible; their looming black shapes against the purple-black of the sky made the whole scene even weirder. I was far past the age of being scared of the dark, but this was the stuff of nightmares.

The noises of the people out in the darkness were amplified. Each sharp clink of glass, or occasional snatches of words, struck through the clawing night like a punch. I was tense and almost jumped when the other two SBS, who I now knew were Karl and Neil, whispered at almost the same time, 'Let's go.'

Mark and Steve stepped off in close formation. Fabian, Paul and I stood silently next to Owen, who, shielding his luminescent watch, waited for the second hand to tick round. I tried to count in my head, as I had in China, but the pressing doom of this place meant I couldn't concentrate past four. My legs were heavy, my head heavier. Fatigue, that I had managed to keep pushed to one side whilst all the activity of the night had been happening, was creeping over me. I wanted to sit down and not get up again. I also wanted a drink. The last buzz, courtesy of the toilet visit, was wearing thin.

'Okay,' Owen whispered at a volume that to my ears sounded like a scream, 'Let's go. Stay close.'

Despite my reservations about trailing at the back, I needed to let Paul and Fabian go in the middle. I couldn't be responsible for losing the man we'd been sent to bring back and I certainly couldn't lose Steve's young protégé in the middle of a necropolis. How would that go down? Not well. I almost laughed at the thought of Steve's face if I had to tell him, 'Sorry, I lost Paul.' Silently I thought, get a grip, Luke. You can't be laughing. To take the edge of, I reached back with my right hand and as quietly as possible brought the zip on the side pocket of my backpack down, tooth by single tooth. Eventually I was able to reach my flask. I painstakingly slowly unscrewed the retained cap. I'd left myself two good drinks in it. That would see me through. I tilted the flask to my mouth and threw my head back. The gin was cold and sweet and harsh and biting on my throat. I steadied my step and kept walking behind Owen, Fabian and Paul who were merely darker shapes in the blackness, even though they were only a few feet ahead.

A final swig and I'd be set. Raising the flask to my lips, I threw my head back, draining the last of the gin before walking right into the back of Paul and cannoning him into Fabian, who fell forward into Owen's legs.

I made a sort of 'Ooof' noise and the flask dropped into the blackness at my feet. My first thought was that I'd never see it again. Fabian let out a gasp and Owen made no noise at all, but having his legs buckled by Fabian, fell forward, sprawling onto the ground. Paul, sandwiched between me and Fabian, fell sideways. He automatically reached out with his left hand to steady himself. Unbeknownst to us, he was adjacent to the sandstone plinth of a monument, carved as a miniature Cleopatra's Needle. The plinth itself was ornately decorated with a waist-high metal fretwork, topped off at regular intervals by spikes in the same shape of the monument. One of those short spikes went straight through Paul's left hand. His scream would have been loud in the daytime.

I was able to see all of the detail of the monument when Owen leapt to his feet and turned on his high-beam head torch.

'What the fu—,' he said at normal volume levels.

'I didn't see you'd stopped,' I said, distracted by Paul, who had not uttered a sound after the initial high-pitched scream, but was biting his lip and looked to be in immense pain.

Owen dug into his pack and produced a first aid kit. He threw it at me. 'Pull his fucking hand off of that and get a bastard bandage round it,' he said, his Welsh accent much stronger and his fury barely concealed.

I wondered why he wasn't going to do it when I realised what he'd seen around the corner of the nearest tomb and why he'd stopped. A dancing pool of light from three hand torches came into view. Owen turned to face it. His head torch showed two younger men, maybe even teenagers, with narrow moustaches and thin shoulders. In the middle stood an older, squatter man, carrying a long crowbar in one hand. The teenagers set their torches on the ground and produced flick knives. The older man shone his torch from Owen to me, then Fabian and Paul, before speaking a flurry of Arabic.

Owen, still facing away from us and towards them said, 'Pull his fucking hand off that railing. We need to move.'

'Ah, Engleesh,' the older man said. 'You should not be here, Mister. Not walk through city of corpses without pay tax. Give me and we shall take fair price. Then you go on. Safe. To see doctor perhaps,' he added and laughed, pointing his torch on Paul and me.

I was grateful for the light. 'Paul, brace up, this is going to hurt.'

He nodded and managed to say through his grimace, 'Just do it. Do it now.'

Fabian and I pulled his hand straight up and thankfully, because the spike wasn't barbed, it came away clean. The first aid kit Owen had thrown at me was trapped securely between my feet and in the erratic light from the older man's torch I could just make out its contents. I grabbed two military-grade field dressings and ripped them open. Meanwhile, Owen hadn't moved, nor had he answered the three would-be robbers.

'You pay now or I have my boys cut you worse than young friend. His hand less problem than throat cut. Yes?'

'Fuck off and leave us alone. Walk away,' Owen said.

Whilst I applied the pads of the field dressing to each side of Paul's hand, I continually bobbed my head back up to check on Owen and our would-be muggers.

Fabian offered under his breath, 'We're screwed. The tomb-dwellers don't just rob people and let them go. This is not good. I could maybe try to tal—'

He was interrupted by another rapid burst of Arabic from the older, squat man. The young man on his right leapt forward. I'd never considered that if you had two people armed with knives, it would be difficult for both of them to attack a single victim at the same time. They'd be in danger of slicing their co-assailant. Unless one came from the front and the other the back. The three Arabs obviously hadn't considered that option, or with Paul, Fabian and I being behind Owen, they'd dismissed it as a plan. Whatever the reason it meant only one teenage boy, holding a knife flat in his right hand and thrusting it forward at waist level, approached the former SBS man. A tiny voice inside my head wanted to tell the kid that he was making a big, big mistake. The rest of me bound Paul's hand tightly and watched the scene to my front, illuminated by Owen's head torch.

As the knife came forward, Owen hadn't moved and I almost shouted a warning, but at the last moment the big Welshman, with a grace and speed I wouldn't have thought him capable of, pivoted on his left foot, turning his whole body ninety degrees to his right. The flash of the knife blade passed in front of him and he followed the motion with both his hands, clamping them around the wrist of the boy. Then he moved forward on his right foot. The attacker's arm bent back towards his own face. I thought the blade, flashing in the torch light, was about to bury itself into the boy's head, but as soon as Owen's right foot planted again, he stepped back on his left and the effect was mesmerising. The boy's feet left the ground and his whole body did a backward cartwheel over the top of his right arm, which Owen still had by the wrist. Landing on the ground with a lung-emptying thud, the teen still held the knife, but with the smallest of downward pressures on a wrist that was now bent at a most unnatural angle, he released it into Owen's care. With one hand controlling the boy's wrist and one holding the knife, Owen straightened up and faced front again. The second teen, obviously not thinking and certainly not processing what he'd just witnessed, launched himself forward.

Owen pressed his weight down fully on the wrist of the first attacker and I heard the sharp crack of bones. He let go of the arm that fell limply onto the ground and faced the second teen. This one was yelling some demented ululation, his raised knife up to head height, obviously going to strike down into Owen's chest. I would have leapt backwards or potentially run away altogether, but Owen went forward, bent slightly, pivoted again on his feet and came up under the attacker's raised arm, his back now facing the boy's chest. He took hold of the boy's raised right wrist with his left hand, smashed his right arm down into the crook of the boy's elbow and took a pace forward. The slightest bend at his waist and shrug with his right shoulder produced another quite stunning effect, or series of effects. The knife dropped from the boy's hand, there was a snap, like a rifle shot, and a loud pop that must have been the boy's arm breaking and either his shoulder, or elbow, or possibly both, dislocating. As for the youth, he executed a perfect forward version of the cartwheel his co-assailant had performed.

I hadn't finished binding Paul's wound and we had two teenage Egyptian knife-wielding attackers on the ground, disarmed, in every literal sense of the word.

Owen, who looked like he had barely moved, shone his head torch on the middle aged man's face.

'No tax. You go away now.'

The man duly obliged and ran.

'How's he doing?' Owen asked.

'I'm okay. Hurts like hell, but I'll be fine. Let's keep going,' Paul answered.

In the sweep of Owen's torch I thought I could see a reflected glint, that might have been my dropped hip flask. It was lost to the darkness when the Welshman clicked the light off and said, 'Okay, stay close and pay fucking attention.'

**

A few hours later, with Mona, Hossam and Tahiya delivered safely to their homes, and the rest of us settled into EgyptAir business seats, I found myself thinking that all our fears about riots and police and the internal security services had amounted to nothing. Being attacked by a knife-wielding idiot … I could have stayed in London for that experience.

26

London, 20th July 2009

Dickie Lessen was apoplectic. His fat red face was positively glowing and I wondered if he got any madder would he potentially, and hopefully, combust. I heard little of what he was saying.

All through his diatribe I was thinking about the possibilities of Mac's idea. I was looking forward to receiving his email. The least I could do was read it.

When Lessen had finished whatever he was yelling at Pat and William and me, we left his office. I was glad to get out of it. The man was truly obnoxious and I had just realised, either didn't know what deodorant was, or simply hadn't used enough of the stuff. He stank.

'Umm, why hasn't he fired us?' I asked.

'I think because he'd have to explain to the members of the Executive Committee why he overruled us in the first place and he'd be ridiculed,' Pat said.

'As it is, he gets to scream and rant at us and no doubt take all the credit for a successful extraction when it gets raised with the bosses,' he added, with not a trace of bitterness. He was calmness personified. As we parted at the elevators, he continued, 'Ignore him. Or better still, learn from him. Yes, the man is an idiot but you can learn as much from bad examples of leadership as you can from good. Anyway, you and William both did a good job. Shame about Paul's hand, but otherwise, it was the perfect little adventure. Any word on him, Luke?'

'Neil, one of William's guys, was a former SBS medic. He dressed the hand properly at the airport and it was fine until we got home. Then I took him to Accident and Emergency. Couple of tetanus shots and they're keeping him in for a day or two, just to make sure there's no infections, but seems to be fine. Straight cut, no internal damage. A few stitches and he'll have a scar to talk about.'

'Well, no way to have planned for a bunch of muggers, that's just the luck of the draw, but the rest of it was clockwork,' William said. 'Thanks, Luke.'

'Yeah … just unlucky,' I agreed, then added, 'No need to thank me. It was my pleasure. Thank you, both.'

He and Pat gave me a cheery wave as I got into the lift. As the doors shut they wandered off in deep conversation. Perhaps they were discussing how long it would be before they quit. He may not have fired us, but Lessen was still in charge. Personally, I intended to read Mac's email when it arrived and if it was a go, I'd tell him I was interested. Depending on the package, I'd take it and then tell my guys I was quitting. Eugene at Cheltenham wouldn't object this time as he didn't need me anymore. Presumably the Chinese bug was doing its job. For now, I'd wait on Mac's email and see how things went from there. Tonight though, there was the small matter of a conversation with Liam.

He was scheduled to finish at nine, so he'd be home early, wouldn't be too tired, would be fairly relaxed. I planned to have a couple of gins to take the edge off when I got home, so that would help me settle into it. On the flight home from Egypt I'd decided I couldn't leave it any longer, and was feeling as good as I could about the whole thing. I figured there'd be tears, maybe a bit of shouting, perhaps he'd storm out. I was wrong about most of it.

**

Liam was home early and was relaxed. I'd had a couple, or maybe a few, gins. The time had come.

'Liam, I think we need to talk.'

'You want to break up with me?'

'What?'

'I've seen it in your eyes, ever since I threatened you.'

'No, that's not true,' I said and realised it wasn't, but equally realised I couldn't tell him why. I'd been about to give him the shove before he had tried to extort money from me. But the thought of saying, actually, I was tired of you before you tried to blackmail me, seemed unnecessarily cruel.

'It is true, Luke. And it's okay. You've been more than kind to me. Especially after all of that … Well, you know … *That*. You didn't have to weigh in on my behalf. You didn't have to involve Tom, or Mark. Especially Mark. You had no idea if he'd stand by you, but he did, because you are fundamentally a good guy. So, please, don't worry about this. I understand.'

I'd prepared myself for tears and tantrums. I was getting tender thanks. It completely threw me.

Liam stood up. 'I'll get my things and leave. It's okay. Friends?'

I stood up and moved towards him. 'Friends,' I said.

He hugged me. I hugged him back. Then he went into the bedroom and began to pack his bags.

I made myself a coffee. I needed a clear head, to make sure I hadn't missed something. 'Do you want a cup of something,' I shouted.

'Yes, tea, please.'

When he'd finished packing, which hadn't taken long as he only kept a few days' worth of stuff at my place, he joined me in the lounge with the London skyline in the background.

'Will you be okay?' I asked.

He gave a half-smile and a snort, but not sarcastically. It was, if anything, apologetic. 'You mean, will I fall back into my old ways?'

'Umm, no, I wouldn't think that of you at all, and I sorely doubt me breaking up with you would force you back into that life. I just mean, you know … will you be okay?'

'Yeah. I mean, I'd be lying if this isn't gonna hurt, Luke. I think you know how much I—' he hesitated, momentarily, 'I like you. So not gonna deny there'll be tears later, but I'll be okay. Especially if we can maybe stay in touch? Have the occasional drink?'

'I'd like that,' I said and discovered as I said it that I meant it.

We drank our drinks in silence and my mind whirled across the conversation, the last few weeks, the things I had been responsible for instigating. The death of Vasile, even though he was a thug. Had that been the right thing to do? I couldn't feel anything towards him. The man had tried to ruin my whole life. The man had killed viciously and used Liam terribly. Not only now, but in the past.

'What was it like?' I asked out loud before I could stop myself.

'What?'

I set my coffee cup down and looked him straight in the eyes. 'We've never spoken about the time after you left the army. When you became … well, you know.'

'A prostitute?'

'Yes. How did you end up there?'

'Are you sure you want to have this conversation?'

'I just realised, I never questioned it when you told me. It was your story and I naïvely figured, these things happen, but, Liam, they happened to you. How?'

'At first, economic necessity. I needed money. Simple as that. And not like most of the girls and guys on the streets. I wasn't into it for drugs, I needed money to live. I was fit and good looking and sleeping rough in Camden. A car pulled up one night and a guy offered me cash to go with him. It was a BMW. I figured he'd be worth a few quid. I negotiated an all-night rate. Thought of a number, doubled it. He didn't even blink. I reckon I could have trebled it. The next morning he gave me an extra hundred as a tip. Went to a café, bought breakfast and a paper. Checked out the classifieds. Thought going high-end with BMW drivers and their ilk would be easier and more lucrative than a tenner for a quick blow job up an alley with some loser of a fat, sweaty business man.'

The image of Dickie Lessen sprang to my mind. I almost gagged at the thought. 'And that was that?'

'No. That was the idea, but it didn't work out. To be high-end, you need a high-end place. High-end clothes, high-end everything. I was on the streets with a few quid in my pocket, but I was still on the streets. Very quickly, high-end became low. Then Vasile picked me up and if you leave aside the end game where he extorted some of the clients, the lifestyle was everything I thought it would be.'

I was amazed. As he'd said that last sentence the twinkle in his eye had returned. 'You were happy?' I asked.

'I was earning four hundred quid an hour. Three grand for an overnighter. Ten K plus for a week's holiday and they paid the expenses. Of course I was happy.'

'Fuck, almost earning as much as me?'

'Ha. But I didn't get the bonuses you get and although I had some regulars, there was the occasional weirdo.'

'Again, just like my job. Some great people, some weirdos.'

'Yeah, but you don't have to jerk off your weirdos, do you?'

The image of Dickie Lessen came back into my mind. 'Ugh, no! That I don't. Thank God.'

'And I'm a fairly fit guy who can look out for myself,' he said.

I thought he was being excessively modest. He was one of the fittest, strongest men I'd ever known.

'Still there were times when I was worried. Scared on occasion. It can be freaky.'

'You sound like it was almost, not perfect, but on balance, a good life.'

He paused and considered the suggestion. 'In truth, it wasn't that bad. But then Vasile fucking wrecked it. He was a mean and oppr— Ah, you know what he was like. I don't need to dredge that all back up again, but yeah, without that prick, it wasn't a bad life.'

I wondered if the obvious had struck him. I wondered if it was about to. He lifted his cup and took a sip. 'Liam?'

'Yes, Luke, that's very formal. What's up?'

'Vasile is out of the picture and won't be coming back.'

He gave that strange half-smile and snort of air from his nose again. Then he drained his cup of tea and stood up. 'Keep in touch?'

I stood too. 'Of course.' He gave me a final hug and left. I'd managed to get through it all without once letting him realise, what the truth really was. I didn't want him as a close companion. I still wanted to spend my life with only one man and I had no clear idea how I would ever be able to move on without him.

By midnight I'd found sleep at the bottom of a Tanqueray No. Ten bottle that had been full that morning.

**

A week after Egypt, Pat walked in to my office and shut the door.

'I want you to see this first. It's due for release tomorrow at midday, but senior managers have been told in advance, so they can assist their people.' He handed me one of the two pieces of paper he held. It was a single page memo with the usual address boxes and details. Not usual was the subject line.

Voluntary Redundancy Package Announcement

'What the fuck? I thought we were one of the best performing banks in the country?'

'We are, but the acquisitions and mergers that we've gone hell for leather on have cost a lot more than we budgeted. Upgrades to teller systems, maintenance of legacy systems, directors to be paid off, literally paid off in some of the more, or should I say less, discerning anti-corruption nations. It all adds up. That and the fact we have about four people in each job role courtesy of buying up whole banks and all their people. Imagine if a football team bought the whole of another one. What would you do with your excess quarterbacks?'

'God love you, Pat. Months we have worked together and still you think I like sport, but I get the gist. Though, I'm not sure why you're telling me this? We definitely need our people. There'd be no cyber security team without them.'

'Yes, but Dickie Lessen doesn't need, or rather, doesn't want me and William. He's going to encourage us to seriously consider taking the package.'

'How do you know that?'

'Because he told one of his best pals, Abby Becker, from HR. Who promptly told one of her best pals and two more pals later, one of them told William.'

'But it's voluntary, you can tell him to piss off.'

'Yes, yes I can. I'm not going to though.'

'Why not?'

Pat handed me the second piece of folded paper he'd been holding. There was a number written on it.

'Seriously?'

He nodded.

'Wow! That's amazing. But you've been with the bank a long time, I mean, I'd expect them to do right by you.'

'Yes, that is true. The thing is Luke, with me and William gone, I wasn't so sure you'd want to stick around answering directly to Dickie, so I figured, as your manager I could do the same to you as he's about to do to me.'

'Umm, okay? I think.'

'I'm here to encourage you to take the package.'

'I've only been here eleven months. Would I even qualify for a package?'

'You would. If you do what I recommend. Oh, and I may have misled you earlier.'

'What do you mean?'

He reached forward and tapped the piece of paper I was still holding. 'That is your figure, Luke. And the first 40K is tax free.'

I felt the colour drain from my cheeks.

'Eh ...' I realised I had stopped, my mouth still open.

Pat chuckled. 'Well, it will be if you do what I recommend. Unless I have missed something and you want to stay working for Mr Lessen when me and William have bailed out?'

'Nope. That is a most definite nope. Go right ahead.'

'If you apply for the package and give them a leaving date of anything after September 15th, then you will qualify. You will be past your one year mark and receive that figure as a pay-out. William and I ran the numbers. It's accurate. The bank is very, very keen to get rid of people, but on good terms. So they don't talk.'

I was shocked, but in a good way. I stared back down at the page. My salary package included a quarterly bonus based on the performance of my team, but it paled in comparison. 'And my guys,' I asked looking past him, through the glass to where the four of them sat.

'They can apply too. I reckon they will once you tell them you're going. If you are going.'

I hadn't received Mac MacLellan's email and although it was only a week, I had dismissed the whole idea of running away to work for the crazy Canadian. I'd once had him described to me as the type of man, who a few generations ago would have sold snakeskins and natural remedies out of a horse-drawn wagon. Lots of promises, but mostly smoke and mirrors. I figured that description was probably correct and that meant if I wanted to continue to live in my apartment, I still needed my job.

This changed the game. This would allow me to leave, take the time to find a new job and stay in my apartment. Cake and eat it.

'Well, what do you think?' Pat asked.

I glanced at the calendar on my desktop. 'If I made it the first of October, I could do the Doha conference. We've committed to it and I wouldn't like to let the organisers down. It's only a couple of weeks more, what do you think?'

'I think it sounds good. All you need to do now is act surprised when Dickie calls you into his office tomorrow and tells you that me and William have applied for voluntary redundancy.'

27

He was cold and hungry. Another day in the Korengal. This one though made him happy to open his eyes into the pitch black of the pre-dawn. For it was finally here. His last full day in the God-forsaken valley and tomorrow, when the Relief in Place had been completed and the unit's responsibilities were handed over to the newbies of the 1st Battalion, 12th Infantry Regiment, he could wipe the dirt and dust and memories of this place away forever.

Dan rolled off his cot and dragged on his boots. The crump of outgoing mortars accompanied him brushing his teeth. He ran through his schedule; chow, handover brief from the off-going night commander, then orientation of the incoming intel guy. Show him the intel feeds that were of most use and where to get the latest information on the tribal factions, then take him through the best structure for briefing the patrols. Finally, deliver the brief for a combined patrol pulled from all three of Bravo Company's squads, who would take all the new squad leaders of the 12th for an orientation patrol up and down the side of a mountain, ending with a meeting in Landigal village. This wasn't a formal Shura, only a meeting with the head man of the village.

A courtesy call to introduce the new guys. Only downside, he and the newbie intel guy had to go along, so that Dan could show him the etiquette and customs he'd need to know for when he attended a formal Shura. Standard Relief in Place stuff. That's why the patrol was, with appropriately dark and morbid Army humour, known as a RIP Trip.

When it was over, they'd return to base, then chow, take part in the nightly firefight, show the 12th how wonderful the Korengal was and then sleep, get up and go home. He was smiling so much he dripped toothpaste all down his t-shirt.

**

Landigal was a shithole, a stronghold of the insurgency, a known weapons cache site, a favourite of snipers and all in all a bad place to go on any given day of the week. It was also, sadly, for each and every one of those reasons, important to make sure the 12th knew their way in and out of it. For, as Dan had explained to Captain Sean Rutter, the Intelligence Officer attached to the 12th, if the United States Infantry weren't attempting to dominate Landigal, then the insurgents would be running the place. Almost as an afterthought he'd added, 'As soon as we leave, they do anyway.'

The outward vehicle transit was uneventful. A couple of sniper shots, an incoming RPG that sailed harmlessly overhead. Dan had forgotten how strange it was to see soldiers ducking and diving like scared rabbits from the dings the rounds made against the sides of the wagons. The 12th regiment's newbies were certainly jumpy.

'Were we like that Morrie?' he asked the Staff Sergeant.

'Yes you were, Sir. Me on the other hand, not for as long a time as I can recall.' More quietly he said, 'Can't wait to see how these boys cope walking up to Landigal.'

The vehicles started slowing and Morrie shouted above the whine of the engines, 'Okay ladies, welcome to the Korengal, look sharp and stay focussed. We want to pass on to you one of the traditions we've developed whilst we've been the custodians of this wonderful piece of real estate. Sergeant Peck, do the honours.'

The Sergeant wedged himself as upright as he could in the cramped compartment and began to recite what had become Bravo Company's de rigueur mantra since the events of January and the devastation of 1st Squad. All the Bravo Company soldiers in the back of the wagon joined in.

'Even though I walk through the valley of death, I will fear no evil, for we have overwhelming firepower and if you shoot at us from a house, we will overflow your cup with MERCY!'

'And don't forget it boys. You receive fire, you answer it with crushing force.' Morrie said as the vehicle stopped.

The squads debussed and shook out into a standard patrol formation. Dan fell in behind Corporal Salla; a huge man who could climb the mountains of the Korengal all day and night and still not show the slightest signs of weariness. He'd been Kracker's direct replacement back in January and Dan had instantly got on with the quietly spoken giant from South Dakota.

'Another day, another dollar,' Salla said, stepping off happily and humming the tune to Green Day's *Nice Guys Finish Last*.

Dan had liked Green Day before meeting Salla, but now he could recognised every song released by the group because the Corporal played nothing else back at base. It was a standing joke throughout 1st Squad.

Dan started to hum along with Salla's chosen tune of the day and with that, almost instantly fell into his patrol routine. Alert and vigilante whilst calm and relaxed. He considered it as normal a routine now as brushing his teeth.

Morrie was coming back down the line towards him. Regardless of the combined patrol being drawn from all three of Bravo Company's squads, 1st Squad's leader was going to make sure all the boys, including Captain Dan were sorted out, in shape and set for their day out in Taliban County.

Morrie checked in with Salla, then walked alongside Dan.

'How's the new intel guy?' Morrie asked.

Dan turned his head to answer. Later he would swear he heard no sound, but there must have been one. What was never in doubt was the combination of blood, brains and bone that coated his face when the sniper's bullet hit Morrie in the head.

28

Doha, 30th September 2009

The applause was enthusiastic enough to tell me I'd nailed my presentation.

I could now kick back and enjoy the Cyber Crime, Forensics and Digital Investigations Conference. So far, it was turning out much as I had hoped. Full to the gunwales with law enforcement, banking and military types. The perfect hunting ground for me, a day away from being unemployed again. Albeit this time on very different terms.

I'd delivered my paper so that it was included in the official conference materials and now I'd delivered my presentation and it had gone over well. We were even being hosted in one of Qatar's newest hotels and I'd been delighted to discover that the bars were licenced for alcohol. The last time I'd been in Qatar I'd been in uniform and the Forces compound, although dotted with bars, had been considerably shabbier than my current surroundings. Although, on the credit side, that compound had been where Liam and I had first met.

It was more than two months since we'd split up and I figured only having slept with him on four occasions since then was fairly good going. We were over, but until I could be with Dan, I had itches that needed scratching. Or in Liam's case almost flaying.

I sat down in one of the designer, high-back chairs in the main bar of the hotel and a waiter appeared almost at the run. 'Large gin and a small bottle of tonic, not poured, please.'

'Make that two. My treat.' The voice was a woman's. I leant out and looked around. She was young, in her late twenties if that. Her brunette hair was shoulder length, and feather cut at the sides. It suited the shape of her face; straight nose, high cheekbones, broad smile and what I noticed most, kind eyes. By the time I'd taken all this in, she had sat down opposite me.

'Don't get up,' she announced. 'I'm Emma Murray. I hope you remember me.'

The name was instantly recognisable, but not instantly placed. I certainly had never met her, I'd have remembered, but I knew her, of that I was certain. To buy myself time, I repeated back what she'd said. 'Emma. Emma Murray.' The act of saying her name allowed the memory to fall into place like a well-played Tetris block. 'You were the head hunter who arranged for me to go to the interview with Pat Harris.' I stood up and offered her my hand. 'I never got a chance to thank you. By the time I was confirmed in the job and rang the recruitment agency, they told me you'd moved on.'

'Yes. In my defence, they were a bunch of narcissistic buffoons. I ended up in a much nicer firm. So how are you? Flying high at Bateleur, I hear? Keep seeing your name in articles discussing the Inter-Bank Task Force. How you were instrumental in establishing it and making it so effective. Go you.'

I felt my face flush red. Unlooked for compliments were my least favourite type of conversation. I stammered out a thank you and then for no good reason said, 'It's changed its name to the Bank Information Sharing Network now.' Thankfully, I was saved from further embarrassment by the waiter returning with the drinks. A long sip of very good gin later, I felt composed enough to ask her the obvious question. 'What brings you here then, Emma?'

'Professional interest. Always on the lookout for good people who I might be able to prise out of their current role and into filling one of my clients' requirements.'

'Bateleur not being one of those clients anymore?'

'That is correct and aren't I the lucky one. What with them rolling out their voluntary redundancy scheme. I doubt they'd be wanting much recruiting done.'

'Quite,' I agreed. 'So tel—,' I stopped as we had started to speak at the same time. 'After you,' I said. 'Please.'

'I was only going to ask, are you still content at Bateleur given their current circumstances?'

'Funny you should say that. Also, I know I was originally head hunted by you, but I hadn't thought to reach out to any recruiters.'

Her face showed that my words had piqued her interest. 'And why do you want to reach out to recruiters, Luke? Are you actively thinking of leaving Bateleur?'

'Yes.'

'Oh, when?'

I looked at my watch. 'In about one day and nine hours. Know of any jobs going in commercial cyber intelligence?'

'As a matter of fact, quite a few. We're starting to see requests from oil and gas companies. Other resource providers, national infrastructure companies and a few others, all asking if we know anyone within the world of cyber intelligence who could start a fledgling organisational structure for them. You could do that, couldn't you?'

The right answer was, yes standing on my head, but modesty kept my response limited to, 'Yes. I could do that.'

'Good. What about you and I sit down when you get back to London and I will draw up a selection of potential roles?'

'Sounds perfect,' I said.

'As for now,' she said, lifting her gin and downing it in one, 'I could do with another of these. Join me?'

I was quite taken with Ms Murray.

**

The following morning, slightly after 8 am, I left the hotel for the airport and thanks to the fact I was still officially a Bateleur employee for one more day, fast tracked through security and took a seat in the First Class lounge. Even though I was still on a business class ticket, my regular flyer status now afforded me some extra luxuries. Like most lounges of its type it had superb food and copious amounts of free booze. After charging my glass I strolled over to the panoramic windows that provided a view across a large section of runway, taxiways, aircraft gates and in the distance, the massive construction effort that was building the new Hamad International Airport. It should have been opening before the end of the year, but it was obviously way behind schedule.

To my left was a heavily secured and cordoned-off section of the tarmac. The military side of Qatar International, used by all the coalition forces in the War Against Terrorism. I stared at the wire and remembered. I'd walked down the ramp of a C130 into that compound on my arrival in Qatar back in 2003. Then, in 2004, I'd boarded my flight home from there. Albeit a typical military flight that went to Basra and Baghdad before it went anywhere near Britain. It all was so long ago and felt like it had happened to someone else.

As I continued to watch out over the airfield, a USAF C-17 taxied off the runway and around to the military apron. By the time it stopped at its mark I had finished my gin and went to get a refill. When I returned, two refuelling bowsers were hooked into the aircraft, providing it a refill too.

I was about to raise my glass in convivial cheers when three 4x4s drove onto the apron next to the C-17 and the aircraft ramp started to come down. I recognised what this was. I had seen it before, back in 2004 when I had been waiting to leave for home.

The vehicles disgorged their cargo of nine US Marines who sprinted to their positions. One Marine to the front, rear and under each wing tip of the large cargo plane. Four more lined up along the leading edge of the ramp where it rested on the tarmac. The last Marine, a Gunnery Sergeant, took up a position just to the rear of the aircraft. I couldn't hear him from where I stood behind the thick glass, but I knew what his words of command would be. The eight Marines positioned around the aircraft sloped their arms and reversed their rifles so that the muzzles pointed down to the ground. This was a formal guard of honour. This C-17 was a re-patriation flight for those killed in either Iraq or Afghanistan. I stood straighter and raised my glass solemnly, for fallen comrades.

**

Dan stood at attention as the Marines reversed their weapons and mounted the guard of honour. A mark of respect for those who had paid the ultimate price for freedom. A warm breeze swept up the ramp and into the hold of the aircraft. Dan relaxed.

He'd requested to be the official escort for Morrie's body. It was an easy request to fulfil. He'd been due to go home on a direct flight out of Kabul, this merely rerouted him. The aircraft would leave Kabul and via Qatar, Iraq, Germany and the UK would eventually set course for home. Dan would stay with Morrie the whole way.

**

I was in the back of a black cab heading home when my mobile rang. A little jetlagged, I didn't check the caller ID. 'Hello?'

'Luke, is that you?'

'Yes. Mac? Is that *you*?"

'Sure is kid. I know, I know you didn't hear from me and it's been weeks.'

I wanted to correct him. It had been almost two and a half months. Instead I said, 'Yeah, I was wondering. How's things?'

'Things are great kid. Really great. Better than I could have imagined. Now tell me, still happy in your job, or do you think you might want to listen to my pitch?'

'I think I'd like to hear your pitch, Mac.'

'Great. That's great. Are you at home?'

'Mmm, if you mean London, then yes, I am. Why's that? Are you coming here?'

'Better than that. Landed about two minutes ago. Wondered if you could take a few days off work?'

I avoided the question. If Mac had a job offer, he didn't need to know I was newly unemployed. I needed to be able to negotiate from a position of power. I suddenly realised just how much Pat Harris had taught me in the previous year. 'A few days? How long were you planning on this interview going for?' I asked, keeping my voice as light as I could, in the midst of wondering what the hell Mac was up to.

'Kinda hoped you would be able to take some time off. I have my private jet on the ground at London City Airport. I'm turning it around and heading back to Ottawa in a little over two hours. I'd like you to come with me. I want to talk to you about what we can do together and I want to offer you a job. Immediate start. I'll pay off any notice periods you have to work or any bonuses you'll lose out on. I'm serious about this and I want you with me. What d'ya say, kid? Want to come work for me at Twenty-Twenty Security Incorporated?'

I heard Pat's voice in my head. 'I'm certainly interested, Mac. Let's see where we're at when we've talked numbers. I can be at the airport in thirty minutes. Is that quick enough for you?'

Epilogue

GCHQ Briefing Notes
For: Bateleur Bank - Group Chairman and Members of the Group
Executive Committee
Date: 8th August 2011

Briefing Team Members: ▮▮▮▮▮▮▮▮

1.   Since July 2009, six of Bateleur Bank's proposed acquisitions in South East Asia and Africa have failed because the confidential and compartmentalised e-mail of ▮▮▮▮▮▮▮▮ was compromised.

2.   Mergers and Acquisition information from secure servers that only the Bateleur Group Executive Committee had access to were exploited by members of PLA Unit ▮▮▮▮▮▮▮▮ under the direct control of the following Chinese Government officials:

3.   Each acquisition opportunity was outbid by Chinese State-backed banks who undercut Bateleur's offers by amounts ranging from $▮▮M USD to $▮▮M USD.

4.   On all six occasions the Chinese banks won each commercial opportunity and have gained significant political and economic influence within these nation states. The long term economic impact of the lost acquisitions to Bateleur Bank is assessed at approximately $12bn USD.

5.   Since August 2009, all research and development (R&D) conducted within Bateleur's Shanghai Data Centre, with particular focus on online banking security, was stolen by the same PLA Cyber Unit and passed from the Chinese Government to Chinese banks. It is assessed that this reduced the Chinese R&D cycle by approximately six years and gave Chinese banks a competitive advantage in online banking internationally for the first time. The long term economic loss to Bateleur with regard to their pre-existing commercial advantage within this market is assessed to be in excess of $24bn USD.

6.   All Intellectual Property (IP) for Bateleur's world leading chip and pin technology for Credit and Debit Card operations has also been compromised. This technology was passed from the Chinese Government and used to help Chinese banks domestically and globally. Significantly, in the incursion of January 2011, the PLA Unit tasked with Bateleur operations corrupted some of this IP and reinserted it into Bateleur's own systems, wiping the original IP and rendering it useless to Bateleur. The combined long term economic impact of this is assessed as in excess of $50bn USD.

7.   The personal information of Bateleur's 210,000 employees globally was stolen by the PLA Cyber Unit and transmitted directly to Chinese Government servers located in ████████████████████. This mass loss of data occurred on 14th February 2011 and included personal debt levels and short falls in personal pensions after a change to Bateleur's final salary pension scheme. The Chinese used this information to socially engineer and bribe over 2000 key Bateleur employees during the spring of 2011 in an effort to get them to sell confidential company information that was not accessible through the Shanghai Data Centre. The actual number of employees compromised and the long term economic loss to

Bateleur remains unquantifiable, but GCHQ assesses it to be in excess of $100bn USD. Significantly, the ███████████████

███████████████████████████████████████

███████████████████████████████████████

███████████████████████

8.   Bateleur, as a former 'Colonial and Dominion Bank', has a significant presence in the former British Empire and still has a major footprint in British Commonwealth countries. Due to this and the instability of many emerging economies, several African governments bank with Bateleur. Through the cyber efforts of the PLA, the Chinese Government stole national economic forecasts for seven of these nations from Bateleur's servers including national debt levels, debt ratios, future agricultural harvest assessments, gold reserve levels and future borrowing requirements. Six of the seven African governments switched their nation's banking from Bateleur to Chinese government owned banks who enticed them with lower borrowing rates and promised free national infrastructure building projects if the countries switched to Chinese government sponsored banks.

9.   Due to banking being a key part of the UK's Critical National Infrastructure, contributing ████ bn GBP to the UK economy in the year 2010, it is pertinent for the bank's Executive Committee to be aware that Bateleur, far from being the only entity targeted, is one of a number across the banking sector and vertices including defence contracting, aviation, retail, e-tail, telecoms, oil and gas and shipping. As briefed by the Home Secretary in March 2011, all sectors of UK Critical National Infrastructure were compromised and the national security posture of the United Kingdom severely diminished. The economic impact to Bateleur as previously shown is significant, but the threat to the UK's national security is incalculable in financial terms.

10.   The commercial arm of the Chinese Government intelligence services, telecommunications company, ███████████, is expected to bid for significant parts of newly developed mobile network technologies forecast to be ready for commercial exploitation in the latter part of this decade. The company already owns

█% of all UK cellular networks and █% globally. UK Government has been advised by all UK intelligence agencies, in cooperation with the US, Canadian, New Zealand and Australian intelligence agencies that Chinese telecommunications companies should not be permitted to take part in critical national infrastructure projects such as mobile communications networks or their subsequent development. Future UK governments are to be updated annually on the critical threat posed.

11.   All intelligence from the UK's Bank Information Sharing Network was compromised in July 2011 when Bateleur decided to provide 'secure' servers to hold the totality of the shared intelligence information. Bateleur's Head of Global Security ordered the servers be moved from London to within the Shanghai Data Centre.

12.   Allow time for questions.

Note to briefing team. Distribute file containing all inter-bank memorandums authored by Luke Frankland and addressed to the Head of Global Security, ████████, that advised against developing, hosting or exploiting any significant bank information within the Shanghai Data Centre and highlight to the bank's Group Chairman that Frankland documented the likelihood of these scenarios occurring.

Post Meeting Notes - GCHQ archive use only.

- On 10th August 2011, Dickie Lessen was fired from Bateleur Bank.
- Following a shareholders Extraordinary Meeting on 12th of August, the CEO and the Group Chairman of Bateleur were asked to resign with immediate effect. The CEO received a £5.4M severance and the Group Chairman £12.3M.
- On 15th of August, during inaugural meeting of revised Group Executive Committee, the newly appointed Group Chairman called Luke Frankland from the board room speaker phone.
- For details of that call, see GCHQ Archive folder 9840-BBNI-11-12-LFA3

To Be Continued

The Luke Frankland Novels

In The Best Interests

Luke Frankland, a junior intelligence officer just home from the Iraq War, finds himself cast into a world of cyber espionage and state-level politics. Out of his depth and with no one in the Government heeding his warnings, he forms a makeshift team and tries to establish who is waging a new kind of war from behind a keyboard. The truth will leave him plunged into an arena he little expected and where the real cost is not measured in 1s and 0s but in human life.

In The Best Interests is the first in the Luke Frankland Trilogy of cyber thrillers. A series of novels based on the real life experiences of the author within the world of cyber warfare and espionage. They will take you on a chilling and personal journey that will leave you wondering where the fiction ends and the facts start.

The first of the Luke Frankland cyber thrillers.

Coming Soon

Twenty-Twenty Hindsight

Recruited solely for his reputation in cyber intelligence, Luke Frankland is meant to lend his name to a cyber start-up venture, host clients and build up the sales value of the fledgling company.

However, when he is targeted by a new type of social engineering he quickly realises that all is not as it seems in the high-tech world of commercial intelligence gathering. Thrust into an environment where corporate advantage means multi-million dollar contracts, he discovers that some within the firm will stop at nothing to protect their share of the profits. In an increasingly dangerous game, Luke must quickly find out who he can trust and who is out to silence him.

The third and most explosive yet of the Luke Frankland cyber thrillers.

Acknowledgements

Yet again, I owe a debt of gratitude to various people without whom this book would not have been possible.

To Peri, for allowing me to love again, helping me to remain focussed and bringing out the best of me in the most tragic of times.

My parents, and my brother Jamie, for your continued unconditional love and unstinting support.

Thank you to author Ian Andrew for his mentorship, wisdom and patience and for editing my nonsense into something readable. Also to his wife Jacki, for her sensible amendments to prospective titles.

To Eric and Neil, for allowing me to use the tranquillity of their Cape Town home to do much of the final work on this book. To sit in their gardens and have Table Mountain as the back drop to my desk was quite the experience.

To the people who helped me research those small details that lend such credence to a story. Thanks to Ksenia and Anastasia for their translations, the information on Kiev's suburbs and their insights into some regrettable (and hopefully diminishing) attitudes towards the LGBTQI community in the former Eastern Bloc. Also to Sara for her help with UK police procedural details and Steve for his advice regarding the banking sector.

To my beta readers Howard and Lewis who gave so generously of their time.

Emma & Monika, my female 'dream team', you are rocks of love and support. Thank you.

A special mention to the teams I lead at Recorded Future in London, Europe, the Middle East, Africa and the Asia-Pacific regions. I could not wish for better colleagues and companions. I'd also like to thank my bosses, Chris, Levi, Stu and Christopher for the support they give me and my teams to achieve what we do.

Finally, I'd like to reiterate the thanks I made in my first book, to the NHS staff at the South Tyneside District Hospital, but especially this time to Dr Topping for her continued monitoring of my health.

Also to Dr R. E. F Cervenak MB BS MRCGP DRCOG at Whitburn Surgery for being the best family GP that Mum and Dad and I could wish for.

Without the care I have received from you all, I would not be here today and the books would not be possible.

Tim
London
March 2020

About the Author

Tim Hind was born in Sunderland and joined the Royal Air Force as a Commissioned Officer in the Intelligence Branch after reading Law at university. He is also a graduate of the UK's Defence Intelligence and Security School.

During his time in the Service he initially focused on the Middle East and then specialised in cyber warfare. He later joined Barclays Bank in a Global Information Security role with stints in the Middle East and emerging markets and subsequently headed up the bank's global cyber intelligence capability.

He then moved to America to lead another cyber intelligence team in his position of Vice President within a start-up cyber intelligence company that was sold in 2016.

Tim now lives in London and is a director of cyber intelligence teams located in Europe, the Middle East, Africa and the Asia/Pacific regions, who service clients globally in the public and private sectors. When not travelling the world for business or pleasure, he enjoys reading biographies, cooking, fell walking and skiing. He is also a qualified scuba instructor and, by his own admission, a commercial aviation geek. Despite all of these activities, he is most happy when at home surrounded by friends and family.

The Book Reality Experience

CPSIA information can be obtained
at www.ICGtesting.com
Printed in the USA
LVHW110527100320
649434LV00004B/235